We hope you enjoy this book.
Please return or renew it by the due date.
You can renew it at **www.norfolk.gov.uk/libraries**
or by using our free library app. Otherwise you can
phone **0344 800 8020** - please have your library
card and pin ready.
You can sign up for email reminders too.

REBEL SKIES

ANN SEI LIN

WALKER
BOOKS

First published 2022 by Walker Books Ltd
87 Vauxhall Walk, London SE11 5HJ

2 4 6 8 10 9 7 5 3 1

Text © 2022 Ann Sei Lin
Cover illustration © 2022 Amir Zand

This book has been typeset in Berkeley and Caslon

Printed and bound by CPI Group (UK) Ltd, Croydon CR0 4YY

British Library Cataloguing in Publication Data:
a catalogue record for this book
is available from the British Library

ISBN 978-1-4063-9959-2

www.walker.co.uk

MIX
Paper from
responsible sources
FSC
www.fsc.org   FSC® C171272

Above the blue sea
I build a boat of feathers
And row through the clouds.

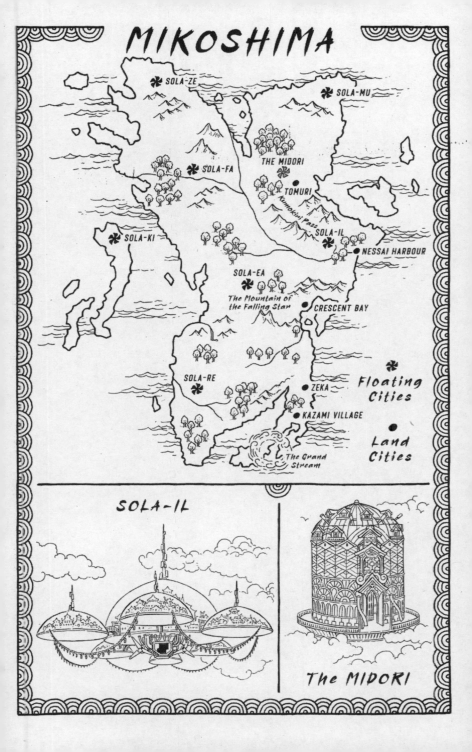

PROLOGUE

WHEN Himura was nine years old, his home town was attacked by a giant tortoise. Whenever he told this story, he made sure to emphasize the "giant" part. Tortoises don't seem frightening until you are leaning out of your window, staring up at the craggy face of a reptile the size of a mountain.

Trees grew from the back of its shell. Its head was covered with moss. Its claws – eating up the ground at an alarming speed – were stained with mud and the remains of animals it had trampled beneath its feet. Roads buckled. The earth shook. Those who weren't fast enough to escape were crushed beneath its body.

Himura remembered the way his fingers gripped the windowsill as the tortoise barrelled through the village. He remembered staring up at its wrinkled face, as monstrous as the living earth. Beneath the layers of soil covering its shell, he could still see the yellowing folds of its body.

Paper. The tortoise was made of paper. A perfect construction of crimp folds and reverse pleats so beautiful Himura could only stare at it in wonder even as it thundered towards his house.

The tortoise's foot swung over the roof of his home, but the snap of wooden beams and the crash of the collapsing ceiling never came. He could not remember the exact order of what happened next; only the sound and the heat. A whistle screamed above him as something struck the tortoise's back, exploding into flames that licked up the creature's body faster than wildfire.

When Himura looked up again, dark ships filled the sky.

Rearing its head back in agony, the tortoise burned and…

The ground moved beneath Himura's feet, jolting him out of his memories. The airship's deck bobbed like a boat on the open sea. Turbines hummed. Propellers churned through the warm summer air. The lights of the capital city twinkled across the ground below, but the night was fading and the first strings of dawn were about to sound.

It had been a long time since Himura had thought about his home town or the shikigami that had been burned down by the hunters. A fiery end befitting a paper beast. No normal person would cry over the death of a shikigami, especially not one as masterless and mad as the tortoise had been, and yet Himura had felt something like grief as he had watched it burn.

It had been such a waste.

"Are you still here?" An annoyed voice drew Himura's attention away from his thoughts. He turned to find the airship's navigator clambering out of the ship's hatch and onto the deck.

As she pulled herself up, Himura noticed that the rings beneath her eyes had grown darker. Both her hair and her kimono were in disarray: one a tangle of knots, the other a wrinkled mess. Sleep did not come easy when one had an entire airship to keep on course.

Himura took a paper square from his pocket and balanced it on the tip of his finger. "I was thinking, Sayo" – without touching it, the piece of paper folded itself into an origami crane – "about a shikigami I met when I was younger. Even though it destroyed my home, it was such a magnificent beast. I wish it had lived."

He flicked the crane into the air and caught it, crushing it in his fist. When he opened his palm, the origami bird was in pieces. With a puff of breath, he scattered the scraps into the air. They billowed over the deck like petals of snow.

Sayo snorted. "You only say that because you're a Crafter. Most normal folk would be glad to see a shikigami burn."

With a flick of his fingers, Himura made the scraps of paper dance around his feet.

Crafter. People had spat that word at him as though it were a curse. Others had whispered it in terror. But when Sayo said the word "Crafter", it was with the scorn of someone who knew Himura and was deeply unimpressed by him.

"Speaking of Crafters" – Sayo's gaze swept across the dawning sky – "you should get going. You'll need to arrive at the *Midori* by sunrise. According to the captain's informant, the girl should be serving breakfast in the main banquet hall. Come back with her, or don't come back at all."

Himura turned his gaze towards the clouds. A single light glimmered against the plum-coloured sky. Though from a distance it looked like a stranded star, he knew the light was coming from the *Midori* – the empire's first and only airborne banqueting hall.

What's a Crafter doing serving breakfast all the way out here? he wondered. What strange twist of fate had reduced someone who could control paper at command, whose blood ran thick with the power of their ancestors, to the life of a mere waitress?

Himura supposed it was a good thing he was saving the girl from such ignoble work. He longed for the company too. Travelling with Sayo and the rest of the airship's crew was like being a wolf among sparrows. It was tiring to be surrounded by people who could never understand the buzz of power in his veins or how the rustle of paper tugged at his heart.

"Don't make any trouble," Sayo warned him. "Just get the girl and go. You'll know who it is when you see her, right? You won't bring back some random maid?"

"I always recognize my own kind." Himura snapped his fingers and the pieces of paper fluttering around his feet swirled upwards. With a flick of his hand, they knitted together into a white bracelet around his wrist.

Climbing onto the ship's guard rail, Himura held his hands out like a tightrope walker for balance. His legs teetered between the deck and the open sky. The city lights swam below him like the lights of deep-sea fish luring prey to their doom.

It was a long way down. Swinging a leg out into the open air, he stepped forward and dropped.

At first there was nothing but the whistling wind. The summer air cut at his skin as he fell. Squinting through his watering eyes, Himura waited until he was a distance from the ship before pulling the bracelet off his wrist.

It broke into a thousand tiny squares of paper that spun in a furious cyclone. The pieces merged together to create a pair of wings, stretching down into tail feathers and folding into talons.

A giant, white falcon formed beneath him. Everything from the tip of its beak to the curve of its claws was as white as snow; even its pupils were invisible against the whites of its eyes.

"Show-off!" Himura heard Sayo shout as he landed on the bird.

Himura smirked. He made no apologies for talent. Holding tight to its feathers, he repositioned himself so that he was sitting astride the bird's neck. It was not like riding an actual shikigami – there was no intelligence in this paper puppet – but the thrill of it was the same.

Carried by the falcon's giant wings, he soared towards the *Midori*, where the banquet hall's red arches and wide golden gates lay open in a salute to the sky.

ONE

WHEN Kurara awoke to the ear-splitting sound of morning bells, her first thought was: *I would burn this whole place to the ground if it gave me ten more minutes of sleep.*

Lights pierced her eyelids as they flickered on. The bells blared against the walls of her box room. Outside, an attendant marched down the servants' hallway, bashing a gong and crying, "Up, up, everyone up! Give thanks to our great Emperor for this beautiful day!"

"Our great Emperor can go suck on a lemon!" Kurara rolled over with a groan. There were no windows in her room, but the glaring electric lights insisted that it was morning.

"Up! Up! Give thanks to our great Emperor that we may see another sunrise!" The attendant's voice echoed through the paper-thin walls. "Give thanks to our great Emperor who protects us from the shikigami!"

Rubbing the sleep from her eyes, the world slowly came into focus: the walls of her quarters, the balls of crumpled paper scattered across the floor, the twin bed on the other side of the room and the person still sleeping in it. A shock of coal-black hair poked out from under the sheets.

"Haru," she called. "Haru, time to get up!"

The lump on the opposite bed shifted.

"Look at the koi pond. The water ... sparkles like gemstones..." Haru mumbled from inside the tight cocoon of sheets. He was talking in his sleep again.

It sounded pleasant. Kurara wondered if he was dreaming about their home, their village. She wished that she could have dreams like that, but all of her memories before the *Midori* were hazy at best: a village in the mountains, a hut by a small pond, blurred faces of villagers that left only a lingering feeling of emptiness like cold smoke after a fire.

"Nessai Harbour. Crab ... big as ... dinner plates..."

No matter how pleasant the dream, there was still work to be done. Kurara plucked a ball of crumpled paper from the floor and chucked it across the room. As it bounced off Haru's bed, Kurara snapped her fingers and the ball froze in mid-air. A pleasant tingle ran through her body, the sensation both exhilarating and soothing. With a flick of her wrist, the ball began to spin, folding with each rotation – crimp, petal fold and pleat – into an origami rabbit.

She was not supposed to do this. The head cook had explicitly forbidden her from any activity that was not cooking or cleaning, but within the walls of her room she

15

was safe from prying eyes. What other people didn't know wouldn't hurt them – and Haru liked her paper animals. At least, when he was awake enough to appreciate them.

At her command, the rabbit hopped across the bed and tugged at a lock of black hair poking out from the sheets.

"Sky cities…" A sleepy hand batted the rabbit to the floor.

Kurara gave an indignant squawk. She scooped the rabbit up, cradling it close before setting it on her pillow.

The attendant banged the gong. Doors along the corridor slammed open as the last sleep-addled servants scrambled down the hallway.

"Haru!" Kurara stalked over to his bed and gave him a firm shove.

At last, a pair of dark eyes peeked out from beneath the sheets.

"All right, all right… I'm up!" Haru groaned.

"Good! Come on!" Kurara tugged him to his feet. They might make it in time if they ran.

———————o———————

The *Midori* was a place built for giants, an immobile castle of feasting rooms and private residences hovering six thousand feet in the air. Its gleaming pearl-glass windows loomed above the clouds. Birds built their nests inside moss-covered cannons while sky fish slipped between the clockwork gears. Large rotor blades cut through the air in the shape of an upside-down halo, the golden rings growing smaller until they tapered to a drill-like point.

Kurara's earliest memories were of those rings. Of the *Midori*'s towering walls and Haru's hand clasped tight in her own as the round hoverpod transported them past the gates. Of a stern-faced man who told them that this would be their new home. At the time, Kurara had not realized that the *Midori*'s gleaming exterior hid a dark and chaotic heart.

"You're late! This is coming out of your pay!" An attendant sneered at her as she arrived just as the breakfast gong sounded. Scrambling to her work station, she hurriedly tied the strings of her apron over her brown work dress.

Servants scurried past her, piling food onto silver trays. Another airship had just arrived and the demands for food and wine were already pouring in. These days, the docks were full of nothing but warships. The conflict in Estia had been dragging on for years – a war that would add another colony to Mikoshima's growing empire – and the soldiers returning from abroad wanted nothing more than to wine, dine and forget about their battles beyond the sea.

Kurara hurried to her station, skidding past mountains of unwashed pots towering towards the ceiling. The fires turned the kitchens into one giant furnace. The stone pillars that held up the cavernous ceiling seemed to sweat beneath the heat. A hundred different smells assaulted her nose: mirin, tōgarashi root, soy sauce and burnt sugar. Bells rang, tea kettles screeched, pans sizzled and plates slipped and smashed against red-tiled floors as the servants dashed back and forth with generously stacked platters of food.

"KURARA!" a voice bellowed. An empty pot sailed through the air, hitting the far wall with a bang that startled the other servants. "For God's sake, girl, where is the plum wine? You were supposed to prepare the plum wine!"

A portly woman marched across the kitchen, brandishing a ladle in one hand and an iron poker in the other. Kurara's eyes widened, her feet snapped together and her limbs arranged themselves into what was commonly known in the kitchens as "Position B". (Hands behind back, head bowed, eyes to the floor: the "I'm sorry, it won't happen again" position.)

"My apologies, Madam Ito, I forgot."

No one had told her anything about plum wine, but there was no point in telling Madam Ito that.

"*I forgot?!*" the woman squawked in a high-pitched imitation of Kurara's voice. Madam Ito's face was red, both from anger and from the heat of the fires. Her black hair, streaked with strands of silver, was pulled into a frizzy bun that wobbled at the top of her head every time she moved. As the head cook, she ruled over the kitchens of the *Midori* with an iron fist and an arsenal of iron pots, which she would often throw at whoever earned her displeasure. Maids jumped in her presence, serving girls fled from her scowls. Even the attendants would tread carefully when in the kitchens, knowing that this was Madam Ito's domain.

Kurara averted her gaze, letting her eyes rest on the pot the cook had thrown as it rolled to a stop just inches from her foot. Its curved reflection revealed a suitably penitent girl, round-faced and pale, with a nose too round and ears too big, and hair that had been cut every few months using the very same pot that now lay in front of her.

"Kurara!"

"Yes, Madam Ito, I'm listening!" She had not been listening.

The head cook's eyes narrowed. The veins on the side of her neck bulged.

"Girl." Her voice trembled with menace. "Do you know who is in charge of these kitchens?"

Kurara said nothing. The price for insolence was fifteen lashes and the head attendant had recently bought a new whip. She had seen him just yesterday morning with it tucked under one arm, his hand curling around its handle a little too affectionately.

"You, Madam Ito."

"And who is it that provides for you, clothes and feeds you, while other much more deserving little girls waste away out in the fields or down in the levistone mines?"

"You, Madam Ito."

"And who was the airheaded fool who forgot to fetch the plum wine today?"

"You, Madam—I–I mean—"

Madam Ito's chest heaved like a ship's bellows.

"I'll go and fetch it right away!" Kurara bowed and hurried out of the kitchens before the cook could throw another pot at her. As she made her way to the door, one of the maids thrust a large, silver tray in front of her.

"Girl, if you're going upstairs, deliver this to the Wisteria Room."

"But the plum wine!" she cried.

The woman shoved the tray into her arms. "Madam Ito is already in a bad mood. What do you think she'll do if this tray doesn't get to the room in time?"

"Clean out the cannons and shoot us into the sunrise," Kurara sighed. It was one of the cook's favourite threats.

"Then go."

Kurara knew a lost battle when she saw one. Taking the tray with her, she headed out of the kitchens, pausing only to reach into her apron pocket to check her crumpled list of chores. Someone had scribbled all over it, making it impossible to read. With a sigh, she stuffed the note back into her pocket.

One day, I'm going to get out of here. One day, I'm going to leave all this behind.

She just had to survive until then.

TWO

WHENEVER Kurara climbed out of the kitchens, she had to pause and wait for her eyes to adjust to the sudden presence of sunlight. The reception hall blinked into focus. A semicircle of golden lattice windows gave a perfect one-hundred-and-eighty-degree view of the blue sky. A domed glass ceiling extended far above her head. When Kurara had been younger, it had felt like the sky itself, beautiful and distant. Now, it merely loomed like everything else inside the *Midori*, making her feel small.

Shadows of clouds floated across the tiled floor as Kurara crossed it. Real flowers bordered the foot of the marble walls: vibrant red and gold orchids, royal purple chrysanthemums and pink lotuses that bloomed as large as a person's head. Mechanical parrots made of steel and stained glass beat their wings among the leafy plants, flying off whenever she approached. There was a coldness to the *Midori's* splendour. It was a beautiful birdcage.

"Rara!" A voice shouted from the top of the curling grand staircase. Kurara looked up to see Haru making his way down the carpeted steps.

"Haru!" She rushed to meet him. "Did you make it to the banquet halls on time?"

"Fifteen minutes late!" The boy thumped his chest.

Such confidence could only come from the very brave or the very stupid, but Haru had a long history of getting away with things no one else could. Gap-toothed, crooked-nosed and with a pair of dark, mischievous eyes, he was awkward and coltish in a way that made others want to indulge him. Letting one's guard down around Haru when he had some half-baked plan in his head was the perfect way to end up sneaking into the food stores at midnight or releasing sky fish into the *Midori's* pipes – activities which always ended with a beating.

From the look in Haru's eyes, he was in the mood for mischief, but Kurara knew him far too well to take part in his schemes.

"Well, since you're here, do me a favour. I need to deliver this to the Wisteria Room, and you" – she snatched the tray out of range as he tried to swipe a sweet roll – "are going to help me get there in time."

Servants were not supposed to use the elevators. The stern-faced attendants who operated them would shoo her away the moment they caught even a glimpse of Kurara's brown work dress, but Haru was different. The other servants often said that he could talk a chicken into buying its own eggs. Kurara had to stamp down on a familiar flutter of jealousy when the attendants opened the elevator doors for him without complaint.

Inside the elevator, Haru pressed the button for the fifteenth floor and allowed the doors to slide shut. Kurara ran a hand along the gold-plated interior as the steel cables hauled them upwards. The metal box was so shiny she could see her own reflection.

"So," she said, finally allowing Haru to take a sweet roll, "why aren't you in the banquet halls?"

When Haru grinned, his mouth appeared too big for his face. The black gap where his right incisor was missing tugged at her attention.

"I was coming to find you! One of the ships just came back from the Grand Stream! The Grand Stream, Rara! And the soldiers have the best stories about it! I didn't want you to miss out on the excitement."

Kurara turned her full attention to him. The world beyond the *Midori* only reached them through the stories the soldiers brought to the banquet halls; tales filtered and distilled into hours of idle, excited gossip.

"Did they see any shikigami?"

"You bet they did!" Haru grinned. Only he could be excited by the possibility of running into one of those paper monsters. "One day, let's visit the Grand Stream too!"

Kurara scrunched up her face. "How about we go somewhere less dangerous?"

The Grand Stream was an area to the very south of the country cut off by eternal storms. It was not just known for being full of shikigami, but for its winds that would tear ships asunder. Soldiers lucky enough to survive the winds returned with hollow eyes and tales they refused to repeat until Haru filled their cups with enough alcohol. It was not a place any sane person should visit.

Haru grinned. "One day, we'll go everywhere!"

One day, yes, one day. That's what they always told one another. One day they'd leave this cage and travel the world. To the Aogaki waterfalls, to snow-capped mountain ridges and green valleys carpeted with flowers. To the ocean where people said the water stretched all the way to the sun. To the very edge of the world.

"One day, we'll go home," whispered Kurara. Maybe if they travelled enough, they would find it again.

Haru's expression turned grim. He only ever frowned like that when they talked about the past. "I told you. That place is in ruins."

"That's all you ever tell me," muttered Kurara.

He always skirted around the topic with an annoying look of pity in his eyes. It irritated her. Haru had memories of their childhood, their home, their old neighbours and friends. She had nothing.

"They found you and Haru," Madam Ito had told her once, *"lying together in an empty barn. There was a great big shaft of wood sticking through his chest. Almost went straight through his heart, it did. He was lucky to survive. Made of stronger stuff than most people. It was almost unnatural."*

Even the head cook knew more about her past than she did! Kurara did not remember the incident. Trauma, Madam Ito called it. The result of whatever had led her to being found in an empty barn with a shaft of wood impaling Haru's chest. Though Haru always denied it, she had never been able to shake the feeling that his injuries had been her fault in some way. Guilt haunted her as much as her missing memories.

"I tell you about the past!" Haru interrupted her thoughts. "I tell you about the rice paddies and the lotuses that used to grow by the village ponds."

"You don't tell me about anything that matters!" she snapped. Inside the elevator, her own anger echoed in her ears.

Haru held a hand over his chest. Over the place the shaft of wood had been. "I don't like talking about things that hurt."

They stood in awkward silence as the elevator continued upwards.

"We could go to the sky cities," said Haru, after a beat. Though he did not say so, Kurara recognized it for the peace offering that it was.

"What about Nessai Harbour?" Kurara softened. She did not want to fight. "You were talking about it in your sleep. Something about crabs."

She pulled the crumpled note from her apron pocket and flicked it at Haru. It bounced off his nose and froze in mid-air. A pleasant tingle of electricity shivered through her body as the note blossomed into a paper crab with brittle, twitching legs.

"Madam Ito said that you weren't allowed to do that outside our quarters," said Haru.

Kurara remembered when he used to delight in her creations, requesting a new animal each night to dance between their beds. She remembered the swell of pride in her chest each time her paper creatures made him laugh. That had been before she had got careless. Before Madam Ito had caught them. Now he only wanted her to do these things in their room.

A prison within a prison, she thought bitterly. Although she knew it was Haru's way of keeping her out of trouble, sometimes she could not help the tiny spark of resentment. It was easy for Haru to say that she needed to stop. He didn't have to fold himself up like origami, smaller and smaller, for someone else's sake.

"We're in a moving metal box. Who's going to see?"

Haru remained unconvinced. Bouncing from one foot to the other, he lowered his voice and hissed, "Remember what Madam Ito said about, you know, people…"

"People?" said Kurara.

"Crafters." Haru gestured to the paper crab floating between them. "People who can control paper."

Kurara remembered the beating more than Madam Ito's furious shouts. The bruises had remained for weeks. Between the pain, she vaguely remembered something about being sold off to the imperial family.

"That's where Crafters go. To serve the Emperor and his children. If you get caught, you'll end up as one of Prince Ugetsu's war dogs. Or as Princess Tsukimi's plaything."

The way Madam Ito had sneered made her think that the princess was the worst of the lot, but Kurara was not afraid. Princess Tsukimi and the rest of the imperial family were a distant threat, the kind of horror story that mothers told their children to make them behave. Kurara was a Crafter. The urge to take control of paper, to move and reshape it, filtered through her veins. Like wanting to run after a long day of sitting still, or the itch to take a shower after spending hours cleaning grease out of the kitchen pipes, the desire built up and built up until she would explode if she did not let it out.

"Seriously, Rara," said Haru. "What if—what if they separate us?"

Never. Before Kurara could open her mouth, the elevator jolted to a stop. The Wisteria Room was on the fifteenth floor, but they had stopped on the tenth. She glanced at Haru. Had the stupid thing broken? It was early morning and the feasts were well underway. There should not be anyone outside the banquet halls to stop them.

"What's—?" she began, but before she could finish her sentence, the doors slid open.

Kurara snatched the crab out of the air and stuffed it into her apron pocket.

A man stood on the other side of the doors. He was young, teetering on the edge of adulthood, though something in his high cheekbones and thick, proud nose made him seem more adult than child. A white bracelet in the shape of a snake wound around his wrist.

Something about him made Kurara's nerves skitter on a knife's edge. His presence was like a thunderstorm striking her spine. The man stepped into the elevator, forcing her to shuffle aside to make room. The doors closed behind him.

Kurara and Haru shared a nervous look.

"Well, what a piece of luck." As he spoke, the man stepped forward so suddenly Kurara had to press herself against the elevator wall so that he didn't step on her toes.

He wore an ominous smile.

"I've been looking for you, Crafter girl."

THREE

THE elevator rumbled upwards as the man stared at her. Fine lines creased the skin beneath his eyes. Though he was perhaps only two or three years older than her, something about him *felt* older. He reminded her of the clerks who visited the *Midori* each year: tall, humourless men who tallied up the wages of each servant and subtracted the cost of room and board, as well as every broken plate or bottle of spilled wine. Kurara had always hated their visits. It was not just their strict demeanour she found frightening, but the unshakable impression that they had sprung from the air just to make her life difficult.

Retreat, Kurara's instincts warned her. The buzzing across her skin had faded to a slight tingle, but it was still enough to put her on edge.

The man took a step closer.

The elevator chose that moment to stop and the door opened on the fifteenth floor. Taking her chance, Kurara grabbed Haru's hand and all but dived for the exit. Haru broke away from her for just a second to place his hands on either side of the elevator, blocking the man from following.

"Sir, please take care around the closing doors." His tone was just smug enough to annoy.

The man tried to push past Haru, but the doors quickly slid shut, closing over him before he could speak.

The pulleys tugged the elevator upwards.

"Come on!" Haru took her hand, pulling her down the corridor. Lost in a fog of growing panic, Kurara could not concentrate on where her feet were going. It took a moment for her to realize that they were heading towards the Wisteria Room.

"What do I do, Haru?" That man was an ill omen. His appearance would lead to nothing good.

"Nothing," said Haru. "Don't worry about it!"

"How can I not worry? That man knew about me! Do you think that he—?"

"He won't take you away. I won't let him."

Haru's grip on her hand tightened. Though he did not look at her, his gaze was stubbornly determined, soothing her panicked heart.

He was still holding her hand when they reached the double doors leading to the Wisteria Room. Soldiers were drinking inside; Kurara could hear them through the walls, their laughter booming like cannons. She squared back her shoulders and braced herself for the flood of noise as Haru pushed his way inside.

The banquet hall was a sea of dark blue air-force uniforms. Men stood around the room deep in conversation. In the middle of the marble floor, a woman danced while entertainers played the koto. Her crimson clothes ignited the air every time she twirled, her bare feet scorching red as they slapped against the polished floor. Purple drapes encased the room. Incense curled towards the canopy ceiling. The Mikoshiman flag hung on one wall – a black spiral surrounded by fourteen moons, one for each colony in the empire. It would soon be fifteen moons if the war in Estia went well.

Kurara had never liked the banqueting halls. They were noisy, stuffy, and the smell of incense was cloying, but right now the mass of soldiers was a comfort. She could disappear here. Become just another faceless servant that no one bothered nor gave a second glance.

Mechanical birds fluttered around the edges of the hall and by the shōchū fountain in the corner. A man in a grey frog-collar suit walked through the crowd, holding aloft a spectacular array of chocolate roses, petals of pink sugar carved into the shape of cherry blossoms and pocket-sized morning glories made of caramel and sesame seeds.

Taking a deep breath, Kurara pushed the tray into Haru's arms. "Here, pass this to the attendant. And don't eat anything!"

Haru took it, but did not move. "Rara…"

"We both have work to do." Her voice betrayed her by trembling. She bit her lip so that it would not give her away further and focused on steeling her gaze.

She was not afraid. Even if her hands were shaking, fear would not conquer her. No one would sell her to Princess Tsukimi or turn her into a plaything or take her away from Haru. She would not let them.

With a reluctant nod, Haru did as he was told, although Kurara had a feeling he was going to duck out of work for the rest of the day to "help" her in the kitchens.

"Did you hear that Prince Ugetsu's ship was attacked by a shikigami on his way back to the capital?" a soldier whispered as Kurara turned around. "Not even the royal family is safe!"

"Heard he was rescued by Sorabito too. That had to be humiliating." One of the soldiers stuffed an almond cake into his mouth. "To be saved by those sky rats!"

"Princess Tsukimi would be dancing in the streets if he died. The Emperor should hurry up and name an heir or one of them is going to murder the other!" another chortled and the other men joined in on his laughter.

Kurara hurried past them. She liked hearing the soldiers gossip, but all this talk of murder made her uneasy.

As she moved to the other end of the hall, someone grabbed her by the arm. She spun on her heel, eyes widening as she came face to face with the man from the elevator.

"What do you want?" The words slipped out before she could stop herself. Such rudeness was not tolerated on the *Midori*.

"To talk," he said. "You're not in trouble. Madam Ito told me about you."

Kurara did not believe that. The head cook was the most wary about keeping Kurara's abilities a secret. She had no reason to tell anyone else.

Unless Madam Ito wants me gone. Was that it? Had the cook grown tired of her and decided to sell her off, as she always threatened to do?

Before she could dwell on the possibility, the man scratched the back of his head and said, "Well, 'told' is a rather generous term. Did you know Madam Ito becomes rather loose-lipped after her fifteenth drink?"

Kurara gawped. All that effort she put into hiding her abilities, all those years of self-restraint, ruined by Madam Ito and a few drinks! Indignation stirred inside her gut, tempered only by unease as the man leaned over her.

"Tell me" – he lowered his voice – "how would you like to leave the *Midori*?"

"Leave?" A one-two punch of terror and elation hit her in quick succession. Kurara was not sure she had heard him correctly.

Could she really leave the *Midori*?

"There is no need to be afraid." Touching his bracelet, the man pulled out a small square of paper. Lifting his index finger, he balanced the paper square on the tip of his nail so that it stood upright. Without prompting, the square began folding itself into the shape of a heron.

"My name is Himura. And I am the same as you."

The same as me.

Understanding hit her as hard as a sky whale. He was a Crafter. Kurara had never met another one before. Seeing him was like encountering a golden tiger. She was

33

excited to find someone like her. And fearful for what that might mean.

Before Himura could continue, someone gave an indignant shout.

"*Excuse me*, sir!" cried Haru. Kurara turned to see him marching across the room towards them.

Before he could reach them, something slammed into the floor above with a thunderous crash. The guests cried in a panic as the ground suddenly trembled beneath their feet.

Then the lights went out and the walls began to shake.

FOUR

THE *Midori* groaned. Kurara fought for balance as the ground tipped to one side. Emergency lights flickered on, bathing the walls blood red. Warning sirens wailed, their high-pitched screams echoing through her skull. Alarmed voices flit through the hall.

"What was that?"

"Did something hit the *Midori*?"

"If it's a cumulous whale, we're doomed!"

Someone pushed past her to brush aside the purple drapes covering the windows. Perhaps it really was a sky whale. Kurara could not imagine who would be bold enough to attack them. The *Midori* had plenty worth stealing, but the number of warships in their docks had always kept thieves at bay.

A flash of white darted through the sky, half hidden by clouds. Kurara caught nothing more than a flicker of a tail before something hit the *Midori* again, making the floor rock beneath her feet. Tremors raced down the walls.

"There! Did you see it?"

"No, it was too fast!"

Another blast shook the banquet hall, this one stronger than before. The ceiling above them split like an egg, bringing a rain of stone and broken wood crashing down. A heavy wardrobe slammed into the ground just inches from Kurara's feet. She scrambled out of the way as it vomited clothes across the floor. Placing a hand over her chest, she tried to calm her frantically beating heart.

"Everyone, leave! Get to the escape pods!" An attendant turned and ordered everyone out.

The entertainers ran for the door, screaming and shoving to be the first one out.

"We have to go!" Kurara hurried to Haru's side. The only thing on her mind was how to get them both to safety. There were not enough escape pods for everyone. They had to get to the docks before they were all gone.

"Wait!" The man – Himura – tried to stop her, but she ducked just out of reach.

The *Midori* shook again. Kurara ran out of the banquet hall, pulling Haru after her. The guests were clogging the grand staircases, but she had not lived aboard the *Midori* for so long without picking up a few shortcuts. Pushing past the tide of people heading in the opposite direction, she slipped through a side door and into the servants' corridor.

"What's going on? Who's attacking?" asked Haru as they dashed down the narrow hallways.

"I don't know," said Kurara, "but we have to go!"

The walls resounded with a deafening boom. The floor was shaking, the world trembling with every second that passed. Panic threatened to overwhelm her, but she pushed the feeling aside. If she gave in, it would drag her under.

"Rara." Haru squeezed her hand. He trembled with excitement. "It's *happening*!" he cried. "This is our chance to leave! We don't have to live the rest of our lives on the *Midori* any more. We can be free!"

Free. Kurara's heart quivered. *Or dead*.

———————o———————

The reception hall was packed with people scrambling for the exits. Plants lay trampled, the windows were shattered and mechanical birds smashed in the rush to escape. Wind howled through the broken windows so loudly that at first Kurara thought there was a monster inside the hall with them.

She could see flames climbing above them. Fat plumes of smoke curled around the top of the grand staircase and towards the pearl glass ceiling. It was only a matter of time before the heat and chaos would cause that ceiling to crack and the *Midori* to collapse.

Someone slammed into Kurara's shoulder, bringing her back to her body with a jolt. Haru reached for her so that they were not swept apart by the crowd, but before she could grab hold of his hand, someone else caught her and pulled her aside.

"Not that way." Himura stood behind her. "I saw an old qipak at the docks when I arrived. If we get there before someone else steals it, we can use it to escape."

His sudden appearance made Kurara jump. The man was as impossible to get rid of as an ink stain on tatami. She tried to shake him off, but his fingers were wrapped around her arm like a vice.

"Sir! Please leave and make your own way to the escape pods!"

Despite Haru's politely worded request, his tone was deep and threatening.

Another loud crash shook the *Midori* to its foundations. The floor above exploded in a shower of broken beams and marble tiles. The crowd screamed as the *Midori* began to tilt to one side.

Himura tightened his grip. "Listen, I will explain everything later. For now, just come with me. *Both* of you!"

"Hey! Wait!" Haru shouted in protest as he, too, was dragged through the crowd.

Ignoring their objections, Himura did not let them go until they reached the servants' staircase. The steps were so narrow they had to make their way down in single file: Himura in front, Kurara behind and Haru bringing up the rear.

There was no point trying to head back to the reception hall now. Kurara forced her legs to move as shadows made twisted shapes against the stone. The shuddering walls groaned.

"Are you afraid?" Haru's wrapped her hand in his, lacing their fingers together.

She did not want to think about whether she was frightened or not. The only thing on her mind was escaping.

Haru squeezed her fingers. "This time, I'll protect you," he promised.

This time? Kurara wondered, but she had no chance to ask. Something smashed through the wall, bringing part of the ceiling crashing down. Stone and dust showered over the steps.

Kurara looked up to see a pair of empty, white eyes staring down at her.

A dragon.

FIVE

KURARA blinked. This could not be real. The dragon stared at her. She stared back, frozen.

Its face was more fearsome than she could ever have imagined. Its alabaster scales and snow-white mane looked like an unfinished sculpture brought to life. Two long whiskers protruded from a snarling snout, sharper than any whip Kurara had ever seen. Its mouth could swallow small ships; its jaws could crush iron. The wind rushed through the broken ceiling, but its paper body held firm. Kurara's throat ran dry.

Not just a dragon. A shikigami.

It did not feel as if she was standing before a living creature, but rather in the path of a hurricane. Something tugged at Kurara's chest. Electricity prickled her skin and sent sparks running through her veins.

"Keep running!" shouted Himura.

The dragon gave a soundless snarl. Its claws pierced the walls, sending bits of stone tumbling past Kurara's head and bouncing down the steps.

"Consume, consume, consume."

A voice resonated inside her, from somewhere deep within her bones. The dragon. It was speaking and its words were inside her head.

"A dying star fell from the heavens, and from that star grew a tree. Humans will have your soul; they eat with their hearts."

Kurara clutched her head. She wanted it to stop. Its voice crashed against the walls of her mind like a creature trapped inside her skull. From the way Himura and Haru also winced, she knew that they could hear the beast speak as well.

The dragon stared at her. Its pupils were non-existent – its eyes were mere circles of white – yet she could feel the weight of its gaze. The scales across its body glinted. There was something beautiful in the construction of its segmented talons, the way the folds of paper cascaded over one another to form its body.

Was it possible to be terrified and enchanted at the same time?

Kurara waited for the moment it would strike, but a sound from above caught its attention. Scales rippling, the dragon launched itself upwards with such force that part of the stairs crumbled and Kurara was blown back into Haru's arms.

"Rara." Haru placed a hand on her shoulder, steadying

her. He looked just as shaken as she felt. "Are you OK?"

"She won't be if we stay here much longer. Keep moving!" Himura bellowed.

For just a second, Kurara caught a glimpse of the dragon again as it smashed through the wall above her and flicked out of sight. She took a step towards it before realizing what she was doing. Was she crazy? She was supposed to be running away from the shikigami, not towards it!

The dragon entered the reception hall. Kurara could hear it thrashing against the walls: metal crashing, glass breaking. Screams echoed down the stairwell.

She swallowed around the hard lump forming in her throat.

"Lead the way."

———————o———————

By the time they reached the docks, most of the ships were gone. Kurara's frantic gaze darted from one empty lot to the next. How were they going to escape?

"Over here!" Himura found the qipak he had spoken of. It was a wingless, brown, canoe-shaped craft, no bigger than a villager's wooden fishing boat, with metal guard rails. It looked barely sky-worthy. The blackened engine underneath the tail was ready to fall off, the sides were dented and the nose pointed slightly downwards, as if predicting the destination of anyone who dared to ride it. Flying out into the battle-torn sky on such a craft was like joining a war armed with the sheared-off edge of a can.

Another explosion caused the ground to shake. Himura started the engine. It ignited in a sudden burst of blue fire.

"We're going out there?" Haru pointed to the aircrafts zipping through the sky.

"On that thing?" said Kurara.

"Will it even fly?"

"Are you sure it won't kill us?"

"The dragon or the qipak?" Haru looked genuinely unsure.

Himura looked weary of their back and forth. "Just get on!"

Haru and Kurara exchanged uncertain glances. After a moment, Kurara crawled onto the qipak, placing herself behind Himura. It was a tight fit. The sides of the aircraft barely came up to her waist while the rest of her body felt dangerously exposed to the open air. Haru slotted himself between them. One hand gripped the guard rails, the other Kurara's hand.

Without warning, the engine suddenly propelled them forward. The qipak sped across the runway and launched itself out from under the *Midori*'s shadow, into a blinding dome of bright, blue sky.

The moment they took off, the dragon burst through the walls. The aircraft shot forward as the docks collapsed behind them. Metal plates and stone pillars crashed to the ground below as the dragon coiled itself around the *Midori*.

The qipak juddered. Kurara's head snapped forward as a pair of sleek white wings unfolded from beneath the craft and the propellers whirled to life, halting their descent.

"Rara, we're flying! We're really flying!" laughed Haru.

"You call this flying?" she cried as the engine spluttered. She was not sure who she was yelling at, Haru or Himura, but she knew that she never wanted to ride a qipak again.

Warships filled the sky in the heated dance of battle. The boom of cannons pulverized the air. Sleek kohanes sliced through the clouds, their wings bright red, as if warning other aircrafts to stay away. They swirled around the *Midori* like birds circling their prey as they opened fire.

The dragon roared as it was hit, but the blasts only seemed to irritate the beast. With a furious growl, it smashed into the *Midori* again, ducking inside where the larger battleships could not follow. Kohanes dived after it. With a snap that echoed through Kurara's bones, the dragon crashed through the bottom of the great banquet hall and then soared upwards, leaving the other ships far behind.

"Rara!" cried Haru.

The *Midori* was breaking apart, the iron structure moaning like some great lumbering beast. The remaining pearl glass shattered in rainbow showers and the docks crumbled. Debris plunged past the clouds: expensive clothes, folding screens, metal pots, shards of china. Steel wings showered over their heads. A rain of broken birds.

Kurara and Haru watched in silence. For years, the *Midori* had been everything. Their home and their cage. As permanent as the sun and as constant as the orbit of the moon.

Now it was crumbling before their very eyes.

It's gone. The realization was not as triumphant as Kurara had imagined. She was glad to see it go and yet it left her with a strange sense of emptiness.

Then something went *snap* behind her.

"Hey, Mister, are you sure you know how to fly this thing?" cried Haru.

Himura's only response was to grunt, but Kurara did not need to know anything about flying to realize there was something wrong with the way they were swooping towards the ground. She looked back. The engine was completely shot, spewing forth a thick black trail of smoke.

They were falling, plummeting past the greying clouds, and leaving the rage of battle far above them. Their descent was shuddery as the craft strained against the force of gravity. Kurara screamed and squeezed her eyes shut, blindly clinging to the guard rails as they plunged down towards the earth.

The qipak juddered and bucked. It skimmed the tops of the trees, throwing leaves into the air like confetti. For a moment, it rose a precious few inches, pushing upwards with renewed life.

Then the engine cut out entirely and gravity claimed them.

Haru shouted as his grip on Kurara's hand slipped. The tips of their fingers brushed against one another.

Then they were ripped apart.

SIX

THEY fell, crashing into the trees. Kurara was tossed out of the qipak. She tumbled down until the back of her dress caught on a low-hanging branch, yanking her to a halt.

The screech of fleeing birds rang in her ears as she dangled there, unable to move. For a moment, all she could feel was the heavy thump of her heart and the sound of her own breath rattling against her throat. Nothing was broken, but everything was sorely bruised.

I'm alive. The realization came as a surprise. Kurara was not sure she quite believed it.

She reached around her back to free herself, but her work dress was caught on the branch. Her fingers scrabbled against the bark until she exhausted herself enough that she resigned to dangling there, graceless and stupid, like a sky fish with its tail fins caught on a lightning rod.

Himura's qipak lay at a distance. Its engine whined like a dying animal. The sky beyond the trees blazed a vicious orange, and the escape pods were nowhere in sight. For a moment, Kurara was seized by the terrifying thought that everyone was dead. That she was alone in this dense, eerie forest.

Just as she was beginning to panic, something rustled in the bushes. A moment later, Haru emerged from behind the trees.

"Haru!" Kurara could not describe the flood of relief at seeing him unharmed. "Thank the Gods! Help me down!"

"Rara! You're not hurt, are you? Where's that guy?" Haru hurried forward, skirting around the smoking qipak. He jumped to reach her. The tips of his fingers skimmed hers, but he was not quite tall enough to pull her down.

"Himura? I don't know," she said. "I'm not sure if he's even still alive."

She hoped that he was. He was a Crafter after all – the first one she had ever met. There was so much she wanted to know. Why had he come to the *Midori*? What had Madam Ito told him? What had he meant when he asked her if she wanted to leave?

Haru sucked in a deep breath and released a small, disbelieving chuckle. "We did it, Rara. We're free! We can go to the Grand Stream! To Nessai Harbour! We're going to have so much fun!"

"Fun?" She shook her head in disbelief. They had been attacked. Their home had been destroyed. How could any of this be fun?

As if reading her thoughts, Haru's smile faltered. "Is it weird for me to be happy? I just saw our only home go down in flames. People are fighting. People are *dying*. Yet all I can think of is that now we don't have to spend the rest of our lives on the *Midori*. I know you don't remember it, but I always missed the ground. I missed the mountains where we were born. The lakes that would freeze over in winter."

As she did every time Haru mentioned something about their past, Kurara tried to remember, but it was as though there was a stone wall blocking her way every time. Haru's words stirred nothing inside her. Only a hollow echo where the missing parts of her memory should have been.

She looked around, taking in the ground for the first time. It was difficult to believe that they had truly fallen so far. Everything around her was so different from the stone kitchen and the clean, airy hallways that she knew. The dense smell of wood filled her nostrils. When she looked up, the sky was so distant.

Another loud rustle caught her attention. Someone was stomping through the forest, heading their way.

"Who's there?" Haru whipped around. As he did, Kurara caught a glimpse of the back of his head. An icy flood of horror surged in her chest. His head…

The back of Haru's skull was partially caved in, perhaps struck by a rock when he had landed. There was a hole at the back of his skull the size of her fist. Kurara could just about see the inside of his head, but there was nothing there. No brains, no blood, just white, empty space.

"There was a great big shaft of wood sticking through his chest. Almost went straight through his heart, it did. He was lucky to survive. Made of stronger stuff than most people." Madam Ito's voice floated through Kurara's mind.

"It was almost unnatural."

What in all of the blue skies was going on? Kurara's heart was hammering so hard she thought it would break her ribs.

"Haru!" Something in her gut was telling her to run before anyone found him like this.

The sound of footsteps came to an abrupt stop. Two dark figures emerged from beneath the trees. Their black uniforms made them look like shadows come to life. The gold decorations on their military caps and the chrysanthemum-shaped buttons of their high-collar jackets glinted beneath what little light pierced the trees.

"Who are you?" Haru shrank back.

The men had the same short haircuts, the same oiled moustaches, and the same disapproving frown. Both carried a large gun and a katana strapped at their waists.

"Watch your tongue, boy!" the man on the right snapped. "What are children like you doing alone in the woods – and with a battle going on right above your heads? This area is off limits. How did you sneak in?"

"We fell from the sky…" did not seem like an answer that would convince the men of their innocence. Kurara

wriggled, heart beating hard. She did not know what the soldiers would do if they saw Haru's injury, but she did not want to find out.

Before she could stop him, Haru glanced back at her. For a few seconds, the back of his head was exposed to the two soldiers.

The man on the left recoiled in horror. "Hey, look at the boy! His head!"

Both men leapt back in horror.

"The boy! Inside his head—it's p–paper!"

"A shikigami?"

Shikigami. The word echoed through Kurara's skull. That was impossible. Shikigami were paper monsters. Creatures that hurt innocent people. Haru was nothing like the dragon that had attacked them. Nothing like the beasts the servants and soldiers spoke of in hushed whispers.

With trembling hands, the man on the right drew his gun. The barrel was three times wider than a pistol, and there was a compartment at the top that hissed as he went to pull the trigger.

Kurara thrashed against the branch. Finally, she caught the back of her dress, ripping it free. She fell, hitting the hard earth with a painful thud.

"Haru!" She was on her feet in seconds.

A loud bang erupted from the man's gun. Kurara did not see the bullet, only the point where it struck Haru in the stomach, knocking him into the tree behind him with such force that the branches scattered leaves across the ground.

"Not that one! You have to use fire!" The man on the left shouted.

Haru stood up, clutching his stomach. Though his expression was pained, he was not bleeding.

"Haru!" Kurara ran for him.

One of the men pulled a match from his pocket. He struck it against the side of his gun, pushed the flame down the top compartment and fired.

Kurara was not sure what came first: the flames or Haru's screams. He dropped to the ground, rolling away from the tree. His arms flailed; his legs kicked out in pain. Flames licked furiously at his body. The smell was familiar. It was the same scent as when Kurara burned the love notes the servants did not want Madam Ito to find, the same as when she was ordered to set fire to all the books the Emperor had branded "unpatriotic".

The flames leapt higher. Haru's agonized wail rang through the trees.

"What are you doing?" All the rage and fear inside her burst from her lips. She screamed until her throat was ragged, until it felt flayed from the inside out.

The soldier who had fired looked at her with cold eyes. "What about that one?" he asked his comrade.

"Kill her too!"

Under the crackle of flames, Kurara swore she heard Haru croak: "Ku–Kurara. Run."

The man struck a match again and aimed his gun at her, but all Kurara knew was that she had to save Haru. She ran to him, throwing an arm over his body in hopes that she could smother the flames, but the moment she touched him, fire licked up her hand and down her elbow. Kurara screamed and jerked back, pressing her burning arm into the dirt until the flames were smothered and died.

"What are you doing? Don't wait! Fire!" cried the soldier.

The smell of smoke was suffocating. Kurara squeezed her eyes shut and waited for the bullet to pierce her chest. This was how she would die, trapped beneath the trees, unable to reach the sky. She would never go on those adventures she and Haru had promised each other, never see the Grand Stream or the sky cities or the hundreds of other places she had dreamed of. She would never go home.

It wasn't fair. She wanted to yell and beat her fists against the ground. This was all wrong.

The men screamed.

Kurara's eyes snapped open.

Himura towered over her, a giant stretching towards the sky. The two men lay on the ground, completely still. She didn't know if they were dead or unconscious. She didn't care.

"Well" – Himura surveyed the dying embers burning across the remains of Haru's blackened, ash-flecked limbs – "this is a mess."

SEVEN

KURARA scrambled to her feet, ignoring the pain that lanced down her arm. She stared in horror at what remained of Haru's body, her gaze stuttering over his broken mouth and the burn marks across his cheek. Like a cracked statue, part of his face had crumbled inwards, leaving deep fissures running across his skin. Only one eye remained. Though he still had both legs, half of his torso was gone, and his right arm was missing.

Kurara covered her mouth to hold back the scream building in her throat. She did not want to keep looking but she could not tear her eyes away either.

"He's a shikigami." Himura stood at a distance from her. His expression was taut, revealing nothing, but the pieces of paper floating in the air around him darted this way and that like restless wasps searching for something to sting. "This shouldn't be possible. I've seen shikigami as large as mountains and as long as rivers, but they've always taken animal forms. Like the dragon you saw – white and, well, papery. This is ... something I've only ever read about. There are old records about shikigami that appeared more human, but I never expected one to look so real."

"No, you're wrong!" Kurara wanted to shout. Haru was not a monster. He was her oldest friend. Her only friend.

"You didn't know?" said Himura. "I was under the impression that the two of you were close."

Kurara glared at him. "We *are* close."

No one else knew that Haru was afraid of fish because he found their eyes creepy. Or that he ate sweet rolls by sucking out the filling first. When they were young and still unused to the pounding sounds of the *Midori*'s engines, they would fall asleep holding hands. Haru could not be a shikigami. There were no secrets between them.

"Do you know where he was from? Anything about his past before he came to the *Midori*? Human-like shikigami were some of the oldest ever created. I never thought a shikigami like this still existed," said Himura. A sickening look of excitement danced across his face, filling Kurara with rage.

"Haru came from the same village as I did! We grew up together!" She furiously blinked back her tears. She was not going to cry here, not in front of someone who was treating Haru like a particularly fascinating relic.

Like a thing.

"So you don't know anything about him." Himura sounded so disappointed she wanted to punch him. "Come here. Look."

He crouched to the side of Haru's body. Kurara did not move. She couldn't. Her legs were boneless, trembling as though she were holding up the entire world. It was only when Himura made an impatient gesture that she forced herself to take a slow, painful step forward.

Inside the cavity of Haru's torso, imitation organs pulsated, beating without any blood pumping through them. Muscles like puppet strings lay attached to the inside of his otherwise hollow limbs. Greenish bile settled in the concave of what was probably his stomach. In the centre of his chest, where his heart should have been, was a discoloured ball of paper covered in dark red lines that wove together to form strange patterns and symbols.

Kurara covered a hand over her mouth. She was going to be sick.

"What you see in there," said Himura, "is the shikigami's core. Imagine it as the brain and the heart wrapped into one."

Kurara did not know what to say. Was that really Haru? Could all those memories, his dreams, the colour of his hair, the gap between his teeth and the way he smiled be reduced down to a simple, tatty ball of paper?

Haru's eye fluttered. For a moment, there was some life in it.

"Rara…" The sound that came from his throat was dry and painful, like he might tear something if he spoke above a whisper. "I–I don't feel good."

"I'm here." With trembling fingers, Kurara touched the burned side of his face, running her thumb over the curve of his eye socket. The skin on the left side was normal, but the right side felt like running her hands over dried leaves. A piece of Haru broke off between her fingers. When she looked at her palm, it was covered in ash and fragments of crumbled paper.

She bit down on her lip to stop herself from throwing up.

"Rara!" Haru's body surged into life, and he gripped her arm so tight she thought he would break it. He could not lift his head to look at her, but his remaining eye turned to stare at her in panic. "The mountains where we lived. The villagers… You asked me to get rid of them!"

"What? Get rid of what? Who? What are you talking about?" Panic whipped a hurricane inside Kurara's chest.

Haru shook his head back and forth. A low, keening sound escaped his lips as his lungs failed him. His shoulders crumbled, clothes sagging. Kurara screamed. She grabbed hold of his kimono, trying to hold on to him as his body collapsed into a mound of ash on the gloomy forest floor.

Deep, deep inside her, she felt something break. It was a small thing. Something she might not have noticed had she not been acutely aware of everything around her in that moment. She did not know what it was, except that she would never be able to fix it ever again.

———————o———————

Someone asked her to stand. The voice sounded so very distant, as if calling out to her from beneath a vast ocean.

"We should go." Himura gestured to the ash on the ground and the bodies of the two soldiers. "After that dragon attack, there will be more soldiers combing these woods for survivors. You don't want them to discover this mess, do you?"

Kurara looked at him with fury. Anger ripped through her like a storm. Her ankle throbbed and her arm felt as though it were still on fire, but she lunged at him anyway, pounding her fists against his chest, hoping to hurt him, hoping that he could feel an ounce of what she was feeling right now.

"You!" she screamed. "This is your fault! Why couldn't you have come sooner? Why didn't you save him?"

Himura said nothing. He only grabbed her wrists and held them until her rage seeped away, leaving her hollow.

"I don't understand," she sobbed. "What am I supposed to do now?"

She was swallowing needles. Every breath was like drinking kerosene.

Himura bent down to retrieve Haru's core from the lump of ash. "I understand your feelings better than you know. I, too, have watched shikigami burn. It is always a shame. The knowledge of how to make more shikigami has been lost for years. What a waste."

"Waste?" cried Kurara. Haru was not a *thing* accidentally thrown out with the trash. Stains on a silk kimono, ink spilled over a carefully composed haiku: *they* were a waste. Haru was a person. The only person that had ever meant anything to her.

"There really is no need to get upset. As long as you still have its core, you can always revive a shikigami."

Kurara froze. Cruel hope pierced her heart.

"If you can make a body, you can slot in the core – like fitting an old engine into a new qipak. Like giving a hermit crab a new shell. It is only the core that is important. No one knows how to make more cores, but bodies are a different matter."

"Then you can..."

"Not I." Himura shook his head, bitterly. "I could make a paper body easily enough, but making one that will work with a shikigami core is no easy task. The only person who can help you now is Princess Tsukimi."

"The Emperor's daughter?" Kurara was shocked. According to the soldiers, Princess Tsukimi was self-absorbed and arrogant. She spent all her time on monstrous experiments, trying to turn children into shikigami or summoning spirits with the blood of her maids. The thought of the princess helping her was as absurd as it was terrifying. Like a rabbit asking a tiger for help.

Himura placed Haru's core into Kurara's open palm. Though it was no doubt made of paper, it was as hard and smooth as a piece of bone that had been polished down into a perfect sphere.

"Princess Tsukimi is an expert in shikigami. Her library holds the world's largest collection of records – books only the royal family are allowed to view," he added bitterly.

"And why would she help me?"

A strange look crossed Himura's face: amused yet bitter, curious but sad.

"Because you're a Crafter," he said. "The Princess is like a kitsune, fickle and unpredictable. You don't know if she'll bless you or bite your head off. There are only two things that can command her attention: shikigami and Crafters. *Strong* Crafters. With some training, you might be powerful enough to catch her attention. I've met Princess Tsukimi once. I know what pleases her. I can help you."

Kurara was not sure what to make of his boast. The *Midori* had taught her to be wary of those who offered help. There was always a catch. No one ever did something for nothing. "You're offering your help? What do you want in return?" she asked.

"Let's make a deal," said Himura.

"A deal?" Kurara clutched her left arm close.

A thin line of smoke erupted from the broken qipak lying a few feet away. Himura gave it an experimental kick. The engine rattled ominously. Frowning, he pushed it upright and began to wheel it out of the clearing.

"If we stay here, we will only run into more soldiers. Let's talk about this somewhere safer."

"Wait! Where are you going?" Kurara staggered to her feet.

Himura glanced back at her. The shadows of leaves danced across his face.

"To the capital," he said. "Are you not coming?"

EIGHT

THE wheels of the broken qipak squealed as Himura hauled it towards the capital. His mind was buzzing. He had left his airship expecting to find a Crafter. What he had found instead was a dragon, a shikigami in the shape of a human and a girl with only a passing understanding of the outside world.

He glanced at Kurara. The girl stared at the ground in front of her. She did not cry, but her eyes were red-rimmed. She was dead on her feet, walking only through sheer determination.

Her mind was probably spinning with all sorts of thoughts. Was it possible to grow up alongside someone without knowing that they were a shikigami?

I didn't know, either, thought Himura.

He might not have known the boy, but Himura was an experienced Crafter. He should have noticed that there was something off about Kurara's "friend", something inhuman.

The lights of Tomuri grew closer. Himura took a square of paper from his bracelet. Balancing it on the nose of the qipak, he made it spin. Bitterly, he wondered if Princess Tsukimi would have been surprised by the boy. With her library of ancient writings, would she have immediately recognized him for what he was?

"You said something about a deal." Kurara scrubbed the back of her arm across her face.

The piece of paper on the tip of the qipak spun faster and faster. Himura was feeling restless. His entire world had tilted sideways, upended, all thanks to a single boy made of paper, but he still had a job to do and a Crafter to recruit.

"I'm with a hunting ship. We need another Crafter for a shikigami hunt."

"Shikigami?" Kurara's expression shuttered.

"Ah, do not misunderstand," said Himura. "Not like your friend. Shikigami like the dragon you saw before. The ones that hurt people. You spent a lot of time among soldiers, yes? You know that the military is putting all their efforts into colonizing Estia and the war there is dragging on. They don't have the time or expertise to take care of rogue beasts. That's where hunters come in. We hunt shikigami and the military pays us for their cores – proof of a successful hunt."

Kurara's expression remained sceptical. "So ... you want me to hunt?"

"Do you know how hard it is to find a Crafter these days? Most are either employed by the imperial family or the military, or they're damned hermits living on the tops of mountains eating nothing but foxtail millet and running at the first trace of another person. You" – the paper dancing on top of the qipak turned to point at Kurara – "are the first Crafter we've found in months."

The qipak gave a loud groan. Himura glanced down to check the fuel tank was not leaking. The land outside Tomuri was nothing but yellow grassland, scorched by the summer heat and dry as a tinder-box.

"We have a big hunt coming up. We need another Crafter to fight. It doesn't matter if you can't even make a paper crane; I'll train you. You help us complete the hunt, and I will take you to Princess Tsukimi and ensure that you get at least an audience with her."

Kurara sucked in a deep breath. The girl did not have many options. Where would she go if not with him? It would be better to stick together. Himura knew all too well how dangerous the world was when one had no money or friends to rely on.

"The princess is staying at the summer palace on Sola-Il right now. She's been banished there until winter after she burned down one of the Emperor's mansions."

"Why did she do that?"

Himura shrugged. "Rumour has it that she was burning the evidence from an experiment gone wrong. Folks say she was trying to create a shikigami and ended up making something monstrous. Whatever the truth is, that's none of our concern. My point is that if things go well, you'll meet her before the summer is out. I'll turn you into a Crafter so capable she won't refuse to see you."

There was a steely, determined gleam in Kurara's eye. "If that's what I have to do to save Haru, I'll do it."

Himura smiled. Flicking the square of paper off the qipak, it spun through the air before looping around him and merging back into his bracelet.

———————o———————

The Mikoshiman flag fluttered above grey walls as the capital finally came into view. Tomuri was a city that was constantly expanding. It had grown even larger since Himura had last seen it, transforming into a vast behemoth that consumed the surrounding countryside.

As the guards waved them through the gate, Kurara's expression transformed from awed to queasy. Himura tried to remember his first visit to Tomuri; how he had felt the first time he had seen the bird-shaped cable cars slicing the sky, the streets aglow with electric lights, the paved roads and crowded market stalls. Everything about the capital was big and bright and loud. Overwhelming for a girl who had lived most of her life inside a floating cage.

The breeze was warm, coloured by the searing smell of fried noodles and soy, overripe fruit and the faint whiff of sewage. The sounds of people singing and laughing carried through the air. Just looking at the overflowing streets, one would never have guessed that the *Midori* had come crashing down barely a few miles away. Their merriment felt inappropriate. Insensitive even. Himura wanted to usher Kurara away from the main streets as quickly as possible.

You have only known her a few hours and you're already feeling protective, a small, critical voice inside his head needled at him. But who could blame him? He had not met another Crafter for so long. She was one of his people.

Himura pushed the qipak past stalls selling rice cakes in ornate lacquer boxes and through litter-strewn side streets.

Shopkeepers gossiped as Himura passed them by. "A shikigami! And so close to the city too! You know, I heard that Princess Tsukimi keeps shikigami chained up in the abandoned mines. Maybe it was one of her projects."

"She's dabbling with things she should leave well alone. Why doesn't she join Prince Ugetsu on the front lines in Estia instead of trying to make monsters? Do something useful for a change!"

Himura decided not to warn them of the soldiers lingering a few paces away. He led Kurara past the last of the stalls. War posters were plastered all over the walls of the city – pictures of handsome soldiers fighting grotesque, demon-like creatures, proclaiming in large red letters: *Do your bit for the empire!* More were stuck to the outside of shop windows. A man dressed in a military uniform patted the head of a weeping orphan above the caption: *The Emperor is father to us all!*

Pictures of Prince Ugetsu beamed at them from the poles of gas-lit street lamps, his moustache finely oiled and his smile as gleaming as the polished buttons of his uniform. A true golden child. It was too bad the prince would never match Tsukimi's intelligence. Perhaps that was why the Emperor had not yet named his successor. It took more than winning battles and looking gallant to rule an empire.

Himura remembered the first time he had seen Prince Ugetsu and Princess Tsukimi together. The only time. Hurrying past the cherry-tree-lined courtyard of Tomuri Castle, hoping not to be spotted, he had caught just a glimpse of the pair. He remembered the way they spoke to each other, each word digging needles beneath nails, searching for a weakness they could prise open with a sharp retort.

He shut off his thoughts before they could continue. Himura did not want to follow that memory. He knew where it led. Dragging the qipak along, he continued past the gates of Western-style manors so large and imposing they looked like explosions of brick and wood erupting from the earth. On the corner of a crossing, the burned-down husk of a building lay smeared with waste, leaving only a half-broken sign that read, *Sorabito cultural exchange*.

"Here we are."

Not far from that burned-down building stood Peacock Blue. It was the only inn Himura ever stayed at when he was in Tomuri. Despite its name, the building was neither blue nor did it look anything like a peacock. It stood in the middle of a narrow street on the outskirts of Tomuri like a sagging cake. The raising blocks had cracked on one side so that the inn stood at a tilt, the doors were battered by the wind and the clay tiles on the roof slipped dangerously, splitting onto the ground in sharp fragments that bit into Himura's shoes. The windows on the bottom floor were all boarded shut.

Kurara stared up at the inn with pinched concern. "This place looks like…" Himura was sure that she was looking for a polite alternative to "a rubbish dump" or "a pit for demons and criminals" – though both were fair assessments.

He had reacted the same way at first, though he had soon come to appreciate the brutal honesty of a place like this. Most inns in Tomuri would charge an arm and a leg for watery miso soup, a futon full of bed bugs, and servants that tattled to the military police. Here, it didn't matter if you were a Crafter, a king or a thief. You could keep your head down and go about your business at Peacock Blue.

Leaving the qipak outside, Himura stepped onto the tilted porch. The woman who greeted them had a hoarse, breathless voice. Wisps of black hair fell from a loose bun to frame her thin, sunken face. Painted flowers bloomed over her eyelids, each petal dotted with a white centre.

"A bird, a meal and a room," he ordered.

"Money." The woman held out a skeletal hand.

Reaching into his breast pocket, Himura pulled out a pouch full of coins and dropped it into her hand. The woman disappeared for a moment and returned shortly with a large, silver crow on her shoulder and a grease pencil in her hand.

The gears on the bird's neck and the bolts on its wings creaked when it moved, threatening to fall apart. It was an old model, definitely not worth the price he had paid, but his airship was not far. It would last the short trip.

Taking a piece of paper from his bracelet, Himura scribbled a quick message. The leg compartment sprang open after some fiddling. He input the coordinates of the ship and released the bird into the night, carrying a single message:

We arrive tomorrow. Be ready.

Interlude

We are of stardust,
Forged and formed from the heavens;
Universe made flesh.

— Sorabito chant

Kazeno Rei was in his natural habitat. Peacock Blue was an inn run by scoundrels and patronized by fellow crooks. He hated the ground, but places like this were not so different from those he frequented on the sky cities. Plastered remains of rotting posters papered the walls – war posters, torn-down eviction notices and adverts for airship parts. The smell of smoke was overwhelming. Men huddled around the card tables, hissing when they lost and chuckling beneath their breath when they won as if afraid a loud noise would make the whole place collapse on top of them.

"Sir, are you going to order something?"

Rei glanced up at the frowning waitress standing by

 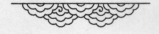

his table. The plum blossom tattoo covering half her face was ruined by her pinched expression. She looked one bad customer away from punching someone in the nose.

"A glass of tenmori-shu," said Rei.

The waitress scrunched up her face in disgust. "That's a Sorabito drink. We don't sell cheap sky-dweller trash here."

Rei raised an eyebrow. "I thought you could buy anything in the capital."

"Not sky-dweller trash."

"Do you know how tenmori-shu is made? Tenmori flowers only grow on the bottom of the sky cities, on the underside of the levitation plates that hold up the entire city. Men tie ropes around their waists and sail down the outside of the city to get them. They hand-pick the flowers while dangling seven hundred feet in the air."

The waitress shrugged, unimpressed. "Order something or get out."

Rei pulled his lips back, baring his teeth in what was arguably a smile. "A bottle of nigori then. And two cups. I'm expecting company."

The woman disappeared and came back a moment later with two barely clean cups and a clay bottle of cloudy liquid. Pouring himself a drink, Rei sniffed at the alcohol suspiciously.

"She didn't spit in it, but she *did* mix it with falcon weed. Just enough to give you an awful case of the runs," said a voice behind him.

Rei did not jump, but his body froze for just a moment.

Pushing the bottle away, he swivelled around.

The old woman standing before him did not look out of place amid the smoke. In fact, she looked exactly like the kind of eerie spectre that would haunt somewhere as run-down as this. Her face was such a mass of wrinkles it was difficult to tell where each began and ended. Though she wore a long, heavy, black cloak over her kimono, when she moved her arm, Rei could see a grotesque belt of paper hands slung around her waist, the fingers grabbing the wrists of the hand in front of it.

Despite the woman's frightful appearance, Rei relaxed. "Don't scare me like that, Inui."

When the woman cackled, it sounded like the wind rattling through hollow bones. She enjoyed the chilling effect her laughter had on people far too much.

A demon. The thought passed through Rei's head as he looked at her. Though those creepy paper hands were not moving right now, he knew that all Inui needed to do was think it and they would wrap around a man's throat.

"Greetings, O mighty leader of the sky people. How are you enjoying the capital?" asked Inui.

Rei frowned. She was making fun of him again. The only thing he was the leader of was Sohma – a ragtag group of rebels fighting for the sky cities' freedom from the empire. He was hardly the ruler of all the skies, though sometimes he did dream of it.

"Tomuri is dirty and noisy and the people are stupid. I wish I had never agreed to meet you on the ground," he grumbled.

Inui chuckled. "Did you like the dragon? It was useful, wasn't it? Why, I don't think the *Midori* lasted more than ten minutes."

Rei's eyes darted around the tavern. Though their corner table was blocked from most prying eyes by a wooden column holding up the ceiling, he wanted to make sure that no one was listening before he spoke.

"It was more destructive than I thought," he said.

Inui took a seat opposite Rei. "The *Midori* was a good test. A floating structure just like a sky city. And an awful lot like Princess Tsukimi's summer palace."

Rei snorted. Smoke wove around the dark silhouettes of the other drinkers. His fingers twitched with the urge to reach for his own pipe, but he had promised his wife he would quit. Besides, his girls were always telling him how awful the smell was, how it stained his teeth.

"Are you sure about this plan?" he asked. "It seems a bit … excessive. Releasing a shikigami just to murder one person."

Even if that person was Princess Tsukimi, she was still a mere human. Setting a shikigami on her felt like crushing a grasshopper with a mountain. Rei was not normally one to care, but the summer palace was located on a sky city. *His* city. He would prefer to use a less destructive manner of assassination.

Inui chuckled. "Murder is such an ugly word. Princess Tsukimi doesn't hide her obsessions. Rumour is that she keeps feral shikigami for experiments. If she ends up dying at the claws of one, I'm sure no one would dare use

 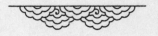

such a horrid term as "murder". No, it will just be a little … accident."

"Is that what Prince Ugetsu said?"

Inui beamed at him.

Rei ran a finger around the edge of his empty cup. If the prince wanted his sister dead, that was fine by him. He hoped they both died. This fight over who would inherit the throne was nothing more than a squabble between two spoiled brats.

But Prince Ugetsu promised that he would give the sky cities their independence. Once Princess Tsukimi is dead, Prince Ugetsu will have a clear path to the throne. And once he's crowned Emperor, he will grant the Sorabito freedom.

After years of struggle, Rei had grown Sohma from a handful of angry young men into a network of rebels ready to lay down their lives for the sky cities. Yet for all the riots and assassinations, the empire continued to grow like a weed that spread across the land. At least Prince Ugetsu promised real change and, if the assassination of his sister went smoothly, one less royal brat in the world.

Inui's lips curled into a yellow-toothed smile. "Don't forget that only a Crafter can hope to control a shikigami. I got it back in one piece after the *Midori* and I'll be around to make sure it behaves. At least, until you leave for Sola-Il."

"And what do you get in return?" asked Rei.

"When I became an imperial Crafter, I was not allowed to choose who I would serve. I much prefer Prince Ugetsu and yet I was assigned to the princess. That insufferable

brat! She treats her Crafters like toys. I would be happy to see her dead." The paper hands on Inui's belt wriggled their fingers.

Rei wondered if that was the truth. Inui did not seem like the kind of person who was easily swayed by petty grudges. He sat back with a scowl. It didn't really matter, as long as he had full control of the assassination plan. He was no one's puppet and he would march to no one's beat but his own.

"You're betraying your master? If you hate her so much, kill her yourself," he said.

"Now why would I take that risk?" Inui's smile was a sharp, pointed thing. "For an assassination to work, there must be an assassin. And people who assassinate imperial brats seldom live very long. This shikigami attack is perfect. Everyone knows about her experiments to create more shikigami. No one would bat an eyelid if she were to die, the victim of one of her own research subjects."

So she and Prince Ugetsu were leaving it to him to do the dirty work. That was fine. He did not care if Inui stayed to help, or to report his actions back to Prince Ugetsu. Rei was used to skulking in the shadows with blood on his hands.

Inui started to stand up when something behind him caught her attention. Rei tensed. He did not look back, but his hand reached for the katana by his waist.

"What?"

"Crafters." She nodded as two guests walked into the inn. A young man and a girl.

"You can tell?"

"I can always recognize my own kind."

Rei turned to watch the pair move through the room. The girl was quite young, perhaps the age of his eldest daughter. He sometimes forgot that Crafters were born and went through childhood like any other human being, rather than just bursting into existence fully formed and capable of slicing a man in two with an envelope.

When Rei was in charge, he would make sure such dangerous people were kept out of the sky cities. The groundlings too. He would rid Sola-Il of all manner of filth. For the glory of the Sorabito, he would do whatever he had to.

"When we have our independence, the sky cities will be a place for my people and my people alone," he muttered. "The groundlings living in the sky can leave or they can die."

Inui laughed. "Do you think the prince cares? Get him what he wants and you can have what *you* want."

NINE

KURARA awoke with her face pressed against the pillow of an old, musty futon. It was so quiet, she could not hear the rumbling of the *Midori*'s engines. Panic seized her. She pitched herself onto her elbows, heart beating fast. Why had the morning bell not rung? Was she late for her shift? She had pots to scrub, heaps of laundry to wash. Madam Ito was going to be furious when she…

Slowly, her vision adjusted to the darkness. Panic ebbed away as her memory returned and the dull, brown walls of the inn blinked into focus. The attack, the shikigami, Himura. Her thoughts tumbled over each other, refusing to leave her alone. The *Midori* was gone. This was Tomuri. She had followed Himura to an inn and fallen asleep as soon as he had set out the futons in their room.

She had watched Haru burn.

Kurara drew a deep, ragged breath and slowly pressed the heels of her palms over her eyes until her heart stopped sounding like a war drum. Though she had never liked her life on the *Midori*, at least she had always known what to expect. There had been a measure of comfort in that. Here, she did not know what the future would bring. What if she could not save Haru? What if she never became skilled enough as a Crafter to impress the princess? What if she did and Princess Tsukimi refused to see her anyway?

What if Haru remained nothing but a paper core inside her pocket?

She shook her head. If she thought about it, she would break, and if she broke, she would be useless, and useless girls were thrown off ships. She had to keep her worries at bay, or else her mind would turn and turn, spinning a web that trapped her inside it.

She was going to save Haru. There was no time for pain.

Grabbing the sheets, Kurara froze. Looking down at her left arm, she knew that something was wrong. The fire had left her skin scarred and numb. She could not feel a thing. Even when she spread the fingers of her left hand over her pillow, she could not feel the hard stuffing.

On the other side of the room, Himura gave a loud yawn. Kurara startled, pulling down the sleeve of her dress to hide her injury. She did not want him to worry about it. Any time spent fussing over her was time they could use to help Haru.

Dressed in a washed-out, brown kimono and a slightly oversized, navy-blue hakama, Himura sat by the window with his legs crossed and arms folded. Dust danced in the weak rays of light breaking through the dirty window, falling gently over his lap.

Kurara was not sure what to make of him now that her thoughts weren't fighting for space beneath the panic of fleeing a sinking *Midori* and the horror of Haru burning. She did not know how far she could trust him, but she did not have a lot of better options.

When she stood up, aches and pains from the previous day curled along her spine. Her shoulders felt stiff and her neck sore from the hard pillow. Seeing her awake, Himura got to his feet.

"Good morning. How do you feel?"

Kurara paused. A close examination of her emotional state felt rather perilous at the moment.

"Like I slept on a rock," she said.

Himura huffed and flung an old, yellowish kimono at her. It hit her in the face. A small pouch poked out from between the folds of the clothes.

"Come downstairs and eat something. I've ordered breakfast." He slipped past her and out of the room.

Kurara dressed and tucked Haru's core into the pouch, which she tied to her obi. The ground floor of the inn was cold and uninviting. The stench of dying smoke hung thick in the air. As promised, breakfast was on the counter. The rice balls were soggy and held together by a limp sheet of seaweed, but she was so hungry she swallowed the first in two bites before quickly polishing off the rest.

Himura was outside, tinkering with the qipak's engine. Caught in the early hours of the morning, the world was frozen in grey light. The streets were so quiet that the sound of Himura unscrewing the qipak's pipes seemed to echo for miles. His bracelet knocked against the metal as he worked. Though it looked like polished bone, Kurara knew that it was made of paper.

"Curious?" He lifted his bracelet to his face when he caught her staring at it. "It's easier than lugging around stacks of paper. And it doesn't make people panic. People get jittery around Crafters. We possess powers normal folk don't understand."

"I don't want people to be afraid of me." Kurara lowered her eyes. She knew what it was like to live like a mouse hoping not to be noticed, folding oneself like origami for fear of taking up too much space.

Himura was not listening. With a grunt, he pulled something out of the engine. The vehicle jerked and the motor gasped before settling into a healthy hum.

"There." He wiped the sweat from his brow and gestured for her to get on.

Kurara gingerly clambered onto the back of the qipak, half convinced that the sky-forsaken thing would just fall apart again, but when Himura kicked it into gear the qipak moved without protest.

Engine purring, the craft picked up speed. The city blurred past her – the lights, the buildings, the columns of steam from trains whistling away. The qipak raced over bridges, beneath the shadows of floating gardens and out of the city gates. Kurara breathed a sigh of relief. They were finally leaving.

As soon as they were free of the city, Himura pulled

the qipak's levers and the wings unfolded from beneath its belly with a rusty screech. The vehicle rose, lifting away from the ground. He reached into the inner pocket of his kimono and pulled out a small flare. Holding it above his head, he fired it into the sky. It arched like a shooting star, bursting into a cloud of coloured smoke high above their heads.

For a moment, there was nothing. Then, slowly, Kurara heard the churning of a ship's engines. Her eyes watered as she peered into the blustery sky. A dark shadow emerged from the clouds, descending upon them like the belly of a whale.

Kurara had seen plenty of airships before, but they had all been military vessels – cliffs of steel that bulled their way through the air by the sheer power of their levistone engines. This was different. This was a ship built not for war but for speed, its sleek hull and tilted red sails designed to slip through the air like a blade cutting through silk.

Someone had painted the ship's name in yellow, next to a thick blob that was most likely a shooting star. Though most of the ship was wooden, the deck was made up of a quilt of different coloured metals nailed together. A battering ram lay strapped to the prow. Twin masts formed an inverted V-shape that stretched at an angle from one end of the vessel to the other. Cannons peeked out from square windows. It was a beautiful vessel, the kind she wished she could show Haru.

With a stomach-lurching drop, the qipak landed gracelessly on the deck. Kurara dismounted. Her gaze travelled upwards to the command tower looming over them. A set of steps that led from the deck to a small balcony halfway up the tower and a square hatch on the floor were the only points of entry into the ship. There was no sign of anyone watching them from the lookout, and she could not see anything past the dark windows of the wheelhouse, but there had to be people about keeping the ship airborne.

"Mr Himura! Back at last!" a voice bellowed. The balcony door flew open with a bang.

Himura whipped around as a man walked down the metal staircase.

A *Sorabito*. Kurara drew a sharp breath. Taller, slimmer and more graceful than their fellow earth-bound humans, Sorabito were the descendants of the very first people who had built the sky cities. This was her first time seeing one – Sorabito were not welcome on the *Midori* – but she had heard all about them. The servants said that they imitated birds and sewed feathers beneath their arms to create real wings. Others claimed that the nails on their feet were as hard as talons, but all agreed that the Sorabito were not quite all there in the head. Too much time in the air made clouds grow in their brains. More sky in their veins than blood.

The man spread his arms wide in welcome. He was willowy and angular, as though constructed from something sharp, with dark eyes and a mouth that curved into an evasive smile.

"Himura, good to see you on time for once. We got your message." He sounded younger than he looked.

A loose, twilight-coloured kimono hung open around the collar, revealing his bare chest.

"Well, thank you for such a warm welcome." Himura did not sound grateful at all. He waved a hand in Kurara's direction. "Let me introduce you. This is Kurara."

Turning to her, the man stared at her through piercing, coal-black eyes. He bowed.

"Welcome, welcome, young one! You may call me Captain Sakurai. A pleasure to make your acquaintance, Miss Kurara. Himura told you all about us, did he?"

"I know that you hunt shikigami."

But not like Haru. Only the bad ones, she reminded herself. Like the dragon that had attacked the *Midori*.

Sakurai's laughter was like a military-grade cannon. "Only the dangerous ones. The army has no time to be chasing around monsters so we do it for them. We hunt shikigami and then sell the cores to the military. It's a profitable business. If you're good at it."

"And are you good at it, sir?" Kurara's question carried a sharp edge. On the *Midori*, she would have controlled her tone. On the *Midori*, she would not have asked any questions at all. But this was not her old home and the part of her that was still raw and hurting was tired of twisting herself around other people's feelings.

Far from being angry, Sakurai's face lit up. His chest puffed out a little. "The best in the seven sky cities," he said.

Kurara wondered about that. She was used to men bragging.

"It's good to have you back." Sakurai turned to address Himura. "I heard about what happened to the *Midori*."

He glanced kindly at Kurara. She looked away. She did not want Sakurai's pity.

"We barely made it out," said Himura. "Some assistance would have been appreciated."

"Ha! You think the military would appreciate a *Sorabito* interfering?" Sakurai's tone was friendly but his eyes were unyielding. "Anyway, come with me and I'll get you settled. Oh, and Miss Kurara?"

He paused at the foot of the steps to smile at her.

"Welcome aboard the *Orihime*."

TEN

PEOPLE were staring at her. Although she couldn't see them, Kurara could feel them hovering around the edges of her vision. Like mice, they would dart out of sight whenever she turned her head. Surely, Himura and Captain Sakurai noticed them, too, though they said nothing and continued to lead her through the ship.

The passageways reminded Kurara of the narrow hallways that the servants would use to get around the *Midori*: clean, functional and flooded by the sharp brightness of electric lights. The wooden walls were warped here and there and the floor was probably a duller colour than it had been years ago, but the corridors were easy to move through.

While they walked, the *Orihime* began to rise. The ground fell away and the clouds moved to curtain her view.

Kurara pressed her hand over the pouch that held Haru's core, squeezing it tight. She had been on the ground for such a short time, but she was glad to be back in the sky if it brought her one step closer to getting Haru's body back.

Sakurai opened the doors to the mess hall. Now *this* was different. On the *Midori*, the servants ate whatever leftovers remained after the guests had finished, feasting on scraps inside empty banquet halls. Here, a food counter with a tray dispenser sat near the door to the kitchens. Chairs stood neatly tucked beneath rows of long metal tables that gleamed in the light.

At the far end of the room, a handful of the ship's crew sat huddled in conversation. More Sorabito. The men were dressed in simple, starched shirts tucked behind the waistbands of their hakama. The women's clothes were a similar jumble; their kimono cut short at the hips and the bottom part replaced by skirts so that their legs could move freely, leather boots tapping at the floor. Their obi looked more like belts – a wide sash of leather that clipped on easily. Kurara was surprised to see any women at all. The soldiers that visited the *Midori* insisted that flying with women would bring bad luck.

The group stood to attention when Sakurai approached.

"At ease." Sakurai waved a hand. "Himura has returned, as you can see. Let us push off. Kenji, find Ichiro and tell him there's a qipak on deck that needs to be dragged down to the hangar. No, better yet, tell him to scavenge it for parts. I have dead relatives that are more sky-worthy than that thing. Momo, go with him."

He watched with satisfaction as his crew darted away to do his bidding. Turning, he searched the rest of the crew for a face. When he did not find it, he frowned.

"Where's Sayo? I told her to be here."

A murmur rose through the crew, silenced only when Sakurai gave them a stern look.

"Tomoe!" His eyes landed on someone at the back, and his face lit up with a smile that promised mischief. "Come here, Tomoe!"

The crew shuffled aside as a girl pushed her way to the front. She was about Kurara's age. At a glance, there was nothing remarkable about her face – her broad nose and almond-shaped eyes would not have made anyone pause – but her hair was a colour Kurara had never seen before. It was deep red, plaited all the way to the bottom of her shoulder blades. Beneath the light, it shone like a river on fire. It had to be dyed, though Kurara did not know what kind of plant could produce such a vibrant colour.

Like the others, the girl wore a modified kimono with the bottom half cut short. A green skirt, pleated and hemmed with white lace, fell to her knees. The strip of bare flesh from ankle to knee was somewhat scandalous. The very sight would have given Madam Ito fits.

Kurara forced herself to look elsewhere, at the top half of Tomoe's pale blue kimono, lighter at the shoulders and steadily growing darker near her waist, and the bright patterns running down her clothes. Birds, birds, and more birds. The Sorabito had an obsession with them. Tomoe's sleeves were painted with sparrows flying between red maple leaves. White doves covered her clip-on obi. A small sheath, etched with crane wings, held a knife close to her side.

Sakurai clapped her on the back. "Kurara, this is Kazeno Tomoe. One of our engineers."

"The *best* engineer." The girl's voice possessed a strange lilt that made her conversation sound almost like a song.

"Tomoe, in Sayo's absence, please give Miss Kurara the tour." Sakurai allowed the girl's boast to go unchallenged.

Tomoe stared at Kurara with a look of pure glee. She dipped her head in greeting. "Welcome, welcome to the madhouse! Kazeno Tomoe, at your service! We of the *Orihime* salute you for having the guts and the stupidity to join our little crew!"

"Kurara. The pleasure is mine, Miss Kazeno." Kurara did not know what else to say. Madam Ito had said that Sorabito were blunt – "*crude and ill-mannered*" were her exact words – but nothing had quite prepared her for this.

"Oh, you don't have to call me Kazeno," said Tomoe. "We Sorabito have city names instead of family names. I was born on Sola-Re, so that makes me a Kazeno. And everyone else who is born in that city also takes the name Kazeno. That's the Sorabito way, you know."

Kurara had not known. Everything she knew about the world came through the filter of servants' gossip and the only things they had told her about the Sorabito were not worth repeating in polite company.

"It can be quite confusing when there's a lot of us around," Tomoe continued. "If you yelled 'Oi, Hoshino!' about five people on this ship would all shout 'What?' right back at you! Ah, the Hoshinos are the ones from

Sola-Il, by the way – although don't let them get started. Once they get going, they'll never shut up about how Sola-Il is the greatest of the seven sky cities and how it has all this *history,* and *'Ooh, isn't Sola-Il just the best?'*"

At her words, the rest of the crew erupted in a flurry of outrage that made Kurara jump.

"Sola-Il is magnificent!"

"No other sky city compares to Sola-Il!"

"Where is your pride as a Sorabito?"

Catching Kurara's attention, Tomoe rolled her eyes and mouthed, *"See?"*

Kurara nodded. *Don't say bad things about Sola-Il.* She stored the information away for her future survival.

Captain Sakurai held up a hand to calm the indignation. *"Tomoe."* There was a warning in his voice.

"Aye-aye, Captain." Tomoe saluted, remorseless, and pushed Kurara out of the mess hall, away from the eyes of the crew. Her lips struggled to contain her grin. Her eyes gleamed with mischief.

"Come on then!" she said. "I'll give you the *fun* tour!"

ELEVEN

THE "fun tour" turned out to be a whistle-stop trip to the most important parts of the *Orihime*. Kurara struggled to keep up as Tomoe rattled off facts and figures that Kurara was sure she would forget by tomorrow.

"There are five levels to the ship," Tomoe explained. "The bottom level is split between the hangar and the engine room. All the laundry shoots, rain catchers and water pipes lead down to the fourth-floor storage rooms. The third level is where the crew quarters, infirmary and lounges are and on this floor you'll find the baths, kitchens and mess hall. Top floor is the deck."

"No escape pods?" Kurara could not help but notice their absence.

Tomoe possessed the brazen smile of an arsonist. "Sorabito live and die with their ships."

Kurara did not know whether to laugh or panic. It was

such a bold, stupid principle to live by and yet it felt exactly like something a Sorabito would say.

She cast her gaze around the hallway. In some places, the metal and wood were a different type or colour where the *Orihime* had been repaired with whatever was on hand. The ship's patchwork appearance was a sign of a place well worn. Well lived. A home so important that the crew would defend it to the death. What was it like, she wondered, to love a place so much you would willingly tie your fate to it?

"This must be quite a downgrade from the *Midori*." Tomoe led her past a small enclave. A sign dangled from a nearby door that read, *Save water! Share a bath!* "Ah, the floating world! Oh, sweet paradise of the skies!"

No, thought Kurara, staring at the frayed cushions of a small window seat beside her. Such wear and tear would never have been tolerated on the *Midori*. Everything outside the servants' quarters had been pristine and cold and empty. *This was not a downgrade at all.*

"I was just a serving girl. I never really got to enjoy it," she said.

"Until Himura found you. Did he sweep you off your feet?"

Kurara pulled a face. Himura seemed more the type to toss her over his shoulder like a sack of rice.

Sensing her thoughts, Tomoe laughed aloud. Her sunny attitude made her easy to talk to. Like Haru, she had the same lazy smile, the same eyes shaped by an intense curiosity, the same restless gaze.

"I know joining a hunting ship can seem scary at first" – Tomoe led her down the steps to the third floor –

"but we're professionals. We've been hunting since … well, since the *Orihime* was first built. Shikigami are amazing, but we can't allow them to hurt people."

"I suppose," said Kurara.

But Haru had been fine. Or had he just not reached that point yet? Given time, would he have turned to violence? No, that could not be right. She needed to believe that Haru had been destined for more than a life of destruction.

"Not all shikigami are bad of course. Akane's a real sweetheart." Tomoe smiled.

"Akane?" asked Kurara, but before Tomoe could respond, a door to a room halfway down the corridor opened.

A thin, frowning woman with thick, black-rimmed glasses poked her head out.

"Tomoe! Captain Sakurai said you'd visit me. He didn't say I'd be waiting for thirty minutes!" Her voice was whip-sharp. Each word carried a sting.

"Registration papers!" Tomoe smacked the palm of her hand against her forehead. "I swear, we came as fast as we could, Miss Fusa! We braved the Hallways of Destiny and conquered the Staircase of Doom to be here!"

Fusa scoffed before turning to bow to Kurara. "This is for you. Your copy of the ship's registration papers and your new ID," she explained in response to Kurara's confused frown. "You might be a groundling, and a Crafter on top of it, but this is still a Sorabito ship and that means we have to make doubly sure the military doesn't have a reason to give us any trouble. I've put together background documents so squeaky clean that no one could possibly object to them. Make sure you can answer any questions about them if a soldier asks." She handed Kurara a small scroll and disappeared into her room.

Kurara untied the corded string. As the scroll unfurled, she saw that they were indeed registration papers, but they were for someone Kurara did not recognize. Her name was at the top, but everything else belonged to a stranger. There was a family name she did not recognize. Her home town was a village she had never heard of. Under "family", there were the names of a mother and father she had never met.

"Aw, Fusa gave you a boring family name!" Tomoe peeked over Kurara's shoulder. "You should have something cool! Like, 'Child of the Midnight Dragon' or 'Goddess of the Star Stream' or something!"

Kurara did not know how she felt about this. Though she did not remember anything about her past, it bothered her to be handed a new one, a fake one, so casually. The wrongness of it weighed heavy in her gut.

They found you and Haru lying together in an empty barn.

That was the only thing from her past that she knew. It probably wasn't important enough to be on any kind of document, but she wanted it there. It was important to *her*.

Her hands brushed against Haru's pouch.

Sensing her feelings, Tomoe placed a gentle hand on her shoulder. "It doesn't mean anything," she assured her. "It's for the military. This is a Sorabito ship and the docking officers will look for any excuse to make life hard for us. Like if there's a family member that's a bit too pro-independence for their liking, or if you happened to have a neighbour that was involved in some crime. Sometimes it's easier just to make something up. It doesn't mean you have to lie to everyone you meet. It doesn't mean that *this* is you now. Plenty of our crewmates have fake families or fake histories. Even me."

Kurara startled. "Even you?"

"My father is a deadbeat. He hasn't had a real job in ten years."

"And that's enough to cause problems for you?"

"That's enough." Tomoe's lips twisted into a bitter smile.

This isn't me. Kurara rolled up the scroll and tucked it into her obi.

Tomoe stretched her arms over her head. An eager grin returned to her face. "Enough of this gloom and doom! Let's get some air!"

———————o———————

The deck was impossibly bright. Sunlight assaulted Kurara's face. A roar of wind beat against her body, snatching the sleeves of her kimono and throwing her hair into her face. In the distance, a pod of cumulous whales drifted past, fluffy, dumb and pregnant with rain. A crooning whine echoed through the air. From afar, the whales looked like oddly shaped clouds.

Despite floating in mid-air, the sky had always felt so distant on the *Midori*, seen only through the bars of the windows. Here it was so close she felt as though she could reach up and bottle pieces of it. The *Orihime* was moving. *She* was moving. Rowing through the skies—

"Say that again!"

Kurara's gaze snapped to the middle of the deck.

A girl in a dark kimono stood beneath the shadow of the red sails, surrounded by three men. Buckets and mops were left out on the deck, abandoned. The men were yelling and gesturing angrily while the girl, perhaps a year or two older than Kurara herself, scowled back with a defiant look.

"I told you to say that again!" she screamed.

The men muttered something too soft for Kurara to make out. The next thing she knew, the girl pulled back her arm, clenched her hand into a fist and punched one of them squarely in the jaw.

The sound of her knuckles colliding with flesh echoed across the entire deck.

"Oh, by the blue skies!" Tomoe swore. "I'm going to get the captain! Stay here and make sure nobody dies!"

"Dies?" squawked Kurara, but Tomoe had already bolted below deck.

The fight was turning vicious. In fact, it had become an all-out brawl. From her vantage point on the balcony, Kurara traced the angular frame of the girl's body, the way she moved like a weapon, turning every swing of her arm and every step forward into a potential attack. Her quick feet darted over the deck and her chest heaved with exertion as she slammed one of the men onto the floor.

The other two grabbed the mops lying around and swung them at her. The girl ducked a blow aimed for her head, but could not dodge the one to the back of her knees. She fell hard. Her head slammed against the deck.

They really were going to kill one another.

"Stop!" Kurara hurried down the stairs.

The girl rolled onto her feet. The man she had previously knocked down grabbed a mop as well and swung it at her. With a roar, she spun around to meet him, fists clenched.

"Hey!" Kurara stepped in between them, flinging her arms out to stop them.

The mop handle struck her burned arm with such force she felt it judder up her elbow. It did not hurt, though. In fact, she felt nothing at all.

Her right arm, however, collided straight into the girl's nose. Kurara felt the weight of the impact, though she could do nothing to stop it. The girl stumbled. Blood poured down her face.

Kurara's horror was matched only by the girl's anger.

"Who in the blue skies are you?" Her eyes lit up in fury even as blood dribbled over her lips and down her chin.

Was this what it felt like to face a lion? From the keen tip of the girl's upturned nose, to the sharp corners of her eyes, to her pointed elbows – every part of her seemed specially designed to inflict damage. Her very presence exuded a furious menace.

Before Kurara could answer, the girl grabbed the front of her kimono and yanked her forward so that their noses were almost touching.

"I said—"

"What is the meaning of this?" A stern voice interrupted them.

The girl let go of Kurara. Taking a swift step back, she performed a salute that looked no less professional for the blood smearing her face.

"Captain Sakurai, sir!"

Sakurai's smile was a terrifying thing to behold. Like watching a hawk smile at a mouse it was about to devour. The men jumped to attention, dropping the mops with a clatter. Sakurai glanced from one guilty face to the next. His gaze settled on Kurara.

"Ah! I see you've finally found Sayo, Miss Kurara."

"Um … yes?" Kurara was not sure what was going on. The bleeding girl glowered at her with the force of a speeding kohane.

Sakurai smiled and placed a hand on the girl's shoulder. "Sorano Sayo, our navigator. She will be your new roommate."

TWELVE

"WHERE did you get this?"
The *Orihime*'s doctor was a silver-haired woman who towered over most of the crew like a pine tree growing among hedgerows. The moment Kurara and Sayo stumbled into the infirmary, her eyes narrowed like a hawk. She swooped towards them, thin hands gripping Kurara with surprising force as she inspected the bruises on her arms.

"From a mop." Kurara jumped in surprise.

The fight had been short. Once Captain Sakurai had appeared, the anger in the air had fizzled out and devolved into a bitter argument of "he-said-she-said" that lasted until evening. Sakurai had let them all go with a warning and an order for Kurara and Sayo to visit the ship's infirmary.

"And this? Where did this come from?" The doctor

pushed up Kurara's sleeves to reveal the mottled burns on her left arm.

"Burned it in a forest near Tomuri. It's fine. It doesn't hurt." Feeling nothing was better than feeling pain, wasn't it?

The doctor frowned at her. Kurara had never had a medical examination before. She had the distinct impression that the woman was mentally slicing her into pieces, weighing up each part of her, and assigning a mark out of ten.

"You're too thin. Eat this," she declared. Straightening, she handed Kurara a plate of stale sweet potatoes, baked in their purple skins and sliced into chunks.

Kurara stuffed one into her mouth. It tasted vaguely of chalk.

"You know, I am bleeding." Sayo took a seat hunched on the edge of an infirmary bed, her head resting in her hands. She looked no less fierce for the wad of cotton shoved up her nose to staunch the blood.

She's my roommate. Kurara forced herself to take another piece of potato. She tried to shrug off the hollow pang in her chest, but it would not leave her. For years, Haru had been her only roommate, but tomorrow she would wake to a world without the sound of his sleep-talking, or the sight of his bedhead poking out from beneath the sheets.

The doctor said nothing. She had moved to her work station and was busy mixing something foul-smelling into a beaker. A little bit of everything went into the concoction — dried herbs, vials of strange, coloured

97

liquids, jars of beetle larvae and things Kurara was sure were ground bones. The contents of the beaker turned a revolting shade of green.

"Dr Yuriha! Are you listening?" grumbled Sayo.

Now that they were not fighting, Kurara had the chance to study her new roommate properly. Sayo's black hair curled above the top of her ears, emphasizing her sharp cheekbones. Her arms were thick, her shoulders bunched with lean muscle. She was rather pale for a Sorabito, who usually saw so much of the sun, but her height and the way she carried herself as if she were walking upon the clouds was typical to her kind.

"Are you done with your food? Good. Now drink this." The doctor handed Kurara the beaker of swamp-green liquid. It smelled like sewage and tasted just as bad.

"W—what was that?" Kurara spluttered. The medicine settled like a rock in the pit of her stomach.

"A tincture to wash away the evil in your soul."

"What?"

"You've eaten birds before, haven't you? On the *Midori*."

Sayo gagged.

Kurara flushed. It was true that she had eaten birds before – servants on the *Midori* did not have the luxury of being picky about what they ate – but on the *Orihime* she might as well have admitted to eating a corpse. She understood enough about Sorabito to know they believed that birds carried the souls of the dead. It was why they left the deceased to be picked apart by carrion, why they shuddered at the thought of putting bodies in the ground or burning them to ash. Kurara looked down at her feet and nodded.

"It's fine," the doctor assured her. "We understand that you're not one of us, but while you're on this ship you'll live the Sorabito way. Come back in a few days for your next dose. You need to drink one of these every week for the next month."

"A whole month?!"

"Do you want your soul to be eternally damned?" Dr Yuriha's eyes narrowed into slits.

"That depends," muttered Kurara. "Do demons make people drink sewage in Yomi?"

"What was that?"

"I want my soul to be saved," said Kurara, dutifully.

"Good." The doctor patted her on the back and let her go.

Tomoe was waiting outside when Kurara finally staggered out of the infirmary.

"How are you feeling?" she asked.

"Like I just drank from a toilet," said Kurara, adding when Tomoe scrunched her face in confusion, "I've eaten birds."

She waited for Tomoe's disgust, but the girl just laughed and said, "Ah yes, the lovely purification process! Sorry I left you on the deck by the way. I didn't think you'd actually step into the middle of a brawl."

Before Kurara could swallow back her nausea to reply, Sayo stepped into the hallway as well. Her bruises were covered with an ointment that smelled of yuzu and her nose had stopped bleeding. She noticed Tomoe and her face immediately reddened, lips twisting into a scowl.

"Tomoe." Her voice was oddly strangled. "Thanks for

calling the captain, by the way. His lecture lasted three sky-forsaken hours!"

Tomoe's grin was as bright as the electric lights overhead. "Anything for you, Sayo."

Sayo's expression shifted towards murderous. The look in her eyes made Kurara want to shrink back, but Tomoe merely laughed, enticed by the sharp edge of Sayo's anger.

"Anyway, I just wanted to check you were all right. Congratulations on surviving your first day! I'll see you tomorrow. You too, Sayo." With a salute, she beat a hasty retreat.

Sayo and Kurara remained standing outside the infirmary. They stared at each other.

"Ugh, sharing a room with a bird-guzzler." Sayo sighed and ran a hand through her short hair. "Groundlings are such trouble."

"I'm not a groundling," Kurara wanted to protest but, well, it was technically true, wasn't it? Anyone born on the ground, no matter where they were from, was a groundling. Even if they could not remember it.

"Well, follow me," said Sayo.

"Where to?"

The girl looked at her as if Kurara had just asked what colour the sky was. "To my – *our* – quarters, of course."

It was almost lights out. The sun was bleeding into the sky, orange light filtering in through the porthole windows. Kurara trailed behind Sayo, down a short flight of metal steps, and through a long corridor lined with paper doors.

Sayo stopped in front of the last door at the end of the hallway. Resting a hand on the side of the doorframe, she exhaled a ragged breath, her anger still present but contained, thrumming beneath her skin. "You shouldn't have jumped in. I had everything under control. Getting the captain involved just makes everything worse."

"Maybe I was jumping in to protect the poor man you punched," said Kurara.

Sayo snorted. "The deckhands are a bunch of babies," she declared as she opened the door.

Her quarters were chaotic. From the small slit of a window, Kurara could make out a slice of the night sky. Bright electric lights made the room glow white, but it was the walls that caught her attention. All four sides were covered with maps, star charts and hastily scribbled weather reports. They coated the walls from top to bottom, taking up every inch of space. As she stepped onto the tatami floor, Kurara noted the tiny coloured tacks pinned to the paper, some in clusters, others dotted sporadically all over the maps with bits of twine tied between them like the briefing room of a war council.

For a moment, she did nothing but take in the walls around her. *If only Haru were here.* She clutched his pouch tight. There was a mountain of things she did not understand about the world, but climbing its peak felt less frightening if he was with her.

Sayo rooted through the closet for a spare futon and shoved the extra bedding into her arms.

Kurara staggered under the weight. "So ... roommates."

If they were going to be living in close quarters

together, she felt she should at least know more about Sayo. Apart from the fact that the girl had a mean right hook and did not appreciate it when helpful people intervened in her fights.

Sayo made a sound as if her very soul was being sucked out through her teeth. "Don't remind me. Let's talk about it tomorrow. It's late."

As if in agreement, the lights dimmed automatically. Kurara set up her bed and slipped beneath the sheets. Sleep did not come easily. The futon was not uncomfortable, but it was not like the one she had on the *Midori*. It was too thick, the pillow was too soft. The sheets smelled wrong too. The *Orihime*'s engines hummed, but they were too quiet, nothing like the noisy churning of industrial levistone burners.

Lying sprawled over her futon, Kurara stared up at the papered walls. With a flick of a finger, she pulled a map of the empire from the wall. It hovered over her, folding into the shape of a lotus flower.

"Lotuses only grow in the mud," Haru had once told her. *"From the dirt at the bottom of clouded lakes, they rise to bloom upon the surface of the water."*

Haru loved lotuses. They reminded him of the ones that grew near their mountain home. Once, Kurara had told him that they were ugly flowers. She had hurt his feelings, she knew, but she had hated being reminded of the gap between them: a distance made up of lost memories that she could not bridge, no matter how hard she tried.

She wished that she could go back and apologize. Had Haru known that he was a shikigami and kept it from her for fear that she would only lash out?

The paper lotus spun above her. Perhaps Haru had been made the same way: fold upon fold forming his hands, the jut of his thumbs, the curve of his mouth. Who had made him and how had he ended up with her? Was he really the ancient being Himura had suggested he was?

She would get to the bottom of this. At the very least, once Haru had his body back, she'd shake him by the ankles until answers spilled out.

Her eyelids drooped. At last, sleep found her and pulled her under.

THIRTEEN

THE *Orihime* was not just a simple hunting ship, but a vessel alive with as much history as any of its human crew. Himura could map out every inch of the airship from the dent where a passing kohane had crashed near the prow to the scorch marks on the cannons. He ran his fingers along crude notches in the wood – marks of boredom and slow nights on lookout. The cargo hold, which had once been a library, still carried the musty scent of ancient pages.

These little flaws were signs of a ship loved by its crew, but Himura had never considered it home. Part of his heart was still tied to the ground, buried in the ruins where a paper tortoise had trampled his home town into the dirt, buried with his parents who used to whisper bedtime stories about their ancestors.

"A long time ago, we Crafters ruled this land. A long time ago, we were so much more than what we are now."

His parents had spoken of ancient Crafters as if they were minor Gods, and died longing for a past they could only dream of. A past that now lay locked up within the books of Princess Tsukimi's library.

Himura's pace quickened through the empty hallways. He clutched a mechanical bird to his chest. The silver gull was too large to fit in one palm. The clockwork gears in its wings were crooked. He looked ridiculous cradling it like a baby, but there was no one about to witness it.

The ship moved in accordance to a precise schedule: pilots in the docking bay by six, maintenance checks by seven, training from three to five then seven to eight, engineers in the boiler rooms on Friday, then the engine rooms on Monday, and the artillery platforms on Saturday.

The crew were clockwork ants in a moving anthill, their whereabouts predictable. Climbing down to the very bottom of the ship, Himura found Tomoe exactly where he expected her to be: in the engine room. She sat against the *Orihime*'s furnaces, pressing her face against the smooth curve of metal.

Engines thrummed. Flames cracked, merrily dancing behind the grille-like mouths of the furnaces. People often thought of the engine room as a sweltering, oppressive place, but Himura enjoyed the darkness and warmth. Though he would have preferred it if there were fewer open flames.

Himura's footsteps echoed against the engine room floor. A trail of snow-white paper danced behind him, forming a line of twittering sparrows. They merged together to make a wolf with rippling paper fur, then a pair of cats that brushed around his ankles. He enjoyed making an entrance.

"Mr Himura, you're up early." Himura could tell by her tone that she was surprised to see him. He had no schedule beside his own. He was mostly left to his devices until it was time to hunt.

"Fix this. It's been flying into the walls." Without warning, he thrust the mechanical gull against Tomoe's chest.

The girl cooed over the bird as though it were a real animal. "Of course it's flying into walls. Its gears are broken, the poor thing."

Himura did not understand why Sorabito were so obsessed with birds – even the mechanical ones. There were many things he would never understand about the crew.

"And how long will it take to fix? I want to send a letter."

Tomoe faked a surprised gasp. "Why, Mr Himura, have you actually made a friend? A pen pal?"

The corner of Himura's right eye twitched. "It's going to the *Hikoboshi*. Captain Sakurai told me they recently picked up a crate of old books from the black market."

"I see. More books about shikigami and ancient Crafters, is it?"

"It's the only way I will ever learn more about my people." There was a chance that none of the old books were the ones he was looking for. Accounts about Crafters were as difficult to find as a piece of lint in a sack of rice, and the few that surfaced were quickly snatched up by Princess Tsukimi. It was a fool's errand, yet Himura could not give up.

"We used to be so much more," his parents had said. *"So much more."*

"You know, Mr Himura, my father used to say that when you let people know what you care about, you let them know your weaknesses." Tomoe fiddled with the mechanical bird's wings. "But I hate him so *I* say, go pursue your dreams! What are those?" She pointed to the papers tucked beneath Himura's arm.

"Sayo's reports. They also need to go to the *Hikoboshi*."

Sorabito ships wrote to one another often, keeping in contact via mechanical bird. There were many dangers out there; storms and shikigami and moody sky whales. Sharing information was how airships stayed safe.

Himura flicked through the papers. Most of it was about weather systems and air pressure. Only the last report caught his attention: *Military ships seen near Kumokiri Mountains and surrounding area. Officers are searching other ships for BOMBs.*

Himura knew from talking with Sayo that "BOMB" was a code word. One could never tell when a military ship with nothing better to do might intercept their messages, so the reports between ships were carefully scrubbed of anything that might upset the groundlings. The military might think "searching for BOMBs" was a funny phrase, but the Sorabito knew what it really meant.

BOMBs meant blast. It meant fun. *Officers are searching other ships for fun.* In other words, they were looking for an excuse to throw their weight around and perhaps pinch a few things while they were at it. He passed the report to Tomoe, who made a disgusted sound.

"Military patrols! Why can't they leave us alone? We're doing them a service by hunting shikigami. They should be more grateful!"

With a snap of his fingers, Himura made the letters fly out of Tomoe's hand, cartwheeling through the air, before he caught them between his fingers.

"What is that saying you Sorabito have? 'Don't let the worms eat you'? If you get angry, you give them an excuse to mess with you," he said, though he felt a flutter of sympathy. Society was a ladder: the imperial family on top, the groundlings below and the Sorabito at the very bottom. Always keeping an eye out for the military – never knowing when a bored soldier would decide to cause trouble – was such an exhausting way to live. When you were at the bottom of the ladder, there was always someone stepping on you.

"Easy for you to say," Tomoe huffed.

"I work for a Sorabito ship, do I not? I'm on the bottom rung with the rest of you."

There was a different ladder for Crafters. They were judged by who they worked for. Joining the *Orihime* meant Himura had less standing than a Crafter in the military and far less than an imperial Crafter serving the Emperor and his family.

"But at least you have a chance to move up." Tomoe unsheathed the blade that she kept by her side.

The tanto was fancier than anything Tomoe wore, the hilt carved with birds, yet she flipped it between her fingers and used the tip of the blade to prise open the mechanical gull's chest compartment, showing no care for such a beautiful weapon.

"I'm only going to say this once," said Tomoe, "but if you ever want to leave us for that royal lapdog lifestyle, I won't blame you. Well, I will, but only because I'll be thinking about all the white rice and beef you'll get to eat. Who would you like to work for? The Emperor maybe? Or perhaps Princess—?"

Paper swirled around him, jerking through the air like wasps. Tomoe flinched. Her hand instinctively gripped her tanto tighter.

"Crafters once ruled Mikoshima. I would never humiliate myself by serving the Emperor and his family. Besides, I doubt they would accept me – I tried to rob Princess Tsukimi once."

A disbelieving laugh burst from Tomoe's throat. "Seriously? Why have I never heard this before? And you lived to tell the tale?"

Himura wished that this was a story he could tell with pride. Instead, he skirted around it like a scab, careful not to poke at the part that bled.

"I lived. I'm here, aren't I?"

Something in his tone caught her attention. Tomoe's eyes were piercing. Whenever she looked at him like that, he always had the feeling she was trying to pick him apart. Running her fingers down the mechanical gull's exposed chest, she shifted the gears back into place and closed the compartment.

"Here" – she handed the bird to Himura – "it's ready to fly."

Interlude

Ah, to be the dirt!
Unresentful of the feet
That tread upon me.
What else is there in heaven
More divine than nothingness?

– from *Citizenship and Devotion*
(approved by the Patriots Office)

"You put it in a crate? Really?" said Rei.

Inui's belt of paper hands wriggled their fingers at him. "Where else do you suggest we keep a giant dragon?"

Her haughty tone made Rei prickle. He had agreed to Prince Ugetsu's deal – freedom in exchange for the death of his sister, the sky cities' independence in return for a throne – yet he still had his pride. *He* was the leader of Sohma. *He* was the one in charge of the plan, not Inui. Her words needled him.

"Fine," he grunted. "It won't struggle, will it?"

Inui moved through Tomuri's marketplace like a spectre, gliding through the crowds untouched and unnoticed. "Even a shikigami that has already lost itself can be somewhat controlled. You need not worry. I have just enough power over it for what needs to be done," she assured him.

Rei was not completely convinced, but then he knew very little about how a Crafter controlled these beasts. He let the issue slide. Whatever she had done to make the thing obey was not his problem. There were more urgent matters on his mind.

"We should concentrate on getting the dragon to Sola-Il," he said. "We'll ship it to the sky cities. I know a man who will deliver anything for the right price. Then I'll—"

"You're overthinking things." The headlights of passing trams flickered across Inui's face. "It will take at least two weeks to reach Sola-Il from here. Isn't there a festival during that time? The *Something* Stars Festival?"

"The Festival of the Seventh Star." Rei frowned. He did not appreciate the interruption.

"Yes, that one. There will be plenty of ships coming and going during that time. Use the festival as a distraction to smuggle the dragon into the city."

Rei bit back his irritation. He did not need the old bat's advice.

"I'll make my decision about what to do once I've seen the dragon," he said, tersely.

As they reached the Tomuri River, the smell of ramen broth wafted into the air, accompanied by the sharp tang of alcohol. The sound of a woman's shrieks echoed across the water.

"Why can't you understand that I hate it here? Everyone is so awful to me. I wish I had never left the skies!"

A woman on the edge of the river bank was screaming at her partner, unaware of the gaggle of onlookers she was attracting. Her accent caught Rei's attention. Sorabito and groundlings didn't always look that different upon first glance, but the moment someone opened their mouth you could tell where they were from.

The woman's rolling Sorabito accent was noticeable despite her screaming. Rei found her shrieks far more soothing than the ugly accents of the city.

"Oh shut up, you damn sky rat!" Someone threw a rock at the woman.

Rei turned away from the scene, leaving the woman to fend for herself. As much as he wanted to step in, he had always told his daughters not to get involved in matters that did not benefit them. Saving the woman would not free the sky cities.

Still, he was in a bad mood when they reached the harbour. Tomuri was an old city, built before the age of airships. To this day, it did not have a sky dock. Airships landed in the water and moored themselves to the harbour like regular boats. The sight made Rei seethe. To force a proud airship to flop into the water like a common fisherman's vessel was nothing short of an insult.

Inui led him past the rows of oil-slicked barges, beyond the cracked stone piers and the ink-black waters to a large, sleek airship bobbing up and down on the waves. None of the lights in the porthole windows were on. The gangway was rolled up and the yellow sails folded as though no one was home, but when Rei approached, someone from the deck called down, "Lady Inui? Rei? There you are!"

Rei recognized that voice. He recognized this ship.

"Nao?"

Ameno Nao made no efforts to hide his Sorabito ancestry. His kimono was covered in large, colourful prints, its sleeves stitched together like a patchwork quilt. With his angular cheekbones and broad shoulders, he was an impressive sight to behold. His ship, the *Hishaku*, was one of the largest merchant ships in the harbour and the perfect cover under which he travelled back and forth from the sky cities to the ground, passing on information to Sohma without suspicion.

Rei's mood darkened. Ameno Nao was useful, but soft. Weak. He always had the impression that Nao put more effort into being a merchant than he did in being a member of Sohma.

He had not expected to see Nao here, and that alone made him scowl.

"Rei! Lady Inui told me the situation. Come! Come inside!" Nao lowered the gangway and ushered them on board.

"It's good to rely on your comrades. I've asked Nao to

keep the dragon inside his ship." Inui placed a hand on Rei's shoulder.

Irritation stirred beneath his skin. Nao was a weakling, but he was one of *his* men nonetheless. Inui had no right ordering him around, making decisions without telling him, bypassing his authority and his plans. It curdled in his gut like sour milk.

Inside the *Hishaku's* cavernous hull, the dragon lay curled in its crate as if in slumber. The front of the wooden box was left open so that Rei could see the dragon up close: its sharp whiskers, its piercing talons, its horns protruding from a long mane of paper fur. Its massive body coiled like a snake. White, paper scales gleamed in the dim lamplight. With Inui around, the dragon was quiet, but Rei found her control over the beast more aggravating than comforting. He did not want to give Inui any more power than she already had.

"Amazing, isn't it?" Inui sighed. A look of longing settled across her face, so different from her usual expression of wicked glee.

"I can't believe I'm looking at a real shikigami!" Nao gazed up at the beast in awe.

"Don't touch it, Nao!" Rei snapped when the man stretched his hand towards the dragon's muzzle. He was angry at Nao for obeying Inui. There was meant to be a chain of command. All orders were supposed to go through *him*.

Nao snatched his hand back. "Sorry," he said, sheepish.

"I just don't want it to hurt you. I care about all my men." Rei smiled through gritted teeth.

Inui's cackling laughter echoed across the walls. "This is the plan: Nao will take you and the dragon to the sky city on his ship. Keep it in its crate and keep the crate in the hull while you're flying. Before you reach Sola-Il, have someone pay off the docking guards to avoid the landing inspection."

Rei sucked in a strangled breath. "I already *told you*, my plan is—"

"Everything is already set. Nao is ready to take you and your men to Sola-Il, isn't that right?" said Inui. Nao nodded, beaming like an idiot.

Rei was going to kill her. He would crush Inui's vile throat and snap her brittle legs.

Everything I do is for Sohma. For the glory of the Sorabito. He repeated to himself over and over until he calmed down. If it brought him one step closer to the sky cities' freedom, he could adapt his plans around Inui's suggestions. He was still the one who had to bring the dragon to Sola-Il after all – the one who had to unleash the shikigami onto the summer palace.

He was still in charge.

"Once we arrive in Sola-Il, we'll need to move the dragon out of the docks as quickly as possible. Sohma owns several warehouses. I'll make sure one is available for us to lay low and wait for the right time to attack," he suggested.

"That's a good idea," said Inui. "See, Rei? You're helping!"

Rei resisted the urge to say something insulting.

 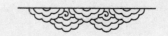

He knew that Inui's smug smile would remain burned in his memory long after she was gone.

"I must be taking my leave now," she said. "I'll head to Sola-Il by myself. I hope to see you there."

"You're leaving?" As much as he disliked and distrusted Inui, she was the reason the shikigami was behaving itself.

"I have to stop by the black market and pick up some books about shikigami. The only reason Princess Tsukimi has not noticed my absence is because she thinks I am collecting a package for her. Whenever her hobbies are involved, she becomes blind to everything else," Inui snorted. "You'll be fine without me. The dragon will remain calm. At least for the two weeks it will take to reach the city."

Two weeks was cutting it close. Rei was sure Inui had planned it this way, giving them just enough time to reach Sola-Il but not enough to try anything stupid like bringing the shikigami elsewhere.

"For Sohma!" Nao saluted. Inui left with a smile, her paper hands waving over her shoulder as she disappeared into the night.

Irritated, Rei reached for his pipe. His daughters would scold him for breaking his promise to give it up, but they weren't here to nag him. Besides, the only child he cared for was his eldest and she hated him for a lot more than his foul habits.

The smoke was soothing. As his nerves relaxed, he imagined himself taking charge of Sola-Il after the

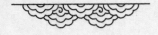 

dragon had crushed the princess. He imagined raising an army against the Emperor, and then Prince Ugetsu. Maybe he would kill them both, maybe he would let them live as second-class citizens within a new, powerful Sorabito empire.

He imagined himself crowned as ruler of the skies.

"For Sohma," he muttered.

FOURTEEN

"*YOU* have only been on the *Orihime* a day and yet you are already starting fights."

Himura cut an imposing figure. Kurara was not sure whether it was his height, his solemn face, or the quiet confidence in his eyes that made him appear so intimidating. Perhaps it was just the thin light of dawn casting pale shadows across his cheeks. It was far too early in the morning. Even Sayo was still asleep.

"Technically, I *stopped* a fight." Kurara stood at the doorway to her quarters.

Himura sighed and handed her a bundle of clothes. "Spares from the *Orihime*. Change and then come outside."

Although Sorabito clothes were much easier to wear than a normal kimono, Kurara's unsteady hands fumbled with the clip-on obi. A cocktail of excitement and nervousness churned in her stomach as she secured Haru's pouch. She had been on the ship a day already, but the real work started now. In whatever time she had before she met Princess Tsukimi, she had to train, to make sure that she earned that audience with the princess. Kurara had always loved making paper dance – the tingle of power through her fingers, the soothing rustle of paper – but this time she was not using her abilities for fun. She was doing it to save Haru.

Stepping out of her room, she followed Himura to the male cabin wing. His quarters were the same as Sayo's, from the heater beneath the window down to the closet in the corner. Instead of maps and charts though, the room was filled with books. Heavy leather-bound tomes, the kind that would kill a man if dropped from a great height, were piled into neat columns against the walls. They were all old and shabby, the covers torn in places, some gutted of pages, some missing their spines. Kurara was not surprised that Himura enjoyed reading. Such a solitary hobby suited him well.

Except he was not alone.

A white fox lay curled up in the corner of the room, lying next to a stack of paper. Everything from the tip of its nose to the end of its tail was as white as snow. Its bushy tail covered part of its face and its four paws were tucked beneath its belly. It lifted its head at the sound of Kurara's footsteps. Even its eyes were colourless.

A shikigami.

She had no time to react. Kurara staggered backwards as the fox lunged for her. Its front paws pressed against her stomach with surprising force, tail whipping from side to side. A dry, papery tongue assaulted her face.

"A girl! A girl!" Its voice echoed in her head, though it did not hurt the way the dragon's voice had. *"Master, look how little she is! A little kit!"*

"Enough, Akane!" snapped Himura, pulling the fox away.

Kurara remained frozen. She knew that shikigami were dangerous. She knew that they were monsters that hurt people. She had seen a shikigami attack the *Midori*. Everything was telling her that she was in danger and yet at Himura's orders the fox dropped onto all fours, slinking away with drooping ears and its tail tucked between its legs like a dog.

So this is who Tomoe was talking about. Kurara remembered that the engineer had said something about "Akane" during their tour.

"You have never seen a normal shikigami, have you?" asked Himura.

"Normal?" croaked Kurara.

Shikigami go mad and kill people. That was what everyone said. The servants on the *Midori* and the soldiers who visited always talked about shikigami attacks, about homes left destroyed and lives lost. Kurara had never questioned it until she'd found out about Haru. She had never thought: *If shikigami hurt people when they lose their minds, then what about the ones that aren't mad?*

Himura stroked a hand between Akane's ears. "Just what did they teach you on board the *Midori*?"

"How to scrub, wash, sew and avoid flying pots."

"Flying pots?"

"They were more common than you'd think." Kurara's mind was still buzzing.

"Then you don't know about how we Crafters used to own shikigami?"

"Own?" Kurara did not think she could hear the word "shikigami" again without thinking about Haru, and the idea that someone could have *owned* him made her gut churn unpleasantly. Her eyes drifted to where Himura's hand rested on the fox's head. Did he *own* Akane?

"Crafter!" Akane, sensing nothing wrong, gave a gleeful yip for no other reason but the sheer pleasure of repeating the word. *"Crafter! Crafter!"*

"So you ... created Akane?"

Himura shook his head. "No one knows what shikigami really are or how they are made. Not any more. Crafters created shikigami many centuries ago but that knowledge has been lost to time. What we do know is that, after many centuries, a shikigami's mind wears away. They lose themselves, forgetting who they are and rampaging through the land, attacking and destroying everything in their path. That is what has happened to most of the ones you hear about today."

He smiled, but his eyes were grim and full of sadness for times gone by. Kurara understood the feeling all too well. It was a yearning for something you had never really known. A nostalgia for a past never lived.

"Once they have lost themselves, we have no choice but to destroy them. That is what we do on the *Orihime*. Here, let me see that core in your pouch."

Kurara hesitated. The memory of the forest flickered through her mind like a dagger. It was her job to protect Haru. She pulled out the core, but kept it at arm's length from Himura. No one else could touch Haru but her.

"Do you see those symbols?" Himura pointed at the pattern of swirling red lines running across the core. "Writing our blood over them forms a bond that makes a shikigami obey us. A bond acts as an anchor that keeps a shikigami from losing control. Without a master... Well, you already know what happens. You saw that dragon at the *Midori*. It had completely lost itself."

"You saw a dragon?" Akane ran circles around Himura's legs. *"Master, why didn't you tell me? Akane wanted to see a dragon too! Why did you leave me behind?"*

The fox flopped onto the floor, as though missing the dragon was the most tragic thing in the world. Kurara could not help but stare. Was this how shikigami were supposed to be? She thought about the ones that had lost their masters, that had been left to wander the land for hundreds of years, only for some new Crafter to impose their will on them. Was it painful? Or were they grateful to be saved from a life of violence?

"Let this little drama queen be." Himura frowned at Akane, who was still rolling about on the tatami. "It's time to get to work."

"Akane will help too!" The fox perked up, dragon forgotten, as it looked at Kurara with a too-human grin.

Kurara was quiet. Her mind was crowded with thoughts of Haru, of him burning in the middle of the forest. She wanted to learn how to be a better Crafter, but she was not sure she could turn around and use those skills to hunt as Himura wanted.

No, she had to be strong. She had seen the dragon that had attacked the *Midori*. Once a shikigami had lost itself, there was no other way.

Himura pulled a piece of paper from his bracelet. It rotated on the tip of his finger, slowly folding itself into the shape of a wolf. Kurara watched, fascinated and envious, as it gave a silent howl.

"Fire is the only way to hurt a shikigami, but it won't just stand there and let you set it alight. That's where we come in. We use paper to restrain shikigami and make sure they do not escape. We protect the crew and the ship, and wait for the opportunity to attack. Any fool with two hands can make origami, but Crafting is the control of paper without physically interacting with it. And paper in the hands of a Crafter is known as ofuda."

The paper wolf became an eagle with outspread wings, then a deer that galloped over Himura's palm.

"Ofuda can do three things: it can change shape and size, it can move and it can become stronger. There is a limit to what you can achieve with only a single piece of paper. However, with preparation and skill, you can work around these limitations. That is what I am here to teach you."

"And Akane!" the fox yipped.

Ignoring his shikigami, Himura flattened the paper deer into a single sheet of paper, held it between his teeth and blew.

The floppy paper suddenly stood needle-sharp. It still looked like paper, but Himura carefully drew it out of his mouth, afraid that the edges would slice his lips. He threw it at the wall.

The sheet whistled as it cut through the air. Hitting the other side of the room, one corner wedged itself deep into the wall. With a look of satisfaction, he stood to retrieve it, holding it out for Kurara to touch. Awed, she reached out a cautious hand. The paper was as sharp as a knife.

Thinking back to the *Midori*, to how pleased she had been by her paper animals, made her feel silly. Her origami creations seemed so trifling in comparison to Himura's power. She had been like a frog content with the water in its well while knowing nothing of the sea.

"How ... how good do I need to be in order to impress Princess Tsukimi?"

"The best," said Himura. "You have to be one of the best."

Kurara gulped. *The best, sure.* It was not like that was difficult or anything.

"First," Himura continued, "you must learn to control ofuda with just your thoughts. Two Crafters cannot control the same piece of paper at the same time. Once you have it in your control, it is yours. Sometimes, another Crafter will say or do something to try to rattle you, to make your concentration slip, in order to seize control of your ofuda. This is why it is important to focus no matter what."

He handed her a stack of paper.

"Show me what you can do."

Kurara could tell from the way Himura looked at her that he would not tolerate failure. What would the crew do to her if she did not succeed? Would they throw her off the ship? Maybe they would not bother touching down at some nearby town and just kick her off the *Orihime* while it was still in flight, hundreds of miles above the ground.

Lotuses only grow in the mud, Haru had told her once. Kurara was a lotus, blooming calmly above the muddy thoughts and worries of her life. She could do this.

Without touching the paper, she concentrated on moving the first sheet on the stack.

A peony. She conjured the image of its petals, the crown of its centre, the gentle curve of its leaves. The corners of the paper lifted and began to fold themselves. *A crab.* The next piece of paper lifted into the air. *A rabbit.* Like the one she used to keep in her quarters on the *Midori*. One by one, they hovered in the air.

Himura stared intently at her creations, as if he thought they would suddenly spring to life if he watched closely enough. "Has anyone taught you this before?"

Kurara shook her head. "Until we met, I had never even seen another Crafter."

Himura's frown deepened.

"Your ability to shape-change is more advanced than I would have expected." He sounded somewhat reluctant to admit it. Before Kurara could feel any pride, he added, "But your ability to move paper is appalling. You need to learn how to do more than make them flutter about."

Kurara's hands tightened around the fabric of her skirt. She could not disappoint him, not if she wanted to keep her place here. Not if she wanted to save Haru.

"I can move more than one piece of paper at the same time!" With a flick of her fingers, she took control of the paper surrounding her. The stack of ofuda jumped. Himura's books catapulted upwards.

Kurara had not meant to move *all* the paper in the room, but every piece flew into the air and out of her control. Lifted by their pages, Himura's heavy tomes crashed into the ceiling with such force they left a small hole above her head. Dust and splintered wood rained upon her head.

"Boom!" Akane leapt to its feet. Kurara made the mistake of catching the shikigami's eye. It jumped at her, paws pressing hard against her stomach as its tongue lolled out between its fangs. *"Boooom! Like a firework! I love you, Crafter cub! I love—"*

Before it could finish, Akane was distracted by more falling splinters. The fox yipped and jumped away, waggling its butt high in the air and crying, *"Boom, boom, boom!"*

Kurara turned to look at Himura, sheepish, as his books clattered back to the ground. "So … imagine the ceiling was a rampaging shikigami…"

Himura did not deign her excuse with a response. Part of his bracelet unravelled to form a long broom with a white bristle top. He handed it to her.

"Get sweeping," he ordered.

FIFTEEN

THE breakfast bell sounded by the time Kurara was done cleaning Himura's room. Her head throbbed as though someone had rammed an encyclopedia into her brain. She wanted nothing more than to collapse on her futon and go to sleep, but when the bells chimed, her stomach growled in answer.

Kurara had never felt like this before – this tangle of frustration, impatience and excitement that got stuck in her throat and occupied her mind. She wanted to hurry up and do all the things Himura could. She wanted to make paper dance the way he did.

Her hunger to learn was only matched by the hunger in her stomach. As she reached the mess hall, there was a sign hanging from the metal doors, proclaiming in large, red letters:

NO GUNS AT THE DINNER TABLES!

Above that, someone had nailed:

NO KNIVES, SWORDS, OR EXPLOSIVES EITHER, PLEASE AND THANK YOU!

Kurara hesitated. She could hear people on the other side. Was she ready for this? Meeting one or two people with Tomoe was one thing, but from the sounds coming through the doors, the entire crew was in the hall.

Her belly growled at her to get a move on. Steeling her nerves, she pulled open the door.

There were twelve people in total, scattered around the mess hall. Kurara recognized a few faces from yesterday. Though the crew was not very large, they were loud enough to match an industrial levistone burner. Men and women eagerly chatted away, laughing aloud as they shared last night's news. Dr Yuriha sat huddled in one corner, gambling with a deck of hanafuda.

Kurara was intensely aware that the crew had noticed her enter. They did not stop talking, but the weight of their stares fell heavy against her as she made her way to the food counter and joined the line for the morning meal.

Breakfast was a bowl of watery okayu and the thinnest sliver of grilled fish. Behind the wooden counter, a buxom woman with black hair that curled silver around her ears gave Kurara a smile.

"Well, well! How do you do, Miss Kurara?" She had a deep, brassy voice, as if she was speaking through a voice pipe. "Madam Chiyoko. Head cook. I'm glad to have you on board!" She slapped an extra fish onto Kurara's bowl.

"Th–thank you." Kurara blushed, unsurprised that the crew already knew her name.

"Are there any snacks you like? I'm happy to make something special for you," the cook continued. "Dried prunes? Dried seaweed? Dried cow tongue?"

Someone at the back of the line coughed loudly.

"Jellied plums? Red bean cakes? Fried squid?"

Before Kurara could escape, a man in blue overalls passed her by with a hearty laugh, slapping her on the back so hard she almost spilled everything on her tray. "Hey, Crafter girl! You're going to help us make lots of money, yes? Distract those shikigami while we shoot 'em full of fire?"

Kurara opened her mouth but she did not know what to say. She felt like an elephant waddling into an orchard full of birds: slow and clumsy compared to the bright, cheerful creatures around her. How she longed for the same easy grace, the confidence that exuded from the crew as they laughed and talked and gambled.

Haru would have loved this. He would have loved to be surrounded by so many new people, living on a ship that would carry them across the country on grand adventures. Though there were so many people in the mess hall, Kurara was lonely without him.

"Good morning!" Tomoe appeared behind her without warning, startling Kurara from her thoughts. "How was your first training session with Himura? Did you finally meet Akane?"

"How did you know I had a training session?" Kurara was happy to let Tomoe lead her to an empty table.

"On a ship this size, word gets around." Tomoe sat in the corner. "If you've got any secrets, better come clean with them now. The crew will find out everything sooner or later!"

At the mention of secrets, Kurara's fingers brushed the edge of Haru's pouch. She did not know if Himura had told anyone else about their deal, but she was not ready to speak about Haru herself. The memories were too fresh.

Before she could say anything, the doors to the mess hall opened once more and Sorano Sayo stepped in, squinting at the light as though it had just insulted her. Her clothes were rumpled and her hair stuck up in odd places.

"Hey, Sayo! Over here!" Tomoe waved. Her elbow knocked against her teacup, spilling hot tea over Kurara's left arm.

Kurara flinched, but there was no pain. Even as she pushed up her sleeve, she could not feel the kimono's fabric brush against her skin.

"Sorry! Sorry! Oh skies, let me take you to the infirmary!" Tomoe paled at the sight of Kurara's scars. A few heads turned to stare at them.

"No, no! This is fine – perfectly fine!" Kurara insisted, embarrassed by the fuss Tomoe was making. "My arm was injured in a fire. I'm all right. Really. It looks worse than it is. I don't feel a thing."

She lifted her drenched sleeve as it dripped hot tea

onto the table. At the very least, she was telling the truth about not feeling anything. Though it was not a pretty sight, she took comfort in the fact that she could still use her arm.

Besides, she did not want to drink any more of Dr Yuriha's noxious potions.

"Don't ruin the new meat on her first day." Sayo slid into the seat opposite Tomoe and poured herself a cup of tea.

Tomoe looked sheepish. "It was an accident, Sayo! Don't frown at me like that – you'll spoil your good looks! Why don't you tell me how your morning was instead?"

Sayo's face resembled an overripe tomato. Kurara had not known a person's face could turn such a vibrant shade of red. The corners of the navigator's mouth turned down into an irritated frown. Tomoe, Kurara decided, was incredibly brave for daring to tease someone who looked two seconds away from murder.

"I've been reading reports about the military harassing passing Sorabito ships," she grumbled. Her gaze doggedly avoided Tomoe's. "Here I am trying to avoid them and all everyone else is doing is pestering me about how quickly we'll reach the Grand Stream."

"The Grand Stream?" Kurara almost dropped her chopsticks. She remembered Haru mentioning a ship full of soldiers returning to Mikoshima via the Grand Stream. He had wanted to go and listen to their stories with her.

Turning to Kurara, Tomoe grinned. "I thought you knew. That's where our next hunt is."

"It's why *you* were hired," Sayo interjected. "For the big hunt."

Kurara's grip on her chopsticks tightened. Himura had told her about the hunt, but he had *not* mentioned anything about it being at the Grand Stream. People said the winds were so harsh they would tear apart a ship within minutes. It was suicide. A death trap.

"There's a really famous shikigami called Suzaku there," said Tomoe. "Luckily, it doesn't leave the area, but no one's been able to touch it ever since it showed up. The winds will destroy even the toughest ship if you're not careful. Trust me, I know. We've flown close to the Grand Stream before."

"That's…" *Suicide. Idiocy. Pure arrogance.* Kurara was not sure which to pick.

"Madness, isn't it?" Tomoe thumped a fist against her chest with pride. Her understanding of the word "madness" obviously had a more positive meaning than Kurara's. "You know, we *saw* Suzaku! Just a glimpse before the winds tossed us back out! It was a bird! A huge bird as big as an airship! Like a phoenix except pure white and, you know, a shikigami. It was beautiful."

Kurara had never heard anyone call a shikigami beautiful before. Then again, the Sorabito had rather odd feelings about birds in the first place. For the second time that day, she wondered if she could really bring herself to fight. The correct response to a shikigami was terror, but Kurara felt only pity. Shikigami that hurt people had to be stopped, but she could not blame them for actions outside of their control.

"It'll be fine!" Tomoe clapped her on the back so hard her face almost went into her bowl. "And after we have hunted Suzaku, let's go to Sola-Il to celebrate!"

Kurara perked up at the mention of the sky city. Princess Tsukimi's summer palace was on Sola-II.

"That's up to the captain," said Sayo.

"True" – Tomoe brushed a grain of rice away from the corner of her mouth – "but you can talk to him about it, can't you? Recommend it? You are our navigator after all. Please, Sayo? Pretty please with an extra five hundred ko on top?"

Sayo's scowl could melt ice. Kurara did not understand why the sight of the navigator's ire made Tomoe beam as though she had hit the right buttons on a combination code only she could see. Or why Sayo looked so exasperated yet did not get up to sit somewhere else. It was like they were performing some kind of strange dance only they knew the steps to.

"… I'll see what I can do," Sayo mumbled into her teacup.

Tomoe whooped. "Yesss! You're the best, Sayo!"

Again, Sayo's cheeks burned tomato red, her expression equal parts pleased and annoyed.

"I'm going back to the control room." She drained the last of her tea before beating a hasty retreat. "There's a storm coming."

SIXTEEN

AS Sayo predicted, the sky darkened and the gathering clouds grew as heavy as cumulous whales. Throughout Kurara's first week and into the next, furious monsoon rains lashed at the windows and swept the deck with so much water it was dangerous to step outside. At night, the raging winds buffeted the ship like a vengeful spirit howling to be allowed inside.

Kurara took shelter inside the heart of the ship, though she could still hear the thunder rolling overhead and feel the winds rock the *Orihime*. Thankfully, her training kept her mind off the storm. She practised three times a day before meals, slipping into Himura's room for her lessons.

Himura was a harsh teacher, difficult to please and quick to criticize, but she appreciated his strictness. Left to her own devices, she would not have known where to even begin. Under his watchful eye, she hurried through the basics of shape-changing and onto bigger, more complex creations – a giant snake that filled the length of Himura's room, the segmented body of a praying mantis, ancient weapons and clockwork puzzles.

Each small improvement came with a spark of excitement, a flash of satisfaction when she finally got a tricky piece of Crafting right. Soon she would become someone strong enough to gain an audience with Princess Tsukimi.

In the darkness of the evenings, as she made paper flowers next to her pillow, she knew that she was not practising this hard for Haru alone. A small, selfish part of her enjoyed her progress for no other reason than that it felt good to get better at something she loved. It was a simple pleasure. One that she treasured.

After the storm had passed, Kurara joined Tomoe outside for some much needed fresh air. A cool summer breeze swept through the *Orihime*'s sails. Weak sunlight warmed the deck, though the skies remained persistently grey. While Tomoe ranted about her last conversation with Sayo, Kurara concentrated on putting the finishing touches to a small, paper pocket watch. Fiddly little details like the gears of a watch or the feathers of a mechanical bird were always the most difficult to make and the most rewarding to finally get right.

"And then I asked Sayo, 'If cumulous whales aren't actually whales, then why do we call them that?' And you know what she said? She said they're molluscs! You know, like slugs! Cumulous whales have that weird translucent skin, right? They absorb air through it. They don't actually have bones. Though they'll rip you apart all the same if you get too close to the pod."

Tomoe nattered on as she tinkered with a small mechanical contraption. Trying to focus on her ofuda while listening to Tomoe talk on and on was, in a way, its own kind of training. Kurara had never met anyone who could talk as much as Haru.

"They have teeth," said Kurara. "Teeth are bones."

Tomoe opened her mouth to argue when the ship's bells suddenly began to ring. As if summoned by the sound, Sayo emerged from the wheelhouse and hurried across the deck. She wore a serious look. More serious than usual.

"What's going on?" asked Kurara.

"None of your business."

"If something happens to the ship, it's all of our business," said Tomoe.

Sayo relented. Kurara was slightly annoyed by how quickly Sayo would tell Tomoe but not her. "The lookouts spotted a ship approaching. A military ship."

Tomoe hissed through her teeth. "Looking for BOMBs?" she asked.

Kurara jumped. *Bombs?*

Sayo nodded. The bells continued to ring as Sakurai strode onto the deck, armed with a handful of papers. Himura was at his side, Akane in tow. He motioned to shoo Tomoe below deck. Kurara moved to follow her, but the captain raised a hand.

"Not you, Miss Kurara," he said.

136

She did not have time to protest. Without warning, a long, silver airship emerged from behind the clouds. Its windows were tinted. A black flag with a golden peony at its centre waved in the wind. Kurara had seen plenty of groundling-made airships before, but only now did she appreciate the difference between military vessels and Sorabito-built ships. Where the *Orihime* was sleek and colourful, the groundling airship was like a cliff of pure steel. Blocky and cumbersome, it pushed its way through the air, engines straining.

Sighing, Sakurai flicked through the stack of papers in his hands. *Registration papers*, Kurara realized.

"Don't worry. It's just a surprise inspection. We can handle a few bored soldiers. Let them throw their weight around. Whimper and cower a bit too. They like that."

Kurara hoped that was all the soldiers wanted, though she could not shake the memory of her last encounter with the military, and the soldiers who had burned Haru alive.

The ship towered over the *Orihime* as it slid into the space beside them. Akane ducked behind Kurara and Himura's legs as soldiers rolled out a gangway, connecting the two decks together. An officer in a dark blue uniform emerged from the opposite ship, accompanied by several armed men. Though he did not appear to need one, he carried a cane, which he used solely for slamming into the ground. His black hair was perfectly shaped like a conch shell, slicked back with all manner of grease. Kurara had met soldiers like this on the *Midori*: sneering little men addicted to the sound of their own voices and the giddy high of power.

The officer took one look at the *Orihime* and sniffed as though trying to rid his nose of some unpleasant smell.

"People say that no one builds ships like the Sorabito. How true that is. No one else builds such junk." His voice was thin and nasal, spoken between clenched teeth as though he was trying to talk without having to breathe the same air as the rest of them.

Beside her, Kurara felt Sayo bristle.

"Welcome to the *Orihime*." Sakurai let the insult slide off him with barely a glancing blow. "I must inform you that my ship employs—"

Without waiting for him to finish, the officer nodded to his men and barked, "Search their cargo! I've heard Sorabito ships passing this way have been sheltering members of Sohma." He turned back to Sakurai with a smug smile.

"Now wait a minute!" Kurara stepped forward, blocking the soldiers' path. "You can't just barge your way on board without evidence!"

The officer's smile lit a smouldering fire in her gut. It burned as she thought of every entertainer who had forced a polite smile for men like him, every attendant who had served them wine in exchange for abuse and the servants who had been left to clean up their mess.

She thought of the crew who had committed no crime except for the fact that they were Sorabito.

Sayo hissed at her, but there was no heat in it. The officer's eyes widened. He walked towards her, loudly slamming his cane against the ground with every step.

"*Stop!*" Akane jumped out from behind. "*Stay away!*"

"Shikigami!" The officer leapt at the sound of the

shikigami's voice. His hand flew to his katana. He drew the sword, steel swinging in the air. The edge of the blade caught the side of Akane's face and cut into the shikigami's cheek.

"Akane!" Kurara stepped between the officer and the shikigami.

The other soldiers scrambled to the edge of the deck, away from the fox. Himura barked an order to freeze, and Akane's body snapped to obey, but its eyes remained wide and full of pain.

"You have a shikigami on board?" Wavering between anger and panic, the officer's gaze shifted from one face to the next before settling on Captain Sakurai. His voice bordered on hysterical. "Where's the thing's master? Where's your Crafter?"

"You'd know that if you actually listened instead of interrupting!" cried Sayo, furious.

"What my navigator means is—"

"Akane was trying to protect me. She didn't do anything wrong!" Kurara crouched next to the shikigami, placing a protective hand on its flank. Fury coursed through her veins. It was not the fox's fault that the officer was a coward.

"Are you the Crafter?" The officer's gaze narrowed onto Kurara. Akane, still frozen in place by Himura's command, stared at her anxiously.

Kurara nodded.

For a moment, she thought that her position as Crafter had spooked him enough that he would back down, but instead the officer reached towards his hip, to the gun holstered there.

Kurara stiffened. That gun… It was the same model the soldiers in the forest had used.

Her throat was suddenly dry. The deck, the soldiers – even Akane and Himura – swam before her eyes. She tried to focus, but all she could see was Haru burning, burning beneath a cage of trees.

Seeing the fear in her eyes gave the officer the confidence to take a step forward. "If you're working on a sky rat's ship instead of serving the imperial family, you can't be much of a Crafter. How did a weakling like you get a shikigami when only the most elite of the royal family's imperial Crafters are given such an honour?" he sneered.

Kurara said nothing. What if the officer burned Akane for this?

Emboldened by her silence, the officer approached her, swinging his cane. His eyes were bright with anger. Himura tried to step between them, his jaw tight as though he were trying to swallow poison, but Kurara pushed him aside.

"*Don't,*" she mouthed. A silent plea. *Don't make things worse than they already are.*

The officer drew his hand back and struck her across the cheek.

Kurara heard Himura snarl, saw Sakurai tense and Sayo flinch as the sound echoed across the deck. She stumbled, her head ringing from the force of the blow.

It was OK, she told herself. This was no different from the punishments on the *Midori*. She clenched her teeth, and swallowed back the humiliation and anger. She had lived beneath Madam Ito's rule for years. Kurara knew how to endure.

"Confiscate half their food and fuel!" the officer barked at his soldiers.

As if struck by lightning, the men jumped to attention, disappearing into the ship. No one said anything or tried to stop them any more.

The officer shifted his focus from Kurara to Sakurai. With a mean smile, he said: "You're heading south, aren't you? If you survive the Kumokiri Mountains, I'll be sure to tell my officer friends to look out for your ship. They'll give you a *warm welcome*."

"Kumokiri?" the captain's tone remained level despite the man's threat. "Has something happened near the mountains?"

The officer chortled. "Are all you Sorabito this stupid? Don't you know a pod of cumulous whales have made their nesting grounds in the mountain mists this year? You know how protective they are around their young. Little birds like you would get swallowed quite easily. It would be a shame to lose such a lovely target—ah, pardon … I mean, ship."

"We will take care." Sakurai bowed. As if the officer had not spent the past few minutes smacking about one of his crew. As if he was not taking half of their supplies.

The ship pulled away. As soon as it disappeared beyond the clouds, everyone moved at once.

Akane, free from its orders to stay frozen, gingerly licked at Kurara's knuckles. It was not until she felt its papery tongue across her skin did she realize that her hands were shaking. She was no stranger to injustice, but it had been a while since she had felt quite so powerless.

"Well, that was stupid of you." Sayo's scowl eased into a grin. "But at least you've got some backbone, after all."

"Are you all right?" Himura grabbed her by the chin, tilting her face up so that he could get a good look at her cheek. "You should have let it go. Never mind Akane. Shikigami forget about pain quickly enough. You'll need to see Dr Yuriha now."

Kurara jerked out of his grip. "But that man – he was so awful! I didn't want to just stand there. Akane could have been really hurt! Don't you care about your shikigami?"

It was so unfair. She wished she had made a swarm of paper wasps chase the officer and his men off the ship, though she knew that would have only made things worse.

Himura's eyes darkened with anger. When he looked at her, Kurara could feel a thunderstorm simmering beneath his skin.

"We need to change our flight plans," Sakurai sighed. "We'll never make it to the Grand Stream on only half our food and fuel. We'll have to make an emergency pit stop, and I want to avoid Kumokiri Pass."

Sayo's jaw tightened. "Surely you don't believe what that groundling said."

"He had no reason to lie."

"But the nearest sky city is—"

"I know." The captain turned to look at the sky, grey with the promise of more rain. "Sayo, set a new course. We're going to Sola-Il."

SEVENTEEN

THAT night, Kurara rolled over on her futon and hugged Haru's core tight. Frustration burrowed beneath her skin, along with a troubled flutter of panic.

They could not go to Sola-Il yet. She was not ready! She thought she would have all summer, and a hunt in between, to practise before reaching the city – and the princess. Though Himura assured her that they did not have to see Princess Tsukimi the moment they landed on Sola-Il – both the princess and the city were not going anywhere – she knew she couldn't wait. She couldn't leave Haru without a body for any longer than she had to. She wanted to save Haru now. If they were going to Sola-Il sooner than expected, then she would master her powers sooner than expected as well. Any other option left a bitter taste in her mouth.

She was not the only one feeling sour, either.

In the wake of the "surprise inspection", Sakurai had ordered their daily meals to be halved. From now on, hot water was rationed so that they could use the fuel to power the engines and meat was to be served only once per week. The mood on the *Orihime* was as foul as the potions Dr Yuriha ordered Kurara to drink, and the awful-smelling ointment she gave her to rub onto her stinging cheek.

Kurara buried her face into her pillow to muffle her groan. She just wanted Haru back. Why did everything have to be so difficult?

"Flying through Kumokiri Pass would be faster. But the whales... That damn groundling..." Sayo's voice drifted through their quarters as she worked past lights out, poring over maps and plotting out their new course by the light of a single oil lamp.

It was no good. Kurara rolled onto her side then onto her back. She could not sleep. Even making a flock of origami sheep leap over her head did not work. The soldiers, going to Sola-Il, meeting Princess Tsukimi – there were too many things on her mind, each worry linking into another in a merry-go-round of misery. She needed a walk and some fresh air.

Slipping out of the room, Kurara made her way to the male cabin wing. Himura was still awake when she knocked on the door to his quarters, lounging beneath his window with a small pile of books stacked beside him. Akane sat by his ankles, softly singing.

"A dying star fell from the heavens, and from that star grew a tree." The fox only knew one song, a lullaby Kurara was sure she had heard somewhere before.

"Couldn't sleep?" Himura closed the book he was reading, placing it carefully upon the stack.

"What were you reading about?" Kurara suddenly felt incredibly childish for coming here. Like a child who needed an older sibling to soothe them after a scary dream.

"Shikigami." Himura placed a careful hand against the hardback cover. "I've been trying to find out more about ones like your friend, but there's so little here. What I need are the books in Princess Tsukimi's library."

"Maybe you can borrow some books from her when we see her."

Himura's expression twisted into a look of pain. "It is her *personal* library. Ordinary people are not allowed to read such things. *Especially* you and I. It's full of manuals on shikigami, accounts from ancient Crafters that once ruled this land. Books the Emperor believes are too dangerous for Crafters to read. What if we became so much more than we are now? What if we used that knowledge to kill the imperial family? Even though that knowledge belongs to us. Even though it is *our* past being kept from us."

There was resentment in his voice. It thrummed like a dark undercurrent beneath his words.

Kurara remembered that Himura had met Princess Tsukimi once. He had told her that Tsukimi was difficult and unpredictable. It made her nervous. It was one thing to train as hard as she could and fail, but if Princess Tsukimi refused to help her for reasons outside of her control … Kurara did not know how she would handle that.

"How did you first meet the princess? Was it that bad?"

Himura's expression shuttered. His eyes gave away nothing. "She asked me to impress her and I failed."

"How did you fail? What didn't she like?"

"I'm in no mood to tell you stories, Kurara. I'm angry with you."

"You? Angry at *me*?" Kurara spluttered. What had *she* done?

Himura was acting no different from usual that at first Kurara did not believe him. It was only when he stood up that she noticed the severe look in his eyes.

"What you did today was stupid. A Crafter should never sacrifice themselves for a shikigami. A shikigami is replaceable. *You* are not."

"If their core remains, I know they can be given new bodies," said Kurara, "but if—"

"There are lots of shikigami out there."

"But none of those shikigami are Akane!" cried Kurara as frustration bloomed inside her chest. She had come here for comfort, not for a fight. "If shikigami are so replaceable, why are you helping me save Haru?"

No shikigami could ever take Haru's place in her heart.

"That one was special," Himura huffed. "Though, in the end, a shikigami is an object created from paper and blood. They're amazing. Fascinating. But ultimately they're simply tools created by Crafters to serve them."

Kurara sucked in a sharp breath. Hearing him say that hurt more than she could imagine. She would rather he had punched her. "If you think what I'm doing is stupid, then don't bother helping me! I'll leave the *Orihime*. I'll teach myself how to become a great Crafter and go see Princess Tsukimi myself!"

"I never said that. You're working yourself up," snapped Himura.

"And you're being pig-headed!"

"*It's late!*" Akane leapt between them, its voice high and loud. The tip of its bushy tail waved in the air like a white flag as it proclaimed, "*Akane will walk the kit back to her room!*"

"Don't dilly-dally, Akane," said Himura.

"*Of course not, Master!*" Akane looked at him as though he hung the moon.

"Getting rid of me?" Kurara stuck her nose in the air. "Fine! I'll leave you to your precious books. Maybe one of them can teach you how to have a heart!"

"Kurara," Himura called as she reached the door. She turned to see him sitting beneath the window again, his nose buried in a book. "Don't oversleep. We still have lessons tomorrow."

Kurara's nostrils flared. Slamming the door shut, she marched down the hallways, fuming. Akane trotted by her side, watching her in silence.

"Himura!" she growled his name like a curse. Hot indignation coursed through her veins. That sky-forsaken man! She'd show him. She would become a Crafter a hundred times smarter and better than he was and then he would have no choice but to listen to what she said.

In the cool darkness of the hallway, she took out a piece of paper from behind the folds of her obi.

It transformed into a paper fox like Akane. Kurara watched it prance across her hand until she calmed down. When she remembered how Himura had tried to put himself between her and the officer, the way he had looked at her with concern after the soldiers had left, her anger wavered, but did not disappear.

"Does it really not bother you? When Himura talks about you like that?" She glanced down at the shikigami beside her.

The fox gave her an odd look. It was nothing like the somewhat thoughtless grin it usually wore. That too-human smile curled around its lips.

"Why be upset? It's true. Akane was made to serve."

Kurara's stomach twisted in knots. It was not the obedience that bothered her – she had lived on the *Midori*, after all – but Akane's willingness to be Himura's puppet. Akane was not an unthinking tool. She was sure of it.

"But you still have your own thoughts and feelings! Himura never ordered you to protect me, yet you jumped in to defend me against that soldier. You have emotions, don't you? And likes and dislikes!"

The shikigami's smile slipped from its face. It appeared lost in thought.

"Akane forgets who it was," it said. *"Memories went goodbye. Now they're gone."*

"What?" Kurara screeched to a halt. "What does that mean?"

Akane was puzzled by Kurara's alarm. *"It is simple. Scrub away parts of the core to scrub away memories!"*

The fox trotted on, but Kurara did not move.

"You mean … you … wiped your own memories?"

"Not Akane! A previous master of a previous master!"

There was no hint of anger in Akane's voice, but the shikigami's calm only added to Kurara's horror.

She had not thought it possible, but then Himura had said that the core was the heart and brain of a shikigami. If humans could lose their memory after a few knocks to the head, why couldn't shikigami lose them too? Her mind turned to Haru. Though she had tried not to think about it, she knew that if he was a shikigami then he must have had masters at one point as well. Back in the forest, he had tried to tell her something. Could it possibly have been related? Kurara could not remember his exact words. By that point, the Haru she knew had been fading fast.

"Why would they do that?"

"Maybe so Akane would not be sad? Doesn't little kit have things better left forgotten?"

Haru burning in the forest. The officer who had taken their supplies. Madam Ito when she was in a rage. Kurara flinched. Yes, there were plenty of things she would rather forget, but that did not mean that she should.

"Did you agree to it, Akane? I mean, was that what you wanted? Are you happy? Are you…?"

The more she thought about it, the more Kurara's mind spiralled. Memories were far too important to be scrubbed away like ink stains. Memories … like the ones Kurara did not have. Like the home she did not know and the lotus flowers she could not remember.

Pain pierced her skull. Who had Akane been before it lost its memories? Who was she?

"*Little kit?*" Akane nudged her with its muzzle. "*Kurara?*"

"Kurara?" She winced when her skull throbbed. "Is that my name?"

Someone had once told her that her name meant both joy and suffering, though she could not remember who. She did not know why her own name suddenly felt wrong, like a coat that had been stretched out so that the sleeves no longer fit. Something hollow and hungry gnawed at her heart. She thought again of Haru in the forest, on the verge of collapsing. What had he been trying to tell her then?

Akane pawed at her leg. "*A dying star fell from the heavens, and from that star grew a tree,*" the fox sang to soothe her. A familiar lullaby that haunted the corridors of her memory.

Interlude

Tie string to the stars,
Let me climb to the heavens.
Oh, I long for home.

– Sorabito merchant song

From the prow of the *Hishaku*, Kazeno Rei looked down upon a multitude of ships. The docks of Sola-Il were vast and cavernous, capable of holding more than a thousand vessels at once. The *Hishaku* entered, guided by flashing yellow lights, and something in Rei's chest swelled. Though he had not been born on Sola-Il, it was the very first sky city ever built. No matter what, it would always feel like home.

The ship landed with a jolt. The entire flight had been an exercise in stress. Though Inui had promised that the dragon would remain calm, Rei had not quite believed her. He had spent most of the flight hardly sleeping, wondering if the shikigami would suddenly burst out of its crate and kill them all.

151

I hope Princess Tsukimi dies painfully. It was the only thought that could bring him comfort after such a nerve-wracking trip. *I hope Prince Ugetsu keeps his promise to grant the sky cities their freedom and then promptly chokes to death on an edamame bean at his coronation.*

At least he had finally reached Sola-Il. Just a little longer and he could relax knowing everything was in place for a grand assassination.

"I never tire of this view." Nao joined him by the guard rails. Though Rei was annoyed by his company, it was Nao's ship and he could come and go as he pleased. He was the one who had transported the dragon all this way. Even if the man was only here because Inui had gone behind Rei's back and roped Nao into this scheme.

"I'll like the view a lot more once the groundlings are purged from it," said Rei.

Nao averted his eyes the way his daughters would whenever he got a little too heated.

Too soft, Rei wanted to sneer. All members of Sohma should be prepared to get their hands dirty. There would be no independence otherwise.

From the ground, dock workers locked the ship into place. A guard in a blue and gold uniform approached them from the side, calling out in a cheery voice, "Greetings, the *Hishaku*. Are you here for the festival?"

Rei tensed. This was not one of the guards his men had paid off in advance.

"Greetings," he replied. "Forgive me, but you weren't exactly who I was expecting."

"Ah yes, all of our other inspectors are busy at the moment. You know what it's like during the festival. Not to worry, we won't keep you from the fun for long," the guard laughed. "Please lower your gangway so we can inspect your cargo."

"What are we going to do?" Nao panicked. There was no hiding a *giant dragon* from the guard. If the man boarded the *Hishaku*, he would find the crate and the shikigami inside it.

Rei glanced up at the docking bay ceiling. Armed men patrolled the rafters along the top of the docks, ready to open fire at the slightest trouble. He had to think fast. Should he insist that the inspection be carried out by the men he had paid off? Or perhaps he could bribe this guard as well.

"Your gangway, please!" the guard called. He was beginning to sound impatient.

"Rei, if they find the dragon, we're as good as dead. Do you know what the soldiers do when they catch Sohma members?" Nao gripped Rei's arm.

"Calm down! You'll give us away!" he snarled, but Nao was not listening.

"They bury them! Alive! In the ground with the worms!"

Their dallying was making the guard suspicious. Rei saw him call over some other men and reach for his gun.

Nao noticed the weapon too. At the first sight of glinting steel, he kicked the gangway down and ran.

"Stop!" Rei shouted. The stupid man had panicked. He was going to ruin everything!

 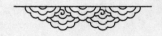

"Halt!" the guard shouted as Nao hurtled towards the docking doors.

The men patrolling the rafters took aim and fired, their bullets barely missing Nao as he careened out of the docking bay. Rei's hands gripped the guard rails as he watched, his knuckles white. He wanted to howl and curse that idiot of a man. This was why he had never wanted Nao involved – the man was an utter coward.

"Stop!" came a stern voice. One of the armed men on the rafters jumped down onto the *Hishaku's* deck. He pointed his gun at Rei. "Put your hands up."

"What's going on here?" A familiar voice interrupted them.

"L–Lady Inui!" The guard jumped. "What are you doing here?"

Rei stiffened. Inui had said that she would meet him in Sola-Il, but he had not expected her to turn up so suddenly. The drab kimono and heavy cloak she usually wore were replaced with a bright, red kimono and a black hakama, but her face was just as spectral as before. A white festival mask of a young woman sat at an angle at the top of her head, like a second face growing from her skull. She looked far too delighted by the sight of the man pointing a gun at Rei's head.

Her belt of paper hands wriggled their fingers at the guard in a manner that would haunt Rei's dreams that night. He dragged his gaze upward to stare at her face. Her sharp, rictus grin, and her light, milky eyes were like those of an ancient beast luring foolish humans into its waiting jaws.

"The *Hishaku* is carrying a very special item for Princess Tsukimi. We cannot keep the princess waiting, can we?" Her broad, false smile displayed a row of yellow teeth.

The guard looked uneasy. "But that man…"

"He's the one who owns the ship. The crew and I are just hired help. Check the ship's registration documents if you don't believe me," said Rei.

Inui waved a dismissive hand. "I'll inspect the ship. He must have had a good reason to run. Perhaps he was late for his leading role in today's parade?" she cackled, far too amused by her own joke. "You should concentrate on finding him. Don't worry your pretty little head about the *Hishaku*. If something happens, I will take full responsibility."

The guard winced but nodded.

Rei led Inui inside for the "inspection". Once they were below deck, he turned around and snarled, "What are you doing here? Isn't this suspicious?"

One of the paper hands on Inui's belt detached itself to flick the hair out of her face. "Come now, I said I would meet you on Sola-Il. Someone has to make sure the dragon performs."

"You didn't mention you would show up in the docks. Here, in front of so many witnesses." Rei simmered with anger. He could not shake the feeling that he had fallen dangerously into her orbit and was being pulled along by her whims.

"Oh, don't be so anxious!" said Inui. "If you must know, I was the one who thought up this whole assassination

plan in the first place. I was the one who approached Prince Ugetsu about it. I know what I'm doing."

Rei's nails dug into the palms of his hands. It did not matter who had first come up with the idea of killing the princess with a shikigami, Prince Ugetsu had entrusted this plan to *him*. The freedom of the sky cities was riding on it.

Ignoring the way Rei's mouth opened and closed in speechless rage, Inui placed a paper hand on his shoulder.

"Leave your men to move the dragon. We should find your comrade before someone catches and questions him."

———o———

The festival was already in full swing. Lantern lights flowed from the port all the way through the commercial hub of the city and down to the wind farms sprouting along the outskirts like giant flowers. Drums beat through the air. Twirling acrobats danced after the procession in black cloaks that glittered with a thousand stars, followed by men breathing fire and women with wings made of steel. Large wooden floats depicting scenes of young maidens riding on the backs of giant birds were beautiful beyond compare. They reminded Rei why he was proud to be a Sorabito.

"This way." Inui ruined the moment by grabbing his arm in her skeletal hand and pulling him towards the alleyways.

The backstreets were narrow and labyrinthine, penned in on either side by towering wooden buildings

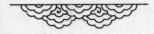

156

that climbed towards the sky. It took longer than Rei had hoped to find Nao. The man was hunched beside a wooden wall, panting for breath. The guards were nowhere to be seen, but before Rei could take another step, Inui suddenly pushed him behind a corner. Just in time to hide from a man dropping out of the sky.

A Crafter landed in the alleyway in front of Nao. Paper wings folded around his back before dissolving into a paper whirlwind that surged menacingly around him.

Another of Princess Tsukimi's imperial Crafters. Rei pressed his back flush to the wall and muttered another curse to the winds.

"Halt!" The Crafter wore the same red and black uniform as Inui. "I saw you running from the guards, fiend! What crime have you committed?"

As he peeked around the corner, Rei heard a voice echo through his head.

"I am here." It rumbled like a growing thunderstorm.

Rei stiffened. A shikigami was speaking.

Footsteps whispered across the stone, as slow and ominous as a hangman's shuffle. From the shadows, a large white tiger appeared behind the Crafter. Though it was completely white, raised marks across its body created the impression of stripes.

"Ruki." The Crafter stretched out a tender hand.

"Who is this, Master? An enemy? Your enemy? What should I do with him? Did he hurt you?" The tiger, Ruki, curled itself around its master. It was twice the size of a regular tiger and had to squeeze its shoulders together

in order to enter the alleyway. It stepped towards Nao. White, unblinking eyes narrowed onto its prey.

"Wait!" Nao shrank back. "Please don't kill me! I'll confess! I have information that will be useful to you!"

That blasted Nao! Rei's heart seized. He gripped the hilt of his katana.

"Shh!" Inui placed a hand on Rei's shoulder and she stepped out into the open.

"Fujiwa. Ruki. What's going on here, you two? Who is this?" She faked innocence. As if she did not know exactly what was going on.

Nao's eyes widened in recognition. He ran towards Inui with relief.

"Lady—!"

"Get away from me!" Inui recoiled. Faster than Rei could blink, she sharpened her ofuda into a blade and sliced through Nao's throat.

Blood gushed from the wound.

Rei turned away from the scene, but he could imagine the look of surprise on Nao's face as his body crumpled to the ground.

"Inui!" The Crafter rounded on her, livid.

"He was going to attack me."

"You were in no danger—!"

"Who was he, anyway?" Inui interrupted him. "Just a simple criminal?"

"I don't know," said the Crafter. "I saw guards chasing him out of the docks. He was up to something. He was about to confess."

"Then you should report this to the princess. I'll ask the docking guards what the matter was."

"Fine," came the cagey reply. "Come, Ruki. Let's go."

Rei peered around the corner again just in time to see the hulking tiger follow its master out of the alleyway. Inui stared after the shikigami with a strange, faraway gaze. Once they were gone, he stepped out into the open. In the distance, the parade continued. Threads of cheery music echoed through the streets, oblivious to the death that had just occurred.

"Poor Nao." Inui crouched by the fallen body. "Well, he served his purpose."

Rei curled his hands into fists so that they would stop trembling. It was not Nao's death that bothered him; he had never liked the man. No, it was the feeling that he had not been in control of anything that had just happened. Not Inui's appearance, not Nao's death, not even the way the other Crafter had been diverted.

Inui stood up, brushing the dirt off her kimono. There were flecks of blood on the front. Nao's blood.

"Oh, come now, don't make that face. I need you to come with me."

Rei seethed. All of this was *his* plan to undertake, his scheme to unravel as he saw fit. He was no one's puppet.

Yet he knew that if he refused, Inui could force him to accompany her and he would rather not be dragged through the streets by her paper hands. He followed her out of the alleyway. With each step, he felt the invisible strings at the end of Inui's many paper fingers forcing him into a dance.

EIGHTEEN

THEY had five days left. Five days. Himura had checked and triple checked the flight plan with Sayo until the girl had snapped at him to leave her alone, yet the the number was always the same. It was not enough time. If Kurara was to learn everything she needed to know before seeing Princess Tsukimi, Himura would have to speed through their lessons. There was no room for failure.

Every hour of training was precious, yet Himura found himself pacing around his room waiting for Kurara to appear. The breakfast hour came and went, the morning turning into early afternoon, and still she did not knock at his door. Minutes passed, each one making him more irritable. Kurara was usually so eager to practise. Was she still asleep? He had told her not to stay up too late.

"Akane, come!" With a click of his tongue, he headed

towards the female cabin wing. He would make sure their lesson was extra gruelling today.

But when he knocked on Kurara's door, only Sayo was there to answer.

"She's playing with Tomoe!" The bags under Sayo's eyes were so dark they looked like bruises. "Could you not bother me? Can't you see I have all these flight paths to calculate? And the fuel! I need to measure our fuel stores!"

Waving her maps like a madwoman, Sayo slammed the door in Himura's face.

"Master." Akane grinned. *"Can we play too?"*

Kurara was playing, was she? Himura breathed in and felt his irritation rise tenfold.

The clouds drifting above the deck were ominously grey. In the distance, Himura could see the mountains the military officer had warned them about – two dark walls of stone shrouded in mist like the gates to a giant's keep. Crooning whale song echoed in the distance.

He exited the ship via the balcony door. As he made his way down the stairs, he heard a gleeful shout.

"Draw!" Tomoe held up a straw basket as she bellowed at the crew gathered around her.

In an instant, four crewmen tossed a copper coin into the air.

Kurara planted her feet in front of Tomoe, her back to the rest of the crew, who formed a semicircle behind her. The moment the coins flew into the air, she spun around. With a single crumpled ball of paper, she knocked the coins out of the sky. Two landed in Tomoe's basket. The other two missed and bounced over the metal deck where they rolled to a stop.

Himura's eyes widened. She had missed the basket, but her control of ofuda was better than he had expected. He knew that Kurara had a knack for shape-changing, but he had not realized until this moment that her talent extended to anything else. She was learning fast.

"Amazing! The little kit is almost as good as you!" Akane whistled.

"That's generous," he snorted. She was not as good as him. Nowhere close.

But, a small voice in the back of his head whispered, *she will be soon*. What had taken him months to learn Kurara was managing after barely a week. She would not just be better. She might even surpass him.

"Draw!" Tomoe shouted again and another four crewmen threw their coins. This time, Kurara only hit one into the basket, but the other three were close, bouncing off the rim.

The crew offered a round of applause.

With a breathless grin, Kurara bowed. She looked pleased with herself. Delighted by the crew's attention. The crew had never asked Himura to play such silly games with them. They would not dare. He was a noble Crafter. It would be an insult to waste his gifts by performing party tricks.

"A long time ago, we Crafters ruled this land. A long time ago, we were so much more than what we are now," his parents had whispered to him. They would have been appalled to see how Kurara used her gifts.

"You're not a damned circus animal," he called out as he marched down the rest of the steps.

The crew stiffened as he approached.

Kurara turned with a disappointed look on her face. "We were having fun."

"We'll arrive at Sola-Il just in time for the Festival of the Seventh Star. Everyone should get in the holiday mood!" said Tomoe.

Himura ignored her. "If you want to join a travelling troupe of performers, be my guest. But if you want to learn how to be a great Crafter, then you'll stick with me," he said to Kurara.

There was something rebellious in her gaze that Himura did not like. He needed to nip it in the bud before it became a problem.

"Leave us!" he snapped at the crew. A single look sent them scattering. He turned back to Kurara. "You are a proud Crafter. Don't disgrace yourself or your ofuda by performing party tricks."

"If I'm a disgrace then what would you call our conversation last night?" Kurara muttered beneath her breath. "Did you know that Akane has no memories from when it was first created?"

Himura lifted an eyebrow. He had not expected this. The emotion in her voice took him aback. He did not understand why she was so upset.

"Shikigami were created to serve Crafters. That is the reason they exist," his parents would whisper at night.

What was the point of getting worked up over Akane's memories? The fox was perfectly fine without them.

"When I first formed a bond with Akane, I thought I could ask it for information about my ancestors, about shikigami, but Akane knew nothing," he sighed. "But what of it? Masters can do as they like. Shikigami have no will of their own. They act like individuals but everything about their personality is created by the symbols on their core. They are not human. They are not *people*."

Besides, he was not a bad master. Even if he was snappy with the fox sometimes, he treated Akane well. That was enough, wasn't it?

Kurara's eyes were bright with anger, but before she could speak, the fox jumped between them.

"Akane thinks that you two shouldn't fight," said the shikigami, glumly.

"Akane is right. We have no time to waste." Himura pulled his bracelet from his wrist. "Meeting the princess is not something you should take lightly. Weakness is an insult and Princess Tsukimi deals with insults very swiftly. Come prepared or don't come at all."

He had not been prepared when he first saw the princess and his pride was still smarting from the encounter.

"Then I'll come prepared," said Kurara.

Himura did not know what to make of the fire burning in her eyes. Pride and unease warred against each other for his attention. Kurara was a product of his lessons, her determination was a reflection of his skill, but he could not help but feel as though she was preparing to race onward, leaving him behind.

When Himura finally turned away, the sun had fled behind the clouds. He walked over to the basket Tomoe had left behind on the deck and picked it up, tossing it high above his head. As the basket sailed through the air, his ofuda darted towards it. With a snap of his fingers, the paper merged to form a hawk that grabbed hold of the basket's rim and swooped towards the deck.

The bird dropped the basket on Kurara's head. She caught it with an offended squawk.

"Since you are quite skilled at shape-changing already, it is time we proceed to lessons on movement," said Himura.

Kurara was not looking at him. Her head was bowed, staring at the deck. Himura felt a twinge of annoyance until he looked down and realized that she was staring at the sudden wisps of white smoke curling across the floor.

No, not smoke, mist. The *Orihime* sailed upon a sea of fog. A rolling haze that blanketed the world from view.

Peering up, Himura could just about make out the side of a rocky wall. They were close to the Kumokiri Mountains, but instead of going around them, they had entered the mountain pass.

But Sakurai said—

Before he could finish that thought, something bumped the ship. Just enough that Himura felt the deck shift slightly. The moment he recovered, there was another bump, harder this time.

"What was that?" he heard Kurara squeak and Akane yip in warning.

Fog brushed against the starboard side. No, that was not fog. Himura's horror mounted as he noticed a large, black eye staring at him from the body of mist.

They had stumbled right into a nest of sky whales.

NINETEEN

WARNING bells rang out across the deck as Kurara felt something else bump into the ship.

"We're under attack," said Himura, grimly. His words made Kurara's heart drop into her stomach. They brought back images of the *Midori* – the screaming, the flames, the shattered windows.

She peered through the darkness until she could just about make out the large, looming rock walls surrounding the ship. The mist was so thick that she had not noticed them when they had entered Kumokiri Pass. Why were they flying through the mountains? Captain Sakurai had said that they should go around.

The air pressure dropped. A pungent, metallic smell filled her nostrils: the familiar scent of a storm. Fog obscured everything except the rock walls, but despite the darkness Kurara could see shadowy shapes move through the mists. Haunting voices crooned in the dark.

Cumulous whales. Kurara could just about make them out if she squinted. Thin, translucent skin, prone to bursting, covered voluminous stomachs that held clouds within them. Black eyes stared dumbly out of flattened heads, fins rowing through the air. On occasion, one would open its mouth, revealing several rows of yellowing teeth.

They had disturbed a pod. The officer had warned them about the nest. The fact that he was right put a foul taste in Kurara's mouth.

When the *Orihime* brushed against a whale, the impact made its body wobble like gelatine. The sack on its belly burst, releasing a sudden downpour of rain.

The other whales responded with gnashing teeth and razor-like fins. A set of humungous molars closed upon the ship's prow, breaking the battering ram clean in two. Sharp fins sheared through the guard rails.

"*Whales! Whales!*" Akane jumped up and down in alarm.

"Take this!" Himura passed Kurara a handful of paper. "And help me!"

"B—but the water!"

"Water does not affect ofuda as badly as fire. Just try not to get the paper drenched!" Himura's ofuda transformed into a school of sleek sky fish with long, elegant tails and wing-like fins. "I was hoping we would have more time to practise first. But it looks like you'll have to learn as we go."

A translucent tail shunted the *Orihime* to one side. Kurara flew back, her stomach colliding with the guard rail. She almost toppled over the edge, but her hands grabbed the railing just in time. She held on for dear life as the ship careened to one side. The rain made the metal slick and difficult to grip.

"What do I do?" she cried.

The mountains kept the ship penned in. Another smack, this time from the tail of a whale gliding beneath them. Kurara heard the wood creak and the metal groan as the impact left a dent in the side of the ship. She looked to the wheelhouse. Was that Sayo she could see directing the ship through stomach-churning turns, trying to shake the whales off their tail?

"Hold out your fingers and make your ofuda follow you. Like this." Himura's paper fish danced around him, darting this way and that as he moved his hands. "Keep your attention balanced between each piece of ofuda. You'll need to make them move as one. All of them."

Kurara copied him. Her paper fish looked just like his, but they did not dart about as quickly or as far as Himura's. Each time they moved further than six feet away, her control wavered and they began to unravel.

A whale slammed into the hull. Kurara fell backwards and rolled across the deck. Her concentration slipped for a moment and her paper fish turned back into plain sheets of paper that were snatched up and thrown aside by the wind.

"Crafting requires focus! If you panic, you will lose control. Remain calm!" Himura shouted over the howling gale.

That was easy for him to say. How was she supposed

to concentrate when she could barely stand? Picking herself up, Kurara snatched her ofuda out of the air and gathered them to her side.

"*Whales!*" Akane barked in warning. The fins of a passing cumulous whale snagged against the guard rails, ripping them off. When the ship groaned, it sounded as though the heavens were being torn in two.

Before they could do any more damage, Himura's paper fish flew right in front of the whales' faces. They danced to and fro in a taunt, then darted away from the ship. Some of the whales peeled back to give chase, their mouths open, hoping for a meal.

"Think of ofuda as an extension of your body. Do you look at your feet every time you take a step? Do you think about your legs when you walk from one place to another? Your ofuda is *a part of you!*" he instructed, dashing to the ship's prow to distract the whales gathering there.

Kurara sucked in a deep breath. Her lessons in Himura's quarters were all well and good, but this was the real thing. She had to protect the ship. There were no escape pods. If the *Orihime* went down, so would the crew.

Her hands were shaking and her heart was pounding as loud as thunder, but she could not let her nerves get the better of her. One by one, her ofuda turned into sky fish. She held out a hand and the fish followed the tip of her finger.

The cumulous whales rushed at her. Their enormous mouths yawned open like gaping chasms.

"Don't draw them towards us!" screamed Himura. "Send them away!"

Kurara ran. The paper fish followed her to the prow. As did the whales. When she reached the front of the ship, she stretched out her hand to send the fish away but, like children unwilling to leave their mother's side, they did not move far enough.

One of the whales dived for the fish, almost taking a huge bite out of the ship.

"Move!" Kurara shouted. Why was this so hard? She stared at her ofuda, concentrating and concentrating, until the back of her eyes pounded and her skull felt as though someone was trying to split it in two.

"Your ofuda is a part of you," Himura had said.

Kurara took a deep breath.

Let go. Stop trying to force it. Let go.

Pouring forth like a broken dam, the paper fish soared into the sky. Kurara did not know whether to laugh or sob with relief. Her ofuda darted around the whales, grabbing their attention and pulling them away from the ship on a merry chase.

"Akane, go and fetch us more paper!" cried Himura.

The fox scrambled to obey.

Haru, you'll never believe this when I tell you! Kurara's ofuda swam through the air. Even though it made her skull throb, she was far too excited to let a little headache stop her. A huge grin spread across Kurara's lips as the fish zipped back and forth across the sky, darting and weaving around the rocky outcrops and the protruding bushes growing on the walls of the mountain pass. The whales no longer seemed so monstrous when she could lead them by the nose.

She was so elated she was not prepared for the sudden, searing pain that burst inside her skull.

"Aki, don't overfeed the fish!" A voice – a memory – echoed in her head. It reverberated in her skull, so similar to a shikigami's voice that at first she wondered whether one was close by. With a jolt, Kurara reared back. Her paper fish crumbled in an instant, scattering into the air.

Enraged by the disappearance of their food, the cumulous whales turned back and rammed the ship. The *Orihime* tilted and the tips of the masts scraped against the rock wall, but Kurara was too dazed to do anything but clutch her head. What was that? A hallucination? A daydream? Though brief, for a moment it had felt as though someone was standing in front of her, speaking to her in a voice that she did not recognize and yet felt achingly familiar.

"Focus, Kurara!" shouted Himura. Though his tone was harsh, the way his ofuda fluttered betrayed his concern.

"No... There was something..." She took a step forward. The world swayed beneath her feet.

A whale lunged for her. A row of yellow teeth, covered in sticky mucus, caught her reflection.

"Get back!" Himura pulled her out of the way before she could become whale food.

"I'm fine! I'm all right!" Kurara gasped. Her head still ached and when she blinked, she swore she saw the shadow of koi fish swimming in water. She forced it from her mind. She had no time to dwell on it. Not when she had a ship to save.

The *Orihime* continued to weave through the mountains, sending Kurara stumbling at every hard turn. Despite the mist, she could see the end of the pass.

Akane returned with a stack of paper in its jaws.

Sunlight peeked through the curtain of rock. Together, Kurara and Himura kept the last of the cumulous whales distracted until the ship made it through the other side. The whales would not linger beyond the mountains; they would not stray from their nests. As the *Orihime* left the pass, the whales retreated into the mountain mists.

Exhausted and drenched to the bone, Kurara turned to look at Himura in disbelief. Pride bloomed in her heaving chest. She had done it. She had helped save the ship.

Himura stared back at her, completely soaked, his breaths coming heavily as well. Something passed between them in that moment. He smirked.

"Not bad," he said.

Kurara was tempted to make a face at him, but then Akane was hurling itself at her back, jumping up and down with a triumphant grin and trying to lick the rain from her face.

"Well done, little kit! Well done! Stupid whales – that trick wouldn't have fooled Akane!"

Laughing, Kurara pushed the fox off her.

There was a loud crack.

"Are they all gone?"

A spyglass rolled across the deck; the lens had shattered where it had hit the metal. Kurara looked up to see Sayo standing in front of her, her eyes wide with fright.

"The whales. Are they definitely gone?"

172

Before Kurara could answer, the balcony door slammed open. Captain Sakurai stood at the top of the steps, his expression grim. Behind him, the disgruntled faces of the rest of the crew peered out from around the door.

"Sayo" – Sakurai's smile was a tight thing, coiled like a spring – "I thought I told you to go *around* the mountains."

TWENTY

THE atmosphere on the deck was pulled as taut as a bowstring. Sayo stood in front of Sakurai, her hands balled into fists, her eyes unable to look anywhere but at the floor. Kurara's legs shook. She was tired and cold and aching all over, but she did not dare move.

"Care to explain just what is going on, Sayo?"

The rest of the crew watched on, silent and indignant. Kurara's nails dug into the flesh of her palms. She had hated it when Madam Ito used to line them up inside the kitchens to listen to her yell at another servant. Even though she was not the one in trouble, the tension in the air made her want to crawl away and hide.

Captain Sakurai did not yell or throw pots. He did not even seem angry, only disappointed, and that was worse. A hundred times worse.

"We're running low on food and fuel." Sayo's words

had to be pulled from between clenched teeth like someone dragging boulders from the bottom of a well. "If we went around the mountains, there was a risk we would run out before we reached Sola-Il."

"And that was a risk I was willing to take." Sakurai was calm, but there was steel in his tone.

Sayo's eyes blazed, defiant. "But I got you through with minimal damage and saved our fuel! We were running half empty. We couldn't afford to waste levistone on a longer flight. I'm a good navigator! I know I am! How many times have I charted a course for this ship without an issue?"

"*You* didn't get us through with minimal damage," said Sakurai. "Himura and Kurara did."

"S–sir—!" Sayo's voice trembled.

"I asked Sayo to take us through Kumokiri Pass!"

A shocked murmur rippled through the crew as Tomoe stepped forward. Her long red hair whipped around her face as she held her head up high.

"Yes, it was I!" She gave a loud, falsetto cry. Her eyes flashed with dramatic aplomb. "I asked Sayo to fly through the mountains so that we might reach Sola-Il in time for the Festival of the Seventh Star! Why, you ask?"

"Tomoe…" Sakurai, sensing trouble, tried to cut her off.

With a twirl of her hand, the girl pointed at Kurara. "It was for her!"

"Me?" Kurara jumped, her boots almost slipping against the drenched deck.

"You!" Sayo scowled.

175

"Yes. Locked on board the *Midori* her whole life, the poor girl has never experienced a Sorabito festival!" Tomoe gestured wildly towards her mesmerized audience. "Does it not bring a tear to your eye? What kind of cold, dead heart must you possess not to feel an ounce of sympathy for our favourite Crafter?"

"*Favourite* Crafter?" muttered Himura.

"Well, comrades, I am not made of stone! I had to make sure Kurara did not miss her very first festival. Whip me! Tie me to the mast! Feed me to the worms! Do what you must, but I won't apologize!"

"Tomoe, by the blue skies, be quiet!" Sakurai shot the crowd a glare when someone among the crew sniggered. He massaged the top of his temples with the look of a man who had walked into the middle of a kabuki theatre just as the lead actor had set fire to the stage. Turning to Kurara, he asked: "Did you know about this?"

"Um…" Kurara hesitated.

She was not friends with Sayo. There were days when they hardly said two words to each other, but Kurara remembered watching how hard Sayo had worked to get them here, staying up in the middle of the night to read weather charts by lamplight and scribble down flight paths. That kind of loyalty was to be treasured.

Behind the captain's back, Tomoe was nodding vigorously.

"Yes?"

Sakurai sighed, his shoulders drooping. "Well, be glad we got through this in one piece. Still, you should know better than to disobey an order, Sayo. And Tomoe, Kurara,

176

I can't have you two doing whatever you feel like. So" –
his gaze swept over the three of them – "all of you will be
punished."

———————o———————

"I wish I'd never said anything."

Kurara's arms ached. The sun beat against the back of
her neck but she could not move. She stood perfectly still,
feet planted against the deck, her hands wrapped around
a piece of guard rail, arms straining to hold it level while
Sayo beat it back into place with a hammer.

This was torture. Nothing short of cruel and unusual
punishment. Captain Sakurai had not pulled any
punches when he had assigned them to repairs. Kurara
was roasting alive. After the mountains and the monsoon
rains, the skies had cleared. As if remembering that it was
summer, the sun scorched the deck. Sweat dripped down
Kurara's face to pool at her collarbone. Her sleeves were
already damp from wiping her brow. Her ofuda, shaped
like an enormous paper fan, wafted the air at her, but it
did little to cool her down. The air was thick, each breath
was like drinking soup.

"Where did Tomoe go?" She glanced across the deck. The
engineer had left to fetch them some "light refreshments"
and had been gone for half an hour. Kurara was not going
to let the girl skip out on repairs. It was Tomoe's fault that
she was stuck toiling beneath the burning sun.

Sayo's face was as red as a tomato, cheeks puffing out
with every pound of her hammer.

"If you have the energy to worry about Tomoe, you have the energy to lift the railing higher!" she barked.

Kurara grunted, arms shaking beneath the weight of the metal rails. Her vision was beginning to spin. Perhaps the heat had also fried her brain because she swore that she could see lotus flowers at her feet.

The deck faded away. She was standing at the top of a grassy hill overlooking a small village.

"*Aki,*" someone called out. "*Aki!*"

"Huh? What?" Kurara jerked her head back. The deck swam back into focus.

Was the heat making her hallucinate? The same thing had happened while she had fought the whales. Was she falling ill, perhaps? She fanned out her ofuda above her head, creating a large parasol that provided a small circle of shade.

"I said," snapped Sayo, "I didn't take us through Kumokiri Pass for the fun of it. I made what I thought was the best decision. Besides," she added beneath her breath, "that groundling said not to go through the pass, and I make a point of not listening to groundlings. They're liars and cheaters, the lot of them! They can't be trusted to tell the truth about anything."

"That's the kind of thing Sohma would say." Tomoe poked her head out of the deck hatch.

Kurara dropped the guard rail in surprise. She darted forward to catch it. As the metal slammed against the top of her forearm, she was glad that she could feel nothing from her left arm. If it had been her right, she would be howling in pain right now.

178

"Where have you been?" snapped Sayo. "Grab a hammer and help or we'll be here from now until we reach Sola-Il!"

"I brought you both dinner!" Tomoe set a plate of noodles between them. *She*, Kurara noticed with a miffed look, was not red and drenched in sweat. "They're a Tomoe speciality: cold beef soba without the beef!"

"So just plain noodles." Sayo took a pair of chopsticks from Tomoe.

"Is that a complaint? Why, Sayo, I take the pain to save you from the worst of Captain Sakurai's wrath, I bring you dinner and this is the thanks I get? You break my heart!"

Sayo gave Tomoe an unimpressed stare. "What were you saying about Sohma?"

"Only that you should keep your opinions to yourself when we reach Sola-Il."

"Is it bad to talk about Sohma?" Kurara set the guard rail aside and joined the others for dinner. If she let the two of them continue like this, they would start bickering in no time. Or rather, Tomoe would say things that would make Sayo blush and snap, which would only prompt Tomoe to keep teasing her in a strange song and dance that had almost become a ritual.

"Well, Sola-Il is part of the empire. And everything in the empire belongs to the groundlings. That's why the mayor and the police on Sola-Il are all groundlings. It's also why Princess Tsukimi can march in and build a palace in the middle of the city without asking us Sorabito first. It's *our* city, but we have no say on how it's run. Talking about a rebel group the groundlings hate is definitely a no-no!"

179

Tomoe flopped across the deck like a cat stretching itself out in the sun. "And during the Festival of the Seventh Star the military police are going to be twice as stressed and short-tempered."

Kurara had almost forgotten that their arrival would line up with the Sorabito festival. She had been so caught up in training that it had slipped her mind completely.

"There's nothing wrong with Sohma," said Sayo.

"I think you're forgetting all the murder. And their obsession with Sorabito purity," said Tomoe, coldly. "In their minds, half-Sorabito should all be shot and anyone who marries a groundling should be executed."

For once, she did not seem like she was joking. Hurt flashed across Sayo's face.

"You don't have to worry, though." Tomoe turned to Kurara. "The military police there are used to making Sorabito cower, but they don't know how to deal with Crafters. They won't mess with you. And Princess Tsukimi has a well-known soft spot for your kind. Though I'm not sure if 'soft spot' is the right word. More like she wants to put a collar around your neck and turn you into her royal lapdog."

Kurara's smile was strained. It was not as though she wanted to hide her plan to visit Princess Tsukimi; she kept Haru's core in a pouch tied to her obi in plain sight after all. She just had not known how to bring it up. The crew hunted shikigami for a living. Even though they only went after the violent ones, would they understand if Kurara told them her best friend was a shikigami? Would they even accept a shikigami as strange and unusual as Haru?

"I think I'm more of a drowned mutt myself," she muttered.

Tomoe's laughter was as bright as bells. Kurara sat back, feeling her aching muscles and the soba filling her stomach. The still, summer air felt much like the calm before the storm.

TWENTY-ONE

"AKI, *we have to run!*"

"Haru!" Kurara jolted awake. Her eyes flew open. She sat bolt upright, her chest heaving.

The detour through Kumokiri Pass had shortened the schedule by a few days. Kurara had spent what little time remained before they reached Sola-Il practising with ofuda, listening to Tomoe's stories about the sky city and trying not to panic.

When she woke on the final day, Kurara was jumpy and restless. She had not slept well, too excited and anxious to close her eyes until long past lights out. Strange dreams had haunted her sleep, echoes of voices clinging to the back of her mind, but when got up she did not feel tired at all. In fact, she was more awake than ever.

It's today, it's today, it's today! Kurara's legs were stiff as she marched to the deck. Butterflies stirred a whirlwind in her stomach. She could not tell if she was excited or nervous, but she was glad to have something to do with the frantic energy bubbling inside of her.

The oppressive summer sun beat against the ship. As Kurara burst outside, the air seemed to waver and bend beneath the heat. Birds screeched high above her head. The ship's sails rolled like red waves, tugging at the strings that kept them secured to the masts, as the sun gleamed against the angled metal with the promise of a long, gloriously bright day.

Himura was waiting for her in the middle of the deck. Ofuda circled around him, rising and dipping like leaves caught in a lazy breeze.

"Kit! Today we will have much fun!" Akane promised, like an overexcited child eager to show an adult its toys.

Kurara nodded as she bounced on the balls of her feet. She was eager to start their lesson – the last one before seeing Princess Tsukimi. There was still so much she had to learn, and she had to learn it all now.

"Do you remember what I told you when you first came on board the *Orihime*?" Himura's ofuda twisted around his body. "Ofuda is capable of three things. Shape-changing."

"Movement," said Kurara.

"And strength," Himura finished. His ofuda formed a solid wall that hovered a few inches above the deck. When he swung his fist into it, it did not crumple. Instead, the sound of his knuckles hitting the paper wall elicited a hollow metallic echo like a gong being struck. "The last part is what makes a Crafter truly powerful.

With paper, you can make a sword sharper than steel or a shield as strong as iron. Watching you distract the cumulous whales, I realized something myself…"

The wall crumpled and curled into the shape of a long pole. Without warning, he struck, swinging the pole with such force that Kurara felt the thrust of the air a second before the pole hit her squarely in the stomach.

"You learn much faster when you are forced to."

Kurara staggered back, winded. That would leave a bruise later. She dreaded the thought of drinking one of Dr Yuriha's nasty potions again.

"Crafting reflects real life," said Himura. "To make ofuda stronger, think of the ship's metal guard rails, think of a sword slicing through silk. Imagine iron, imagine steel."

Avoiding a second blow, Kurara pulled her ofuda together to create a barrier between herself and Himura.

Imagine iron, imagine steel.

When Himura brought the pole down, his weapon hit her shield with a clang. The force of the hit knocked his arms back, and he teetered for a moment on the balls of his feet. Kurara felt it too. The force reverberated through her one good arm. Her left arm, as usual, felt nothing.

Himura grunted in surprise. Kurara blocked another swing to her head. She would become stronger than Himura, stronger than all the other Crafters in the world. Strong enough to impress Princess Tsukimi.

As Himura's pole came down, she turned her shield into a katana and parried the blow. Their weapons screeched against each other.

"*Little kit!*" Akane shouted in alarm.

"Keep out of this, Akane!" Himura ordered his shikigami to stay put.

Kurara aimed a blow at his stomach, but he darted out of the way. Hopping onto the guard rails, Himura gathered his ofuda in front of him to create platforms that hovered in the air. He jumped between them until he reached the highest one, then swung his legs forward. More paper rushed to create a staircase beneath his feet, spiralling upward into the air.

"What's the matter?" He sat cross-legged on the top of the floating steps as Kurara gaped up at him. Holding his head in his hand, he stared down at her with the amusement of a king surveying the rabble below. "Can't reach?"

A sharp bark of laughter escaped Kurara's throat. Her ofuda gathered around her feet and formed stepping stones leading through the air. When she put her weight down, they strained to hold her up, but by dashing up them she could climb just high enough to swing her katana at Himura.

A look of alarm flashed through his eyes as the paper blade cut the air inches from his face. Kurara grinned in triumph. That would teach him to underestimate her!

Himura dropped back to the deck, using ofuda to cushion his fall. Kurara leapt down after him only to find Himura swinging his pole at her. She raised a shield just in time, but the blow was heavier than before, harder, knocking her several steps back from the sheer force of the swing.

Himura was not playing around any more.

They exchanged blows for several minutes, neither one willing to give the other the upper hand. Kurara lost herself to the rhythm of battle and the rustle of paper. Crafting had never felt so exhilarating. It was as if her ofuda was dancing.

Himura flung his pole at her like a javelin, but Kurara had a lifetime of practice dodging pots on board the *Midori*. She ducked just as it soared over her head.

At the very last second, the pole disintegrated into tiny pieces of ofuda, curved around her and reformed itself behind her back.

There was no time to turn. She felt the weapon strike her shoulder then the back of her knees. Her legs buckled. Another blow collided against her left arm. At least this time she felt nothing.

Knocked off balance, she staggered towards Himura. His ofuda returned to his hand, forming the same pole he used to hit her in the stomach. In two quick strides, he closed the distance between them and prepared to strike.

Seeing his arms swing back, Kurara rushed forward.

She curled her left hand into a fist and punched him square in the face.

Kurara did not feel the moment the blow connected. She did not feel anything at all, but she heard the sound of her knuckles hitting flesh, the muffled oomph that escaped Himura's lips as he staggered back.

She froze.

"*Oooh!*" Akane hooted. Bounding in circles around them, the fox cackled. "*Oooh!*"

Himura wasted no time recovering. His ofuda

wrapped around Kurara's ankles. In an instant, it curled up her body locking her arms at her sides and pulling her knees together. She gave a shout of alarm as she toppled over, hitting the deck with a painful thud.

"I won." Relief coloured Himura's words. With a triumphant gleam in his eyes, he grinned down at her. His nose was slightly bloody.

Kurara frowned. He had taken her by surprise. It had not been a fair fight.

She lay on the ground even after Himura released her. Using ofuda was mentally exhausting. Her head felt as if someone had stuffed it with cotton wool. Akane pattered towards her. When the shikigami licked her cheek, she felt only dry paper and pity.

"That's enough." Himura wore an expression of sharp pride as he pulled her to her feet. "You learn fast. Almost too fast, I'd say," he added beneath his breath, barely loud enough for Kurara to catch.

"That's not a bad thing, is it? I need to be prepared for when I face Princess Tsukimi." Kurara dusted herself down.

"No, not bad at all." Himura seemed deep in thought. His ofuda broke into a dozen scraps of paper and fluttered around him, spinning like satellites orbiting a central star. She watched in awe as he formed a paper galaxy – comets darting within the space between his two hands, moons spinning, nebulas expanding and contracting and bursting into stars.

There was something on his mind, Kurara could tell. She formed her ofuda into asteroid belts and moving planets, allowing their creations to mingle. Himura could not command words the way he could control paper, but he was fluent in the unspoken language of ofuda. From the way his paper moons spun in orbit, she knew that there was something gnawing at the edges of his thoughts.

Before she could probe too deeply, Himura pulled his hands away, taking the stars with him. With a flick of his wrist, he divied his ofuda into two halves. Half returned to form his usual bracelet, merging together and hardening against his wrist. Kurara stiffened as the other twelve coiled around her neck to form a thin, white necklace, identical in colour and texture to his bracelet.

With a snap of his fingers, the necklace twisted and morphed. A small, circular pendant formed beneath the necklace. Like etchings in stone, marks appeared on the circle of paper – a face with large, bushy eyebrows, and a moustache that fanned out from its frowning lips, leaving two holes in the centre of the circle where its eyes should be.

It was a daruma – a paper charm that held the dreams and wishes of its owner within its little round body. Kurara had never owned one before but she had seen them in the entertainers' quarters: one-eyed dolls staring down at her from empty shelves. Madam Ito said that you gave the doll an eye upon making a wish and the second eye when that wish came true.

Kurara had never seen one with both its eyes.

"I know we disagree on some things," said Himura.

"That feels like an understatement."

Himura gave her an unimpressed look. She knew he

was trying to address the shikigami issue without getting into another argument with her. "What I'm *trying* to say," he said, "is that we are still both Crafters. I will never turn my back on you. I promised you I would help you and I will. This necklace is a sign of that." He pointed to the daruma. "I'll make sure Princess Tsukimi fixes your shiki—your friend. No matter what."

"Thank you." Kurara fought to keep a soft smile off her face. She was touched. No one besides Haru had ever given her anything. Her fingers pressed against the pendant. She gave the charm its first eye, leaving the other blank, waiting to be filled.

Before Himura could reply, a sudden call of "Sola-Il!" echoed above them from the command tower. "Sola-Il is in our sights! All hands to stations and prepare for docking!"

Kurara jumped. They were early, or had she just lost track of the hours passing? She turned as the crew spilled onto the deck in their excitement. Caught in a cradle of clouds, something glittered against the blue sky.

A sky city. Sola-Il.

Interlude

An echo of joy,
The father of our nation
Smiles down on us all.

– from *Glory to our Empire*
(approved by the Patriots Office)

Inui did not bother with Nao's body. Leaving it in the alleyway for the military police to find, she gestured for Rei to follow her to the military dock.

He bristled as he watched Inui breeze past every docking guard and security check with no more than a flash of paper and a lazy gesture to her uniform. Crafters had it easy. What Rei wouldn't give to make soldiers jump and tremble before him like they did with Inui.

"I could easily use my ofuda to fly us down, but you look like you prefer the comfort of a craft to my paper wings." A dry smirk played on Inui's lips as she guided them both to the ground in an old, military kohane.

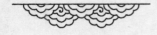

The vehicle landed in Sola-Il's shadow, next to the old levistone mines that had once provided the city with fuel.

The mines were in a state of ruin. Old shacks where workers had once lived lay empty, and broken hoverpods were left out to rust. It was worse inside. The tunnels made Rei feel like a rat trapped inside a maze.

"Relax. No one comes here," said Inui. "These tunnels have been mined almost dry to keep Sola-Il afloat. The only levistone veins that remain are simply too dangerous to extract. All it would take is a single caress of an open flame for this whole cave to explode. Hold that thing steady now. Unless you want to go boom."

She gestured to the lantern she had given Rei at the mouth of the mine. A single candle burned inside the metal holder, the wax dribbling down and pooling at the bottom. The mines beneath Sola-Il were made of narrow, ant-like tunnels that burrowed deeper and deeper into the earth the further one went, splitting off and reconnecting in a manner that made keeping track of their path a challenge. Faint blue lines of levistone glowed softly against the rock wall, casting an icy glow over her weathered face.

"Are you going to tell me what this is about?" Rei held the lantern aloft.

"I told you. It's a surprise." Inui ducked as shafts of wood, intended to keep the ceiling from collapsing, sagged overhead.

"Nao is dead. You killed him."

The lack of air was making Rei light-headed. The

mine stank of wet earth and the metallic tang of blood. He hoped that was the levistone.

Inui cackled. "You would have done the same if you had half the chance. Thanks to me, he did not give away our plans."

True, Rei would have killed him, but that was not what upset him. What made him bristle was how truly powerless he had felt. How everything seemed to play out as Inui wished it. He hated the feeling that everything was spiralling out of his control.

He lifted his lantern to inspect the walls. "Does Princess Tsukimi know you're here?"

Inui laughed. "When it comes to anything other than shikigami, the princess has the attention span of a gnat! You need not worry about her."

Unease stirred in Rei's chest. Was there anyone, he wondered, she was not lying to? What else was she keeping from him? Inui was a woman full of secrets. Secrets that, he had a terrible suspicion, would lead him to his doom.

"And that Crafter?" The man with the giant tiger for a shikigami had not seemed the type to let things go easily.

"You mean Fujiwa? He's probably confiscated the *Hishaku*, I'm afraid. I'm certain your men managed to move the dragon's crate before he reached the docks. But, when the time comes, you'll have to find another way to leave Sola-Il." Inui led him deeper into the cave, further away from the sun and the sky. "Don't worry. Just

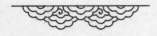 

be a good boy and follow me and all will be well."

Rei seethed. Not for the first time, he imagined wrapping his hands around her brittle, chicken-like neck and squeezing until he crushed her throat.

Not yet. He still needed her to keep the dragon in check. Later. He would do it after the attack.

The tunnels narrowed into a bottleneck before opening up into a wide cavern. Ice-blue stalactites formed spires that hung down from the top of the cave. Though he hated to admit it, there was an ethereal sort of beauty to it. A small fire pit lay in the centre; the bricks were piled up high to form a circle around a cold pile of ash. Cracked paper spheres covered in strange symbols littered the ground. Some were completely crushed; others cracked in the middle as ash and bone leaked out.

"What's this?" Rei came to a stop in front of a large trench – a foxhole filled with yet more ash. Veins of levistone glowed around him.

"One of Princess Tsukimi's labs. You're in the way." Inui shoved Rei aside so that she could access the wall behind him. Her belt separated into a dozen paper hands that latched on to a boulder leaning against the wall of the cavern and pulled it back.

Stone rumbled. The boulder rolled away to reveal a small enclave. Inside, barely touched by the light of her lamp, lay a snow-white bird the size of a large carriage.

Rei's breath escaped his throat. A shikigami. It was chained to the ground by its feet. Paper feathers glowed beneath the light. It was so folded in on itself that he

could not quite tell what kind of bird it was, only that he saw wings, and a beak, and talons. Like the cave, it too was beautiful in a way that distracted from its ability to destroy anyone in its path.

"This is one of the princess's creations. Don't be deceived by its appearance. Though it may look like a real shikigami, it's nothing but a failure. It won't obey anyone, not even Crafters. She'll get rid of it soon." Inui placed a hand on the bird's head. The beast stirred. Rei caught its eye. The fear in its gaze was so human it made him take a step back.

Shadows painted monstrous images over Inui's face. The paper hands floated around her, each one pointing towards Rei.

"There's been a change of plan."

Rei's eye twitched. She was doing it again. Deciding things and not telling him about it, expecting him to dance to her tune. "No, there hasn't. There is no change of plan, because *I* decide what the plan is!"

Inui's mouth twisted into a gleeful smile. Her laughter echoed across the walls. "Little boy, where would you be without me? Could you have attacked the *Midori*? Could you have captured the shikigami afterwards? If I had not stepped in, those guards would have discovered the dragon. Your friend Nao would have ratted you out, and your head would be on a pike right now."

Rei trembled with rage. He could not remember ever experiencing anger quite like it – an incandescent fury that threatened to blind him.

"You owe me quite a bit, don't you think?" Inui continued, airily. "I risked everything to come up with this plan. If not for me, you and Prince Ugetsu would be sitting somewhere twiddling your thumbs, merely *dreaming* of Princess Tsukimi's death. After everything I've done for you, I dare say you could do a little something for me."

A thousand ugly thoughts filled Rei's head. "And what is it that you want?"

It had been a mistake to come here. He had forgotten that being alone with a Crafter was like being alone with a rabid wolf. One never knew when it might lunge at your throat.

"The dragon," said Inui. "Do you know how I have kept it calm all this time? Of course you don't. You know nothing about Crafters or shikigami do you?" Inui said before Rei could answer.

He bristled.

"I have a bond with it. Though its mind might be broken and its spirit difficult to control, my blood is on its core," she said. "It's mine."

"Mine." At the sound of that word, the shikigami suddenly jolted to life. It lifted its head in alarm and hurled itself against its chains, trying to escape.

"Although I've always wanted a shikigami, I was willing to sacrifice the dragon for the good of the plan. However, now another opportunity has presented itself."

Inui looked at the bird in disgust. Her paper hands yanked the shikigami chains, forcing it back against the rock wall.

"I've tried several times to form a bond with this one, but even with a blood bond it just won't obey me. There's something wrong with its core, something missing. So let's make a switch. Use this shikigami for the attack on the summer palace instead and I will keep the dragon. If you set the bird loose inside the palace, I guarantee it will cause the same havoc the dragon would. You will still be able to kill Princess Tsukimi and I will finally have a shikigami more deserving of myself. Everyone is happy."

Rei backed out of the enclave. He did not know how Crafters were given their shikigami, but it was odd that an imperial Crafter such as Inui did not have one. Especially when that other Crafter had such a large and impressive tiger to serve him.

"If you want a shikigami so badly, why don't you ask your princess for one?"

Inui chuckled. "I have a … reputation for going through shikigami too fast. The princess stopped giving me any after the fifth one died on me. Shikigami are so *precious* after all."

Five shikigami… Rei shuddered. What did one do to get such beasts killed?

"It's only natural for a Crafter to want a shikigami. They belong to us. I would say we're not really Crafters without one." Inui yanked a feather from the bird's wing. The shikigami squawked in pain and tried to peck at her eyes, but she paid it no mind, twirling the paper feather between her fingers as though it were a fascinating toy.

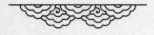 

Rei could not do this. The last of his patience snapped. Sohma was his, this plan was his, independence would be his — but Inui would ruin everything. The woman could not be trusted.

"No." He took another step back, almost tripping over the trench in the ground that was half hidden by the ash covering the floor. The lantern swung in his hands as he steadied himself.

"You can't refuse." The paper hands hovering above Inui began to advance upon him. Beside her, the bird thrashed and its chain creaked.

"You need me."

Rei lifted the lantern to his face. "I need no one. You can burn in Yomi."

Just as he threw the lantern towards Inui and onto an exposed levistone vein he heard the sound of a chain snapping. Rei did not stick around to watch the bird break free. He ran for cover, dropping into the foxhole just as the shikigami crashed through the top of the cavern and flew away. A moment later, the world around him exploded.

TWENTY-TWO

KURARA'S breath caught in her throat. Forgetting her training for a moment, she rushed to the edge of the deck. Her hands fluttered across the daruma pendant around her neck. They were finally here. At last, she would have her chance to see Princess Tsukimi.

As the *Orihime* drew closer, Kurara understood why the crew called Sola-Il the "Pride of the Skies". The city grew upon circular plates, forming six domes that were arranged in the shape of a cherry blossom. The central dome was connected to the surrounding ones with bridges that arched like rainbows. Thin panes of pearl glass stretched over the city like a transparent shell. Navigation towers, standing like imposing ivory shards, pierced the sky.

Beneath the city lay an uninhabitable jungle of

cables and chutes: giant engines that kept the city afloat. Rotating solar panels glimmered like scales. Churning wind farms spun their pinwheel blades. Bright banners streamed in the wind with the city's motto blazing across it: *The Sky Is Here*.

"Haru…" Kurara clutched the pouch tight as she rushed to the front of the ship.

They had finally made it.

Her moment of sharp joy was swiftly replaced by an intense sense of loss. They had not made it. *She* had made it. Haru was not here to see this with her. He was not here to grab her hands and point at the rain catchers gleaming in the sun or the school of sky fish in the distance. There was no debate about what they should do first or eat first or see first, no excited chatter, no squeals of delight.

Despite the crew around her, she had never felt more alone.

"All hands to stations!" the lookout cried.

The crew dispersed to prepare for landing. With a curt nod, Himura patted Kurara on the shoulder before heading below deck with Akane.

Now she was truly alone.

Kurara stood at the prow, gazing down at the city. From her bird's-eye view, she could see the lakes and fields, the sprawling buildings stacked on top of one another like towers, winding up towards the sun. Cable car wires sliced the sky. The smoke from factories rose to the air and hit the glass panes of the dome. They were coming in close.

There was so much to take in. Even the area around

Sola-Il intrigued her. Mines lay in the city's shadow, far below on the ground. From a distance, they looked like long scars pulled taut across the cracked skin of the earth. Military barracks clustered around the site, their tiny red roofs were the only splashes of colour against the tired brown huts and mining lodges.

A sudden explosion of light blinded her eyes, followed by a deafening *BOOM!*

A rush of wind hit her so hard that for a moment she thought that someone had tackled her. Her ears rang. The ship rocked like a boat in a storm as the burst of light enveloped the world for a moment before fading back to blue sky.

Kurara looked down. Plumes of thick, black smoke rose from the mines. Below, what had once been a series of snaking warrens was now a crater. Chunks of stone had been flung into the barracks and lodges. From out of that chaos, a white eagle shot upwards, soaring past the *Orihime*.

A shikigami.

The *Orihime*'s bells began to ring in alarm. Sunlight hit the shikigami's wings in a way that made them seem to glisten like scales. Every feather was rendered in exquisite detail, its beak curved to a point so sharp it could pierce steel. Its blank, white eyes carried a look of intelligence – and ferocity.

It was coming this way.

TWENTY-THREE

THE bird's stubbed talons grabbed hold of the side of the ship. The eagle was larger than a horse, its mouth big enough to swallow a child whole. Guard rails screeched and bent beneath the pressure of its burned and half-broken feet. Kurara dived to the floor just as the rush of air from its wings blew over her like a cannon blast.

Its alabaster eyes fixed Kurara within its gaze.

"Run away, little one." Its voice echoed through her head, loud then soft then loud again, pressing against the walls of her skull as if it could crack open her head with the right combination. It stretched its enormous, trunk-like neck across the deck. Its shadow was a mountain looming over her. *"Humans are hungry. Eat your flesh with their mouth; eat your soul with their eyes. Consume, consume."*

The *Orihime* performed a stomach-churning drop. Kurara felt all her organs jump several inches and her feet lift from the floor. The ship was retreating from Sola-Il, drawing the shikigami away.

"Kurara! Get down!" The balcony door burst open. Sayo stood at the top of the steps, holding a large cylindrical gun like the hand-cannons the *Midori* used to shoot fireworks into the sky.

Sayo lit the fuse and aimed the hand-cannon at the eagle. Sparks ate the string all the way down to the flintlock. As Kurara made a dash for the balcony stairs, the eagle swooped towards her, talons outspread.

"Fire!" screamed Sayo.

Kurara clapped her hands over her ears as flames burst from the barrel of Sayo's gun. Even at a distance, she could feel the heat licking at her back. Waves of hot air pulsed against her face. Behind her, the eagle screamed. Burning paper made a terrible crackling sound.

Furious, the shikigami shed its burning feathers to keep the flames from spreading to its core. Lumps of ashen paper scattered across the deck, filling the air with the stench of smoke. With a scream, the bird lunged at Sayo. Kurara rushed up the balcony steps, pushed the navigator inside and swung the door shut. The shikigami smacked straight into the metal, leaving a dent the size of a cannonball.

"Let's go!" Kurara grabbed Sayo's hand and ran.

The ship was a hive of frantic activity. The crew rushed back and forth, delivering gunpowder and cannonballs to the artillery rooms where the cannons were rigged to the floor. Kurara spied Tomoe with the rest of the crew. Her hair, tied back into a long plait, swished from side to side as she packed gunpowder into the cannons' hungry mouths.

"Sayo! I thought you'd be flying." Tomoe's eyes widened as she noticed them.

"I'm on my way there." Sayo shook off Kurara's hand, as if she had not been holding on to her like a vice mere seconds ago.

"Smoke!" Someone shouted. On cue, the men and women manning the cannons pushed smoke canisters down the muzzles, lit the fuses and clapped their hands over their ears.

The cannons boomed. The echoing snap and recoil of the heavy artillery tore through the ship. A fine grey mist erupted across the sky.

The eagle glided past the windows, through the veil of smoke, and darted towards them.

"It's coming this way!" The crew backed up just in time as the giant eagle punched its head through the wall, tearing through the portholes and tossing cannons aside in a blast of broken wood. Clinging to the side of the ship, the bird thrashed its head inside the room, its beak snapping at the crew.

Kurara pulled her ofuda into a long chain and whipped it towards the shikigami. When the eagle grabbed the chain in its mouth, her paper wrapped around its beak and clamped it shut. The eagle writhed this way and that but she held it fast, waiting for the crew to retreat. When the shikigami pulled its head back, Kurara loosened the muzzle, the paper darting back to her side and transforming into a battering ram that she then slammed into the eagle's chest. The bird screeched as it was knocked back.

"Stay away!" Putting all her strength into the next blow, Kurara hit the shikigami again, hard enough to dislodge its talons from the side of the ship. Before it fell, its head lunged forward, clamping its beak around Kurara's left arm, and dragging her out of the ship like a worm yanked from its hole.

Tomoe and Sayo called her name, their voices panicked.

The eagle's beak sunk into her skin. She was lucky that she could feel nothing from that arm, even as her bones snapped beneath the pressure and she was dragged through the air. Feeling the muscles in her shoulder beginning to tear, she scrambled for purchase with her good arm, her fingers closing over a fist of paper feathers.

Kurara's legs bicycled through the air as the eagle dragged her through the sky. The earth was so far below she could not fathom how long it would take to hit the ground if she fell.

Her ofuda swirled around her. The rustle of each piece of paper calmed her nerves. They stretched and grew, merging together to form a long pike.

Imagine iron... The weapon hovered in the air, just above her head. Kurara angled it at the shikigami's eye and let it fly.

The pike hit true. Crying in pain, the eagle jerked its head back. The next thing Kurara knew, she was falling. Without a second to lose, she summoned her ofuda to her. The pike pulled itself out of the shikigami's head and returned to her side, crumbling into a dozen pieces of paper as it did so. Like a flock of tiny white birds, they gathered on the deck and ballooned out into the shape of a large mushroom. Kurara landed on her ofuda, the paper inflating to break her fall.

She tumbled onto the deck. Wind lashed against the ship, the air heavy with the smell of gunpowder. The shikigami dived towards her once more. As Kurara pushed herself up, her bad arm suddenly gave way. There was an awful cracking sound as it snapped beneath her weight.

She sucked in a sharp breath.

Her arm had broken clean off.

TWENTY-FOUR

A few feet away, what remained of her limb lay on the deck looking like crumbled plaster. The wind blew flakes of skin from the inside of her arm like ash caught in the breeze. Her vision blurred. She was not bleeding, though she did not understand how that could be. Her remaining hand clutched at her sleeve, closing around nothing but fabric. Her arm was on the ground in front of her. Her arm. On the ground.

The shikigami shrieked at her, talons extended. Kurara could not move. She knew that she had to get out of the way but none of her limbs would work. In one last, desperate attempt, she pulled down the cushion of ofuda that had saved her from the fall and remade it into a shield, praying that it would be strong enough to withstand the blow.

A second before the shikigami was about to strike, a blur of white knocked it away. Akane was hanging from the giant eagle's throat, its hind legs dangling in the air as the bird reared its head back.

The eagle shook Akane off and dived on top of the fox, holding it down with a single, giant talon. The fox howled and writhed as the eagle's beak pierced its tail.

"Keep it distracted, Akane!" Himura burst onto the deck. His ofuda whirled around him, paper flowing together and merging into a long spear which he sent flying towards the beast. As the eagle turned its head, the spear soared through the air and pierced its wing with such force it sent the bird flying backwards, pinning it to the deck.

The eagle shrieked. Himura walked towards it, his ofuda dancing around him. Another spear tore through the eagle's other wing. Paper chains lashed themselves to its feet and pulled.

The bird struggled, wings flopping miserably on the ground. Its screams echoed through Kurara's bones. Its eyes were blown wide. She recognized that look. She had seen it in the boy soldiers who visited the *Midori* after their very first battle, their expressions haunted by things they had seen.

"You're not mad; you're afraid," she realized. The thought was like a thunderbolt striking her from the heavens. It split everything she thought she knew into pieces.

As Himura approached, he struck a match against a piece of hardened ofuda.

"Himura, wait!" she shouted.

In one, fluid motion, Himura tossed the match at the shikigami.

Akane leapt clear as the eagle went up in flames. With the last of its strength, it surged forward, wings tearing against the spears. Parts of its body were soot black, crumbling with each flap of its wings. Feathers and skin fell away, revealing the hollow parts of its body. Its legs broke beneath its own weight.

"Run, little one, run!"

Kurara stared in horror as the shikigami writhed against the deck. Why was it telling her to run? The eagle was the one in danger.

Himura's spears hovered in the air, ready to strike again.

"Run, before they—"

The spears pierced its chest, severing the cords that tied the shikigami's body to its core.

Like a puppet whose strings had been cut, the eagle flopped to the deck and lay there, limp and unmoving. Himura lifted a boot and stomped out the flames before they could reach the core. As the last of the fires petered out, he turned and strode towards Kurara.

"Stay away!" She scrambled backwards, pushing herself further against the guard rails. He could not see her like this. Without her arm. Without blood.

"What happened?" He hurried forward, ofuda whistling around his ears in concern. "Are you injured?"

There were many times on the *Midori* when Kurara had wished that she could sink into a hole and hide. None of them compared to how she felt now.

A foot away from her, Himura came to an abrupt stop. His gaze fell on her detached arm then on Kurara herself, clutching the empty fabric of her sleeve.

"I don't know how it happened! I don't know what to do!" Her face burned with shame. This was what she got for keeping secrets – for lying when she said that she was fine. Madam Ito always said that little girls who lied had their tongues cut off in the fifth level of Yomi. Perhaps they lost their arms too.

Crouching by her side, Himura pulled back her empty sleeve until he could see what remained of her arm. She flinched and tried to bat him away, but he stopped her and continued to pull up the fabric.

From the curve of her shoulder, her skin looked normal enough, but as it travelled down towards her elbow it became whiter and whiter until it reached the broken stump of her arm. At the edge of her elbow, where the limb had been severed, her flesh was the colour and texture of chipped plaster.

Paper. She was made of paper.

TWENTY-FIVE

HIMURA'S fingers trembled. He let go of the sleeve as though it had burned him.

Kurara pushed him away as she doubled over, throwing up onto the deck. Strangely, the sight brought him a moment of relief. Until he remembered Kurara's friend, and the network of paper organs inside his otherwise hollow body, his paper stomach filled with bile.

"You're a shikigami too?"

That was not possible. Her friend was one thing, but Kurara could use ofuda, she got into fights, she had opinions and fears and hopes of her own, she was just so … so human.

There was a churning feeling in his chest, but he did not recognize it as panic until he heard Kurara gasp for breath. The sound brought him back to his senses.

He had to keep a grip on his emotions. He had to do something before anyone else found out.

Himura pulled her to her feet. "Make yourself an arm. You know how."

There was a storm inside him. His ofuda was a turbulent whirlwind spinning around his body.

Kurara gathered her ofuda to make another arm. It slotted into the hollow of her elbow and she bound it there, wrapping more ofuda in a band around the joint. It was clearly made of paper, the colour of the rest of the skin had not transferred down her newly formed limb, but it was better than nothing.

Himura made his way to where her broken arm lay. Before anyone else could see, he stomped on the arm until it was no more than clumps of paper scattered by the wind.

As soon as he had destroyed it, he turned back to her.

"Himura," she said, so quietly it was almost lost to the wind. He had no idea what expression he was wearing, but he knew how he felt – lied to, tricked, and humiliated as everything he thought he knew crumbled around him.

"Master, are you all right?" Akane came bounding onto the deck.

"Akane, did you know about this?" he snapped.

The fox stopped short, recognizing the anger in his voice. *"Master?"*

The side of one temple was beginning to throb. Was Akane lying to him too? Purposefully playing dumb? No, that was impossible. A shikigami could not lie to its master any more than it could disobey an order.

He grabbed Kurara's wrist. Her good one. The one that looked like it belonged to a human.

"Let's go." He dragged her inside.

Below deck, Himura was greeted by a buzz of frenetic activity. The crew rushed this way and that, harried but relieved. Despite the work left to do, there was a celebratory mood in the air.

"Mr Himura! An unexpected but successful hunt!" They called as they saw him enter the hallway.

"Another core! And we weren't even prepared to run into a shikigami! Are we the best hunters ever or are we the best hunters ever?"

Their joy only made Himura's mood even darker.

"Miss Kurara, my heart stopped when you got dragged out of the ship like that! Are you all right? You look pale," someone asked.

She did look pale. In fact, she looked like a strong gust of wind would send her tumbling. Himura placed a hand on her shoulder and tightened his grip.

"She just overdid it. She needs some rest." He waved off the concern, pulling Kurara away as he did so.

The crew were crudely nailing planks of wood over the holes in the hull and covering gashes in the wall with canvas.

"Busy like bees." The fox watched the crew work. In its eyes, everything was too interesting to be ignored. It had to be exhausting to be so constantly upbeat, but then Himura supposed shikigami did not grow tired the way humans did.

So why did Kurara look a second away from collapsing?

They made it to his quarters without being stopped by anyone else. Kurara did not wait for him to drag out the futon. She all but collapsed in the corner of the room, using the wall to prop herself up.

"What's going on?" She sounded half delirious, caught between panic and exhaustion.

"I don't know." Himura did not realize how tense he was until he had to prise open his jaw to speak.

"Then why are you so angry?"

His fingernails dug into the flesh of his palms. He had thought Kurara was a Crafter. He had thought they were the same. He had cared about her.

You were a fool, a small voice sneered at him. *How did you not notice she was a shikigami?*

"Were you lying to me? This whole time?"

"Of course not! I didn't know!" she cried.

"How could you *not* have known?" Himura felt his anger rising. "It's your body, isn't it? Are you trying to tell me that in your entire life you never once bled? Never cut yourself on a kitchen knife? Never got into a fistfight with someone? What about your blood each moon?"

"Madam Ito said I was just a late bloomer!" Kurara's cheeks coloured crimson.

Himura's head spun. Wasn't that blush proof of blood rushing to her cheeks? If he tried, could he convince himself that he had just imagined everything? That Kurara was really a human, after all?

No, the truth was power. He could never turn a blind eye to it, no matter how tempted he was to do so.

"Of course I've been injured before," Kurara was

213

saying, her words increasingly frantic. "But just bruises and welts and small nicks. I wasn't allowed near the knives. I've never seriously cut myself! Maybe that's weird to you, but that's the truth!"

She's lying. It was one thing to not know anything about her friend, but how could she not know about herself?

But then what did he really know about shikigami? Only what little his parents had told him and the things he had read about in books from the black market. Books that could be fake. Or wrong. The only reliable information was in Princess Tsukimi's library. Only she would know for sure what Kurara was.

A surging rage filled him. Why was the princess allowed to know and not him? He was a Crafter – that knowledge belonged to his ancestors, his people – and yet he knew less than someone who thought of his life as a hobby. He knew less because Princess Tsukimi kept that knowledge locked away from him.

"A long time ago ... we were so much more than what we are now."

If only he had managed to steal Princess Tsukimi's books ... he would never have been caught unaware like this.

"I ... need to attend to other matters," he ground out between clenched teeth. As hard as it was, he held his frustration in careful check. "We'll discuss this later."

As soon as he was outside his quarters, Himura buried his fist in the wall. He hated this. The not knowing. The feeling that there were secrets he was not part of.

"Master." His shikigami nudged the back of his hand.

"Shut up, Akane." He was not in the mood.

The ship gave a jolt. The *Orihime* was moving again. From the window, Himura watched as they approached Sola-Il's docks. Doors at the bottom of the city opened up like a gaping mouth, and the *Orihime* soared through the entranceway into a long, metal tunnel.

The docking bay was filled with ships. Flying over them was like flying over a box of twinkling jewels.

Men in brightly coloured jackets guided the ship into a docking space. The *Orihime* shuddered as it descended, finally coming to a jolting stop on the landing bay. Two large towers of scaffolding rolled towards them, locking the ship into place. Dock workers in blue uniforms helped to anchor the *Orihime*. Above, guards in bright gold and blue patrolled the top, peering down at the docking floor from time to time like twinkling sparrows.

Akane nudged his thigh.

"Little kit passed out. Didn't want her to crush it."

A pouch dangled from its jaws. The one Kurara always kept tied to her obi, the one that held her friend's core.

Himura took it. The core was heavier than he remembered. He slipped it out of the pouch. The paper was as hard but delicate as a shell, dented slightly where some of the blood markings had smeared.

This was what was inside Kurara too. Inside Akane. They did not have hearts, just a ball of paper that determined who they were and what they liked. They were not *real* people.

"Himura!" Sakurai called.

Himura jerked his head up to see the captain making

his way towards him. Sakurai wasted no time on greetings.

"We need to discuss repairs." His smile was as taut as a bowstring. "It's not looking good. At least we have the eagle's core to sell."

Of course, thought Himura. They were hunters, after all. He looked down at Haru's core. How much, he wondered, was this one worth?

"Master?"

"Stay here, Akane," he ordered the fox. Before turning to follow Sakurai, he slipped the core back into its pouch, tying the strings to his obi. "I'll hold on to this."

Akane watched him go. If Himura did not know better, he would have thought that the fox disapproved.

It does not matter, he reminded himself. *A shikigami only has to obey.*

TWENTY-SIX

A gentle breeze brushed against Kurara's cheeks. She blinked, wiping away the grit from her eyes. The world around her was hazy; like an unfinished painting, its corners blurred and the colours ran into each other. Where was she? Kurara felt the answer creep around the corners of her memory, just out of reach.

She looked around from her position on the edge of a wooden porch. Behind, sliding paper doors opened to a barren room. A well-pruned garden sprawled before her. Moonlight shimmered over a small pond as paper fish flicked their lazy way beneath the surface. The sky above was the colour of ink. Anaemic clouds spread thinly across the sky as snow fell like powdered sugar, coating the garden in frost.

"Aki…" A voice was calling her, nostalgic and yet unfamiliar. Her chest ached like a wound. She did not know why, and not knowing made it hurt all the more.

"Aki." Someone touched her shoulder.

Kurara turned to see a boy her age crouch beside her.

"Are you feeling any better now, Aki?"

She blinked. "Haru?"

"Is this what you really want?" he asked.

Kurara did not know what Haru was talking about. It had been so long since she had seen him – really seen him. She just wanted to hug him, but when she tried she found that she could not move.

Instead, her lips parted. As though someone else was in control of her body, words tumbled out of her mouth unbidden.

"I thought about it. I'm sorry to leave you behind, but I can't see any other way." She grabbed his hand. He was warm, as if there really was blood flowing through his veins. His fingers gently prised hers off.

"If you do this, you won't be Aki any more. You'll forget everything."

The room was beginning to blur around her. "I know," said Kurara as the stars began to fuse into one. "And I'm sorry."

———————o———————

Kurara woke with a start. As the world came into view, her breathing steadied and she realized that she was in Himura's quarters.

She sat up, groggy. Her head ached.

What had she just seen? It had felt like something more than a dream, worse than a nightmare.

A shikigami... she remembered. *A shikigami attacked and then I—*

Her whole body jerked as she looked down. Her left arm was as white as paper yet as solid and strong as real flesh and bone. The fingers on her right hand trembled.

I'm a shikigami too.

But what did that mean? A thousand questions tumbled through her head all at once. She took a deep breath. Was she only imagining her lungs filling with air? Her stomach churned. Was she only imagining the queasiness in her gut as well? She did not know. She could not think beyond the cloud of fear that filled her mind.

Her elbow knocked against a stack of books, tipping them to the floor. Outside, the door opened and Akane trotted in carrying a black glove between its jaws.

"Little kit is awake!" It sounded as sunny as always. As if Kurara was not slowly losing her mind. The fox placed the glove on the tatami, beaming with pride. *"Put it on! Akane found it for you!"*

Kurara picked up the glove. The material was thick but soft, made of some kind of animal skin. When she put it on, it reached just past her elbow.

Of course they had to keep this a secret. No one could know about this. If the crew found out that she was a shikigami they would – well, she did not know what they would do but she did not want to find out either. Would Himura become her master? If not, would she eventually lose her mind? Would the very same people who greeted her in the morning and smiled when they passed in the hallway be the ones who ripped her core from her chest?

I am a lotus, she told herself as her heartbeat thundered in her ears. *I am a lotus sitting above the water. The murky world below does not affect me. I am a lotus, a lotus, a lotus.*

"Akane." She curled her legs up to her chest. This was all too much. "Help me!"

Sitting beside her, Akane rubbed its papery face against her cheek. *"Don't cry, little kit. Now, now, don't cry."*

Kurara could not help it. She had not felt this wretched since she had lost Haru. She was scared. Everything she thought she knew had been ripped apart, and she did not know how to deal with it or what she should do next.

"What's wrong with me?"

"Nothing," said the fox. *"Little kit is like Akane!"*

"Shikigami have no will of their own," Himura had said, but now Kurara was certain that it could not be true.

Here was Akane, comforting her because Akane was kind and good and so much more than Himura made the fox out to be. Shikigami had their own desires, their own personalities – they were no mere objects. She was a shikigami and still she desperately wanted to save Haru, to improve her use of ofuda, to explore the world. To find that elusive place she had once called home and all the forgotten memories wrapped up with it.

Nobody had ordered her to feel this way. Everything that she felt, everything that she believed, her thoughts, her personality, they belonged to her. They were not something written down in blood by some long-dead Crafter. Her nails clawed at her arm until red welts appeared, but when her nails finally pierced her skin, though the welts remained, no blood bubbled to the surface.

Kurara quickly looked away. Her gaze shifted to the books around the room. Perhaps they held the answers to her questions, but then again everything Himura knew about shikigami were from these books and he had not known a thing about her or Haru. What did he really know? What could those books teach her that wasn't lies?

"Why am I so different?"

Akane did not answer. Instead, it hummed a familiar song. *"A dying star fell from the heavens, and from that star grew a tree."*

Kurara let the lullaby wash over her. She was a shikigami. She was not a human. Not a groundling or a Sorabito but a being created from paper. The reality of it sank to the bottom of her gut like a stone. Perhaps it was not so bad. After all, this just meant that she was like Haru.

Her hands reached for his core. Her stomach lurched when she realized that it was not there.

Haru's pouch was missing.

With an alarmed cry, she ran her hands over her stomach, around her sides, and over her legs. She scrambled at the clasps of her obi, pulling it off so that her kimono fell open. Jumping to her feet, she rummaged through the pile of books and tossed them aside.

Haru was gone. His core was missing. What if she had dropped him? No, she would never have been so careless, but – but it had been so chaotic at the time. If the core had slipped, she would have never noticed. What would she do if she had lost him? How could she be so stupid?

"Haru! Where's Haru?"

The fox's expression shifted into something unreadable.

"Akane gave your friend to Master for safe keeping."

A wave of relief made Kurara's knees weak. She sank to the floor, her panic ebbing away. Her hand came to rest on her necklace, on the daruma Himura had made for her.

Thank goodness. Haru was safe with Himura. She did not know what she would have done if she had lost him.

TWENTY-SEVEN

KURARA could barely hear herself think over the sound of repairs. Hammers beat against the ship's hull, a constant rhythm that had become the background symphony to life on the *Orihime*.

A part of her felt guilty for not lending a helping hand, but she had more pressing worries at the moment. She wanted to find Himura so that she could get Haru back and plan their audience with Princess Tsukimi, but she also wanted to talk.

She could not recall everything from her conversation with Himura, but she remembered that he had been upset. It was difficult to blame him. Kurara remembered when she found out about Haru. Discovering that he was a shikigami had hurt, not because he was not human but because it felt as though he had not trusted her enough to tell her the truth, that perhaps they were not as close as she had believed.

It had made her feel like a fool.

Now Kurara could appreciate how Haru must have felt in his last moments. Whether he had known about being a shikigami or not, she knew he had never intended to hurt her. If only she could convince Himura of the same thing.

Kurara wandered down hallways littered with debris, past creaking scaffolding and long gashes in the walls. She poked her head into the mess hall and stopped by Himura's quarters more than once, but he had disappeared. The deckhands she questioned as they hurried past her did not know where he was. It was as if Himura had become a phantom, disappearing from everyone's sight. Even Akane did not know where its master had gone.

"Did he say anything to you?" she asked the fox.

Akane shook its head as it trotted by her side.

After combing the entire ship, Kurara found herself in front of the captain's quarters. The door was open and she could hear Sakurai deep in discussion.

"How far can we fly on what we've got?" He sounded more serious than Kurara had ever heard him. He was sitting by his desk with his back to the window, his face obscured in shadow.

"To the next sky city." Sayo's voice came from somewhere within the room.

"And the ship?"

Tomoe flipped through the notes in her hands, her back to the door. "I'd give it two days at most to replace all the broken guard rails. The hull and other parts of the ship will take maybe a week. Problem is, we're low on cash. In fact, after restocking all the food and fuel that officer stole from us during his 'inspection', I'd say we're flat out broke."

Just then, Sakurai spotted Kurara at the doorway. He smiled, gesturing for her to come in.

"Miss Kurara! I heard you took a tumble during the fight. How are you feeling now?"

Kurara pushed the door all the way open and stepped inside. Tomoe and Sayo turned to look at her.

They did not know what she was. How could they? Her paper arm was covered. She looked perfectly human. Acted and sounded like one too. There was no reason for anyone to suspect anything was amiss and yet, when their gazes came to rest upon her, Kurara could not help but feel as though she was walking a very careful tightrope that could snap at any moment.

Don't be ridiculous! It's all in your head, she chided herself. Snapping her attention back to the task at hand, she swallowed around the hard lump in her throat and asked, "Have you seen Himura?"

Sakurai shrugged. "He just left, actually. In quite a rush too. Never thought he'd be one for a festival, but he ran off as quick as a speeding kohane."

Akane made a sound, as though being left behind amounted to nothing short of cruel betrayal. Kurara bit into her lip. Of all the times for Himura to disappear!

"*Anyway*" – Sayo cleared her throat, loudly – "we need to buy more fuel. We might have enough to take us to the next sky city, but nowhere near enough for the Grand Stream."

"Well, at the very least we do have something to sell." Sakurai reached into his desk and pulled out a shikigami core. It was the one from the eagle that had attacked them. "Tomoe, you know the city well. Where is the nearest military outpost?"

"There's a Patriots Office in the restaurant district," said Tomoe.

"Good. Get a good price."

"You're going to sell the core?" Kurara sucked in a sharp breath.

Sayo looked at her as if she had grown another head. "We are hunters, you know."

Kurara knew this, of course, but everything felt different now. How much did they get for a core? What was the price of a soul?

"Yes, of course," she croaked. She could not be angry at the crew. They had told her what they did and she had been fine with it, telling herself there was a difference between Haru and Akane and the monsters that attacked people. Telling herself that the shikigami they hunted could not be saved anyway.

Even if that was true, it was a sad and pitiful fate.

Sakurai waved a hand. "Dismissed."

With a heaviness weighing on her shoulders, Kurara followed the others out of the room.

"Hey, Kurara." Tomoe caught her before she could leave. "Want to come with me to the Patriots Office?"

She shook her head. Ever since leaving the *Midori*, Kurara had never had a pleasant encounter with the military and the Patriot's Office was just a fancy name for the place where men did all the empire's paperwork. It would be crawling with soldiers. Besides, she had more important things to worry about.

"I have to speak to Himura first." Her mind did not have space for anything else.

Tomoe shrugged. "All right, but you've never celebrated the Festival of the Seventh Star, have you? I know things seem all doom and gloom, but you gotta unwind or you'll go grey before you're thirty! Why don't we all go together? You're in too, right, Sayo?" she called as Sayo passed them by.

"And Akane!" The fox bounced up and down.

"Of course, how could anyone forget you, Akane?" Tomoe leaned down to stroke the fox's head.

A shikigami is not a pet! Kurara wanted to snap. Her anger was so bright and sudden that it caught her off guard. Where was all this rage coming from? With every breath, she could feel it heaving at her lungs, wrapping around her throat like vines threatening to strangle her.

"At the festival, there'll be food! And fireworks! And fun games!" Akane's tongue lolled out between its teeth in excitement.

Sayo snorted. "We're not little children. Why would anyone get excited over another stupid festival?"

All this talk of festivals and fun made the irksome feeling in Kurara's chest grow. It was all so trite. There were a thousand things more important than some festival. Princess Tsukimi's summer palace was near by. Himura had disappeared. She was a shikigami. She was a shikigami. She was a shikigami.

"You two go together," she managed to say through clenched teeth.

"But—"

"I have more important things to do!"

The moment she snapped, she regretted it. Tomoe took a sharp step back, eyes widening. Sayo glared at her.

"Hey, *groundling*! Don't take your moods out on Tomoe!"

"S–sorry…" Mumbling an apology, Kurara swiftly turned on her heel. Akane bounded after her.

"What's wrong with her?" she heard Sayo grunt as she hurried away from Sakurai's quarters.

"It's OK. Looks like it will just be the two of us then," said Tomoe.

"I never said—"

"Oh, come on! It'll be a date! Wait for me here! Once I'm done, I'll come back to the ship and then we can go together to…"

Kurara's pace quickened until she could no longer hear them. She just needed to find Himura. Then everything would be OK.

Interlude

Do not walk the earth
For you are of cloud and sky;
The earth is unclean
And the eyes of the heavens
Shall not stand impurity

– from *The Thirteen Decrees of Tenyo,*
Sorabito religious text

The cavern was blown open. When Rei finally lifted his head to peek out of the foxhole, all he found were smouldering rocks and an opening in the cavern's ceiling so big it looked as though a giant's fist had crashed through the top.

Pulling himself out of the hole, he staggered to his feet. A loud ringing echoed in his ears. He looked around.

Rocks and pieces of levistone lay scattered everywhere on a bed of ash. Stumbling forward, Rei made his way to the small enclave where the shikigami had been chained.

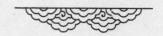

Despite the light streaming in from the ceiling, it was difficult to make out anything. The walls had caved in, filling the enclave with rock. If Inui had not been blown apart, she was buried beneath the debris.

A small laugh bubbled at the back of his throat. His ears were still ringing. Rei let himself collapse against the rocks, his giggles turning into stomach-clenching roars of laughter.

He had killed a Crafter and survived. He had burned her, crushed her, blasted her into pieces. *Good riddance!* he thought. The old bat had deserved everything she got. It served her right for trying to use Sohma. For trying to use *him*. This was what happened to people who dared to cross him.

What if Prince Ugetsu finds out? The thought crossed Rei's mind for a moment. Inui was the one who had helped arrange the deal between Rei and the prince. The old bat had no doubt reported back on everything Rei had said and done. What if the prince took Inui's death as a sign of betrayal?

A dozen worries gnawed at the back of Rei's mind before he quickly squashed them. Well, in that case, he supposed he had better make doubly sure Princess Tsukimi died.

The ringing faded as he made his way out of the mines. The ground was not a pretty sight – long scars ran across the land, the mining huts and bits of equipment blown apart, the debris scattered in a perfect ring from the point of explosion. Rei found the kohane Inui had

used to fly them to the mines. It was still in one piece. Setting it upright, he headed back to the city.

———————◦———————

Rei was calmer by the time he returned to Sola-Il. The streets bubbled with talk of the shikigami's sudden appearance. Its freedom had lasted only minutes before it had been burned down by hunters.

How fortunate. Hysterical laughter threatened to steal Rei's breath all over again. His clothes were singed. His heart pounded. But the Gods were smiling upon him today.

It was good to be alive. To be home. Rei stopped for a moment to breathe in the recycled air and admire his city.

The domes stretched over the entire city, regulating the temperature and atmosphere so that it was cool in summer and warm even in winter. Building stacks lined the road, each level piled so haphazardly on top of the other that parts jutted out or tilted precariously. By all rights, a soft breeze should have sent them toppling, and yet they remained, gravity-defying, growing upwards as if the city's domed ceiling was a challenge to be met. Flowers bloomed from the balconies, spilling down the sides of the wood in a carpet of vibrant orange, rich purple and burning crimson. Fresh laundry was left out on poles between the buildings, fluttering in the sun.

How the city filled him with pride.

He made his way past the city's massive rain catchers and towards the hub. With Inui out of the picture, his thoughts turned back to the assassination. He could finally move the plan forward exactly as he wished.

The military police were out in full force in case of trouble and Rei's pace quickened. It was easy to disappear into the crowd. Like the swelling sea, the hub was an ever-changing maze of shops and street stalls. A singing vendor indicated where one could buy a range of exotic sky fish. Beside him, large posters splayed on the walls declared: *Madam Tai's Tea Shop — over seven hundred flavours of tea! Lucky Red Emporium! Today: Crab-sumo. Twenty-ko bet minimum.*

Rei tried not to touch anyone as he struggled through the crowds. The marketplace was brimming with traders from all over the empire – not just Sorabito, but Northmen with spices from the empire's distant colonies and wools from the east. Groundlings running around like rats. The streets reeked of them.

A ramshackle workhouse with thick blue windows sat on a quiet corner of the hub, away from the hustle and bustle. Someone was leaning against the sagging door. To the casual observer, he was no one special, but he was just who Rei wanted to see.

"Yuzo." He approached the workhouse. "Is everything ready?"

"We transported the dragon to one of the warehouses for now. We've removed the beast from its crate and chained it up." The man gave a jerky nod and handed

him the register of ships that had docked at the city port within the last week. Without Nao or the *Hishaku*, Rei and his men would have to make their escape on one of the ships in the dock. Rei accepted the file, taking a moment to quickly observe the young man.

When he had recruited Yuzo, he had seemed like the wild type that would gladly walk into a rain of bullets for the cause. Now, dark purple circles lined his sunken eyes. He looked as though he had not bathed in over a week and his kimono was rumpled and stained.

"What's the matter?"

Running a hand through his thin hair, Yuzo sighed. "Nao gave his life to distract the groundlings. Do you know what happened after the parade? Do you know what they did to Nao's body after he was caught?"

His haunted look deepened.

"They buried him!" Yuzo spat. "They *buried* him under the dirt where the birds cannot reach his soul! He pulled the strings to get us here. Now look at what has become of him."

Ah, poor Nao. Rei would have felt sorrier for him if he had not been such a coward. Nao had chosen his fate the moment he ran.

Striding forward, Rei gripped Yuzo's shoulders. "That is exactly why we are doing this! Nao deserved so much more than this, and yet what have those groundlings done? Look how they desecrate our dead. They cannot even let his soul rest in peace! Nao was one of us. He was a friend! That is why we cannot stop. Because *they* will not stop until they have crushed our spirit and turned

us into obedient puppets of the empire! That is why we exist – why Sohma exists. We will not stop until every last groundling rat is eradicated from our city!"

He could not allow his plans to be ruined by weak morale. As he spoke, he could see his words beginning to take effect. Yuzo nodded, his confidence clearly swelling.

"By the way" – the man faltered as Rei released him – "a few hours ago, the dragon began squirming. I don't know how long it will stay calm. We need Inui to come and get the blasted thing under control again!"

Rei clicked his tongue in annoyance. He could not tell Yuzo that Inui was dead – that would only make the man panic – but without the old bat they had to act fast. It would do no good if the dragon started attacking his men.

A frustrated sigh escaped his lips. He flipped open the docking register. Scanning the list of ships, his eye caught on a familiar name. The Gods truly were smiling upon him today.

"The warehouse where you've stashed the dragon … it is the one right by the summer palace, isn't it?" asked Rei.

"It is," Yuzo confirmed.

That was good. Rampaging shikigami were like enraged bulls. They always attacked whatever was closest.

"Wait here!" Pressing the register into Yuzo's chest, Rei hurried back through the hub and towards the docks.

He arrived just in time to see the gates open. People poured out of the docking bay and into the paved streets.

Rei darted through the crowd, studying each face that passed. She was here. She had to be – the solution to all his problems.

Before he could reach the docking doors, he caught sight of a familiar swish of red hair in the corner of his eye. The girl made her way from the docking bay down the main road.

The Gods truly were guiding him.

Rei's heart matched the pace of his footsteps as he fell into step behind her. How long had it been? She still looked the same as when she had left home – her rebellious red hair shining in the sun, almond eyes full of fire, the tanto he had given her by her waist.

Unaware that she was being followed, the girl headed through streets lined with food stalls and towards a large grey mansion at the top of the road.

The Patriots Office was an ugly building full of ugly groundlings. You could tell that it was not Sorabito-made. It looked completely different from the thin wooden structures around it – a gated mansion of dull, grey stone sprawling outwards instead of upwards like the Sorabito architecture around it. Statues of tigers rather than birds decorated the entrance; a black iron fence surrounded the grounds. The long, rectangular windows adopted a brutal appearance.

The men standing on guard wore high-collar black uniforms with golden peony buttons that glinted in the light like the eyes of demons. They glared at the girl when she approached. They questioned her longer than usual,

but eventually let her through. Though not without a snide comment and a snigger.

Sky-forsaken worms! Rei kept his distance, imagining shoving the tip of his katana down one of the guard's throats.

He idled by the side road, out of the guards' sight, and waited. When the girl re-emerged, she wore a small pouch full of ko at her side and a thunderous expression.

Rei followed her through the streets and down narrow alleyways. Old men slept in tiny booths carved out of the side of building stacks. He waited for her to drift away from them, down quieter roads where no one would see him. Washing lines dangled overhead, swaying in the artificial wind.

The smell of overripe fruit drifted out of a nearby window, reminding Rei of the peaches his daughters gave him in attempts to buy attention, before they learned that the only thing he was interested in was whether they were willing to gut groundlings alongside him.

"I know you're following me. You saw me coming out of the Patriots Office, didn't you?" The girl suddenly stopped. Without turning around, her hand drifted to her tanto. Rei was not sure when she had noticed him following her, but she made sure to remain a good distance from him. "Well, I have bad news. I sold a shikigami core to them and the damn groundlings gave me nothing but pocket change. Those liars had the nerve to claim it was a bloody dud!"

Rei chuckled at the thought of being mistaken for a petty thief. His plans were so much greater than mere robbery.

At the sound of his laughter, the girl whipped around. Her eyes widened.

"Hello, Tomoe." Rei smiled at his daughter.

Tomoe gaped at him.

"Let's have a chat."

She stiffened. Her hand remained on the hilt of her blade. "A chat? About what?"

"About how you are going to help me kill Princess Tsukimi."

TWENTY-EIGHT

HIMURA cut through the crowds, past stalls twinkling with cheap jewellery and booths where men lined up to shoot cork bullets at gliding targets. People barely touched him: his body twisted out of their way, side-stepping the careless gaggle of children running in front of his feet. The pouch, and the core inside it, dangled at his hip, weighing down his body and his mind.

Those who noticed the white bracelet around his wrist gave him a wide berth. Others avoided him for the simple fact that he was obviously not a Sorabito. Himura wondered if Kurara would experience the same thing when she finally stepped out into the city. As soon as the thought came, he squashed it.

Turning away from the crowd, he headed down narrow alleyways and past the darkened windows of empty building stacks. He needed to be somewhere quiet, somewhere with space for his thoughts.

His feet took him to the outskirts of the summer palace. A large lake surrounded an even larger floating rock on which the palace was built. Blue lines of levistone, embedded deep inside the rock walls, glowed in the darkness. Water flowed over the edges and spilled down into the lake, creating a curtain of waterfalls.

"*Impress me,*" Princess Tsukimi had said with a mocking smirk when he had asked her for a royal favour all those years ago. Himura wondered if Kurara was prepared for the kind of lashing the princess could dish out. Not that it mattered to him anymore. Kurara could go and beg for the princess's help on her own.

His fingers brushed the pouch. The core at his side was probably more valuable than anything the *Orihime* had ever hunted before. It was the core of what was perhaps one of the first shikigami ever made. If Kurara showed it to Princess Tsukimi, it would certainly impress her. Maybe it would please her so much the princess would give Kurara anything she wanted – her friend's body, all the white rice she could eat, the royal jewels. Power. Knowledge.

Himura stepped back for a better view of the summer palace. It was well guarded. The floating rock was a natural obstacle that most people could not overcome, but then he was not "most people".

He pulled off his bracelet. Paper swirled over the ground. His ofuda formed a pair of wings, stretching into talons and tail feathers, cascading upward into a curved beak.

He had not made a falcon of this size since the day he had left for the *Midori*. The bird lowered its neck and Himura climbed on. With a single beat of its powerful wings, it took off into the sky and soared over the palace. Carefully tended gardens extended below him. Trees, dwarfed by the tiered pagodas beside them, stretched their branches towards Himura as if to snatch him from the sky.

The guards in the towers spotted him immediately, turning their cannons towards him. Before they had a chance to blow him out of the sky, Himura slipped off the falcon's neck and dropped onto the palace grounds below. The bird crumbled and reformed into a cushion beneath him to soften his fall. He landed right in the middle of the gardens, spooking a man who had been sitting in front of the koi pond, feeding the fish.

"I seek an audience with Princess Tsukimi," he said before the man could do more than jump.

"What rudeness!"

It was Himura's turn to be startled. He had not noticed the white crow circling above him, staring down at him through its blank, beady eyes.

"Master, allow me to peck this man's eyes out! The nerve of this nobody to demand an audience with Her Imperial Highness!"

"Not yet, Yui." The Crafter waved his crow back. He was a heavy-set man a full head and a half taller than Himura, with feet that stomped across the ground as though he wanted the earth to tremble in his wake. A tingle of electricity danced across Himura's skin in a greeting of power that allowed Crafters to always recognize one another. Each of the man's fingers was adorned with paper rings.

The man held a hand up, waving off the guards running towards them. Slipping off one of the rings, he transformed it into a short blade.

"You there!" he addressed Himura. "Tell me why I shouldn't gut you like a fish? If you don't, I'll—"

"What's this, Goro?" A calm voice came from behind Himura. A voice he remembered.

Himura had never seen a man so large jump quite so high. Whipping around, the Crafter cried, "Please, Your Imperial Highness, stay back! It's nothing but an intruder. Perhaps—"

A firework rose through the sky, bursting into a shower of green light that illuminated the faces around him.

Princess Tsukimi was as beautiful as a lioness; half her allure came from the feeling she could devour you whole. When she smiled, it was only to expose a flash of her pearl-white teeth. Her long, black hair was as dark as night, sweeping over her shoulders and down to the small of her back. Though there was a Crafter with a knife behind him and a shikigami that wanted to peck out his eyes above, Himura's gaze remained fixed on the princess. He knew which of the three was truly dangerous.

Himura remembered the first time he had seen Princess Tsukimi. Even as a child, it had been easy to vault over the walls of Tomuri Castle with nothing more than a handful of paper. He had stolen his way into the castle, sneaking through the bushes and hovering over nightingale floors like a ghost, before slipping into the royal chambers. He had seen Princess Tsukimi with her brother earlier and expected her to still be in the courtyard, but the princess was there, inside her room, reading at her desk.

Instead of calling the guards, she had smiled and asked him what he wanted.

And Himura, like a fool, had told her.

"Is this what you want?" She had dangled the book she had been reading in front of his nose. It was a small leather-bound tome with a dark red cover. *"I'll give it to you if you want, little boy. I've read this one so many times I know its contents by heart."*

Princess Tsukimi had worn a viper's smile.

"But first, impress me."

Blinking back the memory, Himura schooled his face into a blank expression. Princess Tsukimi lived to provoke. The more upset one was, the greater her triumph.

"My, my, a stray dog has wandered before me. Are you looking for a home, stray? A new master? Would you like me to pet and feed you?" The princess's voice was like the jingle of bells – light and purposefully mocking.

"Do you remember me, Princess Tsukimi?" he asked.

The princess stepped in front of Himura. Fireworks illuminated half her face in golden and red light, leaving the other half hidden in deep shadows.

"Should I?" She raised an arched brow. He had her curiosity, but there was still no recognition in her eyes. "What's your name?"

She did not ask; she demanded, as if every answer to her questions should be given to her by right.

"Himura."

"Himura," Princess Tsukimi repeated, as if sampling the taste of his name.

The pouch tied to his obi weighed him down. The core within felt like an anchor.

"I am here to seek an audience with Your Imperial Highness. I wish to ask for your royal favour," he said.

Princess Tsukimi laughed.

"Sure. I don't mind listening to one of my loyal citizens! Let no one say that I don't care about my people! Especially a proud Crafter such as yourself!"

Her smile was the same as it was back then.

"But first, impress me."

TWENTY-NINE

KURARA had hoped that Himura would return soon. Sola-Il was vast and she did not fancy her odds of tracking him down out there in the middle of a crowded festival.

Yet as night settled into the bones of the city and he still did not return, Kurara knew that she would have to try her luck. Akane remembered the places Himura liked to visit. With the fox's help, perhaps she could find him after all.

The doors to Sola-Il opened like a mountain splitting in half, spilling starlight into the docks. As Kurara stood in line to leave the docking bay, she observed the gaggle of families who were also eager to step into the city. Young couples returning from visits to relatives, starry-eyed groundlings touring the sky city for the first time, merchants loading crates onto hovercrafts and traders arguing with docking officers over the contents of their cargo all shuffled their feet as the procession inched closer to the exit.

Kurara clutched her token close. The small square of wood dangled on a thin cord, identifying her ship and the space where the *Orihime* was docked.

Guards waved her through. As soon as she was outside, she drew a sharp breath. The city sprawled before her, winding upwards to the domed sky. The stream of stars shone across the night in a long, glittering streak of twilight blue. Something welled up inside her. When she breathed in, her chest felt full.

"Festival! Fun! Let's go to the city, little kit!" Akane tugged at her sleeve.

"Don't get lost now."

Kurara turned to see Sayo leaning against the wall of the docks, arms folded and lips pressed into a frown. She looked different, dressed in a dark blue kimono patterned with bright red and gold maple leaves and a matching red skirt with a white lace trim. Silk sparrows rested on the embroidered branches of her yellow obi. It was the brightest thing Kurara had ever seen Sayo wear, but it was not just her clothes. She had done something to her hair, Kurara was not sure what, and her face ... was that rouge?

"I thought you were going to the festival with Tomoe?" Sayo's appearance had her almost tongue-tied. She reminded Kurara of those woodblock prints of female ronin riding hovercrafts into battle – fierce and beautiful.

Sayo's cheeks coloured. "Tomoe isn't back yet. We agreed to meet back here after she was done at the

245

Patriots Office." She glanced at the bruised colour of the sky. "It's getting late."

Kurara remembered her earlier outburst and felt guilty all over again. "I'm sure she'll be back soon," she said.

Something in Sayo's expression shifted. The tension in her shoulders uncoiled.

"Do you think so?" she asked, almost too softly for Kurara to catch. "Do you know what the Seventh Star festival is all about?" She pointed to the sky. "That star there is the Weaver. And that star is the Cowherd. The Festival of the Seventh Star is all about reunion. When a shoal of sky fish build a bridge for the two stars to see each other again."

"Romantic!" Akane bounced up and down. *"It's a love festival!"*

"It's about reunion," Sayo insisted, but her cheeks were flushed.

If tonight was a festival of reunion, perhaps that was a good sign. Parting with Sayo, Kurara headed straight for the lantern-lined streets. The roads were packed with makeshift stalls, the tall building stacks festooned with banners. People squeezed past pop-up shops selling brass trinkets and tiny china birds.

Where would Himura go on a night like this? She tried to remain focused as a thousand different sights and smells pulled at her attention – the aroma of fried eel that made her stomach rumble, the bright red and gold fish swimming about in large tanks of water, stalls selling mechanical owls and street entertainers spinning sugar into star-shaped clouds. It was all so wonderful, and so

246

very lonely. Twinkling, coloured lights demanded her happiness, but Kurara could not bring herself to smile. There was a crushing weight against her chest. Her first trip to Sola-Il should have been with Haru.

She wanted him back.

Soon, she told herself. The summer palace was so close she could see its shadow stretch over the streets. The thought of facing Princess Tsukimi was a daunting one, but she would not let that stop her. Whatever she needed to do, she would do it.

Fireworks suddenly exploded within the dome, the dying sparks and the smell of smoke falling back to the ground. Was it so late already? Kurara hurried through the streets, hoping that she would spot Himura, or even just another member of the *Orihime* who might have seen him.

She was so absorbed in her search that at first she did not notice that she was the only one moving freely through the crowds. When she looked around, she noticed that people were avoiding her, staring at Akane with distrust.

Kurara was ushering the fox closer when someone soared out of the window of the building stack above and crashed on top of a fabric stall just inches from where she stood. Women screamed. Splintered wood and bolts of silk went flying everywhere. A second later, two men in black high collar uniforms ran down the steps from the second floor of the stack.

"You want to say that again, sky rat?" The first officer – a pudgy man with a large handlebar moustache – seized the man who was lying on the ground and shook him by his kimono.

"*Little kit!*" Akane tugged at her sleeve when Kurara took a step back. Its voice, the way it rang through people's heads, was unmistakable. The military police and the Sorabito sprang apart to stare at Kurara, wide-eyed.

A bolt of terror zapped through her. She remembered the soldiers in the forest, their golden buttons glinting, their hands on their guns as they burned Haru's body to cinders. Kurara watched as the military police raised their hands …

… and saluted.

"This man was disturbing the peace, my lady." The officer who spoke sounded like a child who had just been caught with dirt on his clothes.

It took a moment for Kurara to understand what he was saying. *My lady*. No one had ever called her that before. She stared at them, but they were not looking at her. They were looking at Akane and at the paper daruma hanging from the white necklace around her throat.

They thought she was a Crafter. One of Princess Tsukimi's.

As soon as it hit her, something vicious snarled through her gut. She wanted to make a fool out of these men, to frighten them just as she had been frightened when they had appeared in the forests below the *Midori*. To lord it over them like the man who had taken the *Orihime*'s supplies.

"I see. And what was he doing exactly?" Kurara placed her hands on her hips, her tone as harsh as she could muster.

The officers stood a little straighter. "Getting drunk. Harassing others, my lady!"

Kurara sniffed. "You smell like sake too."

They said nothing, but their eyes darted around the road in search of an escape.

"Who is the officer in charge of you?"

"M–my lady, please, we were only—"

"Bullying some poor man. Yes, I can see that. Did you have to throw him out of the window? Who will pay for all this?" Kurara's hand swept over the ruined stall.

The officers began to sweat.

"What's going on?"

Before Kurara could enjoy their panic, another man approached. A tingle of static played across her skin as he came closer. The scarlet of his kimono was broken by the black hakama tied at his waist and an expensive black haori over his shoulders. Chrysanthemum-shaped fastenings on the lapels glinted beneath the light. A white cuff dangled from his right ear.

Behind him stood a tiger so massive it could crush the market stalls with a single swish of its tail.

Kurara sucked in a sharp breath.

An imperial Crafter. A real one.

THIRTY

HIS sweep of ink-black hair matched the hue of his eyes. He was handsome, yet something about him was uncanny to look at. One had the feeling that nature had no part in forming his face, but instead a committee had selected a mishmash of good-looking features and arranged them together. He looked like one of the toy soldiers the empire sold to children.

Kurara eyed the oversized tiger looming over him. Unlike the man, there was nothing toy-like about it.

"He was disturbing the peace." The soldiers pointed to the Sorabito.

"The military police were harassing me! Can't blame a guy if he bites back!"

The Crafter took one glance at the situation and said in a stern voice, "Leave. All of you."

"Sir, my stall!" The owner of the broken fabric stand

began to complain, but she was silenced with a look. The crowd quickly dispersed, as did the drunken Sorabito and the two officers, each one scattering in a different direction. Kurara took the opportunity to sneak away as well, but the enormous tiger stepped in front of her, its body blocking the entire street.

"Hello. I'm Akane!" The fox bounded towards it. The tiger backed away with a look of alarm and disdain, like one suddenly confronted by a particularly bouncy cockroach. Kurara glanced at its enormous frame. Its hulking presence was intimidating, yet she could not help but admire the construction of its body – how the pleats and folds overlapped to form its powerful legs and broad face.

"Calm down, Ruki," said the Crafter when the tiger hissed at Akane. He turned to Kurara. "I've never seen you before. Where are you from?"

"I'm a hunter on the *Orihime*, sir." She stood a little straighter.

"And what were you doing just now?"

Kurara steeled her nerves. She may have been caught pretending to be something she wasn't, but she had also stopped the soldiers from harassing an innocent person. That was something she would not apologize for.

"Those men had no right to throw their weight around like that! I was trying to teach them a lesson – it's not my fault they mistook me for one of Princess Tsukimi's Crafters."

"Impertinence!" The tiger's growl shook Kurara's body. She clenched her teeth together and hoped her expression

did betray her fear. How easily its massive paws could crush her like a bug. Akane put itself between the two of them, though the tiger paid it no attention.

"I'll let you go with a warning this time," said the man. Kurara released a short sigh of relief. "Don't cause any problems while you're here. You may be a Crafter, but that doesn't give you permission to stir up trouble." He turned to leave, gesturing for his shikigami to follow him away from the festival stalls.

"Wait!" Kurara ran after him. When she had imagined arriving on Sola-Il, she envisioned herself walking up to the summer palace with Himura by her side, the two of them discussing how they would petition the princess for help. Not once had she imagined bumping into an imperial Crafter and his shikigami, but she was not about to let the opportunity pass her by. She would get that audience with Princess Tsukimi no matter what she had to do.

"You work for Princess Tsukimi, don't you? Please, will you let me see her?"

"Princess Tsukimi doesn't just see anyone!" the tiger growled.

The Crafter held a hand to his shikigami's muzzle, calming it. "Why do you want to see her?" he asked.

"My friend – he – I have this core—" She reached for her pouch only to remember that it was not there. She bit her lip. "I want to ask the princess for help remaking a – a shikigami's body."

A look of understanding crossed the man's face. "Ah, you had a shikigami and it got injured, I suppose? My comrades would say you should just get another one, but shikigami don't grow on trees. And I understand what it's like to get attached." He glanced at the tiger by his side and laid a hand on its rippling paper fur. "But what makes you think the princess will help you?"

"She likes our kind, doesn't she? I heard that Princess Tsukimi is always interested in meeting new ... Crafters." Kurara swallowed down the thought that came next: was she still a Crafter if she was also a shikigami?

"The princess is interested in Crafters that can impress her."

In the distance, the city clock tower struck the hour. Beneath the shadow of the building stacks, a group of Sorabito tumbled out of a nearby bar, their cheeks rosy with joy. A woman staggered out behind them. For a split second, when their eyes met, Kurara glimpsed the well of hostility beneath her intoxicated stare.

"Rot in the earth, Crafter! Empire's dogs!" The woman hurled a bottle of sake at them.

Anyone within ten feet of the bar scattered. The tiger roared in outrage. As the bottle soared towards them, Kurara's ofuda slipped from around her neck. Paper twirled through the air and folded itself into a white falcon. It shot towards the bottle and snatched it out of the air, dropping it right into Kurara's outstretched palm.

"What makes you think I can't impress the princess?" The falcon landed on her shoulder before crumbling back into her usual necklace.

"We're the best hunters in the empire!" Akane yipped.

253

The Crafter lifted an eyebrow, his expression halfway between amusement and surprise.

"*That woman is running,*" his shikigami warned them. The woman was indeed running, or rather stumbling away, as terrified onlookers scrambled out of her path.

"Let her go. It's not worth arresting a drunkard." The Crafter's eyes did not leave Kurara's face even when his shikigami growled with displeasure. "I didn't introduce myself, did I? Fujiwa Tokiyuki. This is Ruki," he said.

"Kurara." She gestured to Himura's shikigami. "This is Akane."

Fujiwa's gaze narrowed. He looked at her as if he was sizing up a pig on market day.

"Very well," he conceded. "I will take you to the princess. If you can keep up."

Interlude

By the stars we live,
To the stars we shall return;
All else is but dirt.

— Sohma motto

Rei knew many things about his daughter. More than she was willing to admit. He had no doubt that he could convince her to work with him. Tomoe was a smart girl – Rei did not raise idiots in his household. No matter her opinion on Sohma, she was too intelligent to be unreasonable.

"Come with me." He turned away without waiting for her to follow. Just as a loyal dog would track a snake through the grass, he knew that she would go with him to find out what he was up to, if nothing else.

As predicted, Tomoe cursed beneath her breath and fell into step behind him. They looped around the hub, climbing up and down the many stairs that led past

building stacks and through narrow alleyways. Military posters wallpapered the sides of houses, the painted faces of beaming soldiers overlapping into a sickening collage. Vacant temples, empty of the Gods they had once held, slouched over the roads, gathering dust.

"Not even our Gods are safe," sighed Rei. "Look what the groundlings have done to our city. Do you remember—?"

"I don't care." Tomoe's tone was unforgiving. "You're not going to drag me all around Sola-Il on a sightseeing trip, are you?"

Rei tamped down on his anger. Tomoe had always been a bit too outspoken for his liking.

"Your mother will be relieved that I ran into you. You know she and your sisters worry about how you're doing on that ship."

He was pleased when Tomoe flinched. *Find the vein and stab deep.* When it came to family, he knew how a sharp word at the softest point could inflict the most damage.

Along the bank of an artificial lake, a line of warehouses stood back to back, engulfed in the shadow of the summer palace. People seldom lingered in the area, put off by the constant darkness. Sohma had bought out the place a long time ago. On the surface, the storage houses were somewhere for merchants to keep their goods in the short term – one day they held boxes of tinned fish, another day crates of mechanical parts – yet when Rei needed them they were the perfect hide-out.

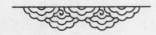 

"No doubt you have heard, since you fly everywhere, about the attack on the *Midori*." Rei lifted the storehouse shutters.

"A shikigami attacked it." Tomoe stepped inside, warily.

Upon first glance, there was nothing odd about the warehouse. Shelves stretching across the dim stone floor were lined with neatly stacked crates full of canned food and clay tableware. Rei pushed one aside. It rolled back to reveal a trapdoor. He heard Tomoe's breath catch as he unlatched the door and pulled it open. Beyond the hatch lay a staircase that plunged into the darkness below.

"After the attack, do you know what happened to that shikigami?" He began to climb down the steps. Miniature lights embedded into the walls illuminated his descent.

"It disappeared." Tomoe hesitated before following.

The staircase ended in front of a discreet metal door. There was nothing of note around it, only stone and a small electric lamp hanging next to the hinges. Pausing just long enough to give her a meaningful look, Rei walked inside.

"We managed to keep it down for now, but it won't be long before it starts going berserk."

"*It?* What are you—?" Tomoe stopped short. As her eyes adjusted to the darkness, she finally saw it: a giant, white dragon lay curled into a ball, tied and bolted to the ground with chains designed for holding a ship in place.

As Rei approached, the beast strained against the chains. It was a marvel how a creature with such blank eyes could glower so hatefully.

"This dragon was … a gift. After the *Midori*, my comrades and I smuggled it through the docks."

Tomoe was pale. "You were responsible for the *Midori*? And then you brought a shikigami you cannot control *here* of all places! Surely even you realize how dangerous this is! Who knows how long before it escapes and wrecks everything! You're endangering the entire city by keeping it chained up down here!"

"It will be worth it in the end. As long as we Sorabito have our freedom, as long as the princess dies, as long as it gets rid of all the groundling worms in our city, it will all be worth it!"

His daughter shook her head. "*Nothing* is worth risking innocent lives!"

That was about the reaction Rei had expected. Tomoe was smart enough to know that the way groundlings treated the Sorabito was not fair, but lacked the guts to make the sacrifices necessary for change. She was like every other spineless coward. Full of empty talk and useless complaints, but without the stomach to act.

Well, now he would force her to act.

"That is why I am asking you for help. You have experience killing rampaging shikigami. You can ensure that the damage does not spread, that it is contained to the princess's summer palace, and by killing it you can be a hero. I will even let you keep the core. I'm sure you could use the cash," he said.

Tomoe's nostrils flared. "Or you could not do that and just destroy it now while you still can!"

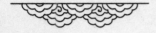 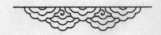

He gave her a disappointed look. Women were so weak-willed. He wished that his wife had given him sons. "Tomoe."

"No." She stood firm. "No, I don't want to hear it."

"It pains me to see my own flesh and blood content to be shackled by our oppressors. The groundlings hate you and yet you smile as they spit at you – a good little sheep all too happy to trot to the slaughter."

Tomoe clenched her hands, just as she used to as a child whenever she didn't get her way. "I – No. No. I'm tired of having this argument with you."

Rei walked towards the dragon, his steps echoing against the stone. The shikigami shifted and snarled at him in warning.

"Everything I do is for the good of the Sorabito."

Tomoe glowered at him, furious. There was a mix of anger and exasperation written across her face, an expression that he recognized from her younger days when she would stomp her feet and growl whenever her mother told her that she could not play in the shipyard. It had been a risk bringing her here. She could run and tell the military police. Well, she could try, though Rei hoped she would be smarter than that. It was always a shame when a parent had to bury their own child.

"I fail to see how endangering Sola-II will do anyone any good, least of all the Sorabito!" she spat.

Rei let her anger slide off his back.

"We will release the shikigami at midnight, just as the festival reaches its height. The Princess will be inside the

   259

summer palace at that time, away from everyone else. Whether you choose to do something or not is up to you, but know that if you do not, you will be responsible for the destruction that follows."

Tomoe gave him a steely look. "What if I destroy that shikigami now?"

"Do you think that you can?" Rei eyed the tanto she kept sheathed by her obi. He had given her that weapon – a beautiful blade he had hoped she would use to slit the throats of the groundlings that stood in their way.

His hand purposefully drifted to the hilt of his katana. Tomoe's gaze followed it. He knew what she was thinking. She was assessing the likelihood that she could cut into the dragon's chest while it thrashed, pull out its core and escape before he cut her down.

"Well?" he baited her. "Are you going to try?"

THIRTY-ONE

FUJIWA was fast. Even with the help of Akane's sharp nose and even sharper eyes, Kurara struggled to keep him in her sights. Swinging onto Ruki's back, the Crafter grabbed the paper fur at its nape and let the shikigami's powerful legs carry him through the streets.

People dived out of the way in terror at the sight of the tiger tearing down the road. Though Fujiwa's presence atop Ruki eased the worst of the crowd's fears, a shikigami under control was a shikigami nonetheless. The sight of any paper beast was still terrifying to behold.

Akane was not big enough to ride, though the fox had suggested it. Instead, Kurara hurtled down the road, cutting through twisting alleyways and past forgotten shrines. As she raced after Fujiwa's retreating back, her ofuda transformed into paper tiles that hardened to stone. When she stepped on them, the tiles sank beneath her weight then bounced up like a springboard, lending her a burst of speed as she was launched down the street.

"Take the alleyway to your left!" The fox occasionally barked out instructions.

Akane had visited Sola-Il before with Himura and still remembered some of its shortcuts. At the shikigami's suggestion, Kurara used her ofuda to pull herself up to the top of the building stacks and raced along the roofs. Paper flew ahead of her, forming platforms between the buildings, making ropes with which she could swing across the streets, and staircases that led to taller rooftops.

It was easier to keep an eye on Fujiwa from above and there was no one to get in her way. From up here, she could see Ruki leap over a stall and bound towards the bridge connecting Sola-Il's domes together. Scooping Akane into her arms, Kurara jumped down.

Her ofuda gathered on the street below and inflated into a giant balloon to cushion her fall. She landed outside an auto-parts store, next to a line of copper-coloured kohanes and other antique-looking aircrafts chained to metal posts.

"Kurara?"

As she released Akane from her grip, Kurara turned to see Sayo sitting outside. She looked terrible. Her eyes were red-rimmed, her face splotchy. Her short hair was sticking up at odd angles as if she had just crawled out of bed. Tomoe was nowhere in sight.

Their eyes met, but Kurara had no time to stop. With an apologetic nod, she dashed after Fujiwa's retreating figure, over the connecting bridge and into the next dome where the streets were adorned with festival decorations.

The summer palace sat upon a wedge of rock that floated several miles in the sky, suspended between the ground and the top of the dome. Its imposing shadow fell over the surrounding land, swallowing the area in darkness. As Kurara stepped closer, her gaze swung up in awe.

Flowering cherry trees grew between the many tiered buildings and pagodas standing upon tall, stone foundations. At the four cardinal points, the water spilled over the edge of the rock, flowing into the lake below. Tearing her gaze away from the palace, Kurara found Fujiwa and Ruki waiting by the edge of the water.

"You made it." Fujiwa wore a small, impressed smile. "Forgive me for causing such trouble, but if you were not good enough to keep up, then it would be better for you to not see the princess. She has no tolerance for weak Crafters."

Kurara did not care what the princess tolerated. Her lungs burned. She was annoyed that she had been forced to play this stupid game, guilty that she had left Sayo when the girl looked like she had been crying and tired from using her ofuda so much. All she wanted was Haru. Why did everything have to be so difficult?

"Are you ... going to let me ... see Princess Tsukimi now?" she managed to speak between heaving gasps.

Again, Fujiwa sized her up.

"Very well," he said, with a small smile. "Come with me."

Fujiwa's ofuda created a delicate path over the water, allowing them to cross without getting wet. Kurara followed him towards the centre of the lake, her senses alert for any other "tests" he might try to pull. Behind the curtain of water lay an elevator – seemingly broken. There was no power, and no pulleys strapped to the box, but Kurara noticed the paper lining the bottom and more stuffed into the cracked walls.

Akane nudged her on. As they squeezed together to make room for Ruki's hulking frame, Fujiwa took control of the paper lining and lifted the elevator into the air.

For several minutes, there was only darkness. They moved through the centre of the rock, the elevator groaning from the stress of their weight. Kurara worried at her bottom lip. This was it. She was going to see Princess Tsukimi – alone.

The elevator led them right onto the palace grounds. Kurara thought the *Midori* had been lavish, but nothing could compare to the summer palace. Red-tiled buildings sprawled across the flat surface of the rock. Statues of stone dragons stood upon the spine of the roofs and curved around the eaves. Whereas the Sorabito built tall, the palace was built wide, designed to occupy as much of the rock as possible. Small gardens dotted the grounds, filled with koi ponds and bridges that arched over trickling streams.

Despite the palace's splendour, Kurara could not help but feel as though she was stepping into a lion's den. They passed a pair of watchtowers on either side as the guards opened the gates into a large garden. Kurara sucked in a deep breath. A sand path, the grains perfectly raked into straight lines, led up to a sprawling red building with a green-tiled roof, four floors high. This was it. She was here.

Haru. Again, her hands wanted to clasp his core, and she had to remind herself that he was not with her at the moment.

"This way." Fujiwa led them up the steps into the building and right into the path of a young woman hurrying down the wooden hallway.

"You're back, Tokiyuki." The woman wore the same crimson attire as Fujiwa. Her ofuda was a simple drop pendant resting on her collarbone. "Have you heard anything from Inui yet?"

Fujiwa shook his head. "I'm afraid she still has not returned. I'll ask Princess Tsukimi if I may search for her myself."

The woman looked troubled. "You might have to wait a while. Her Imperial Highness is busy."

Fujiwa frowned. "Busy?"

"She's in the middle of a big project."

Akane tugged at Fujiwa's sleeve. *"Want to see princess!"* it demanded.

"Of course. I promised, didn't I?" Smiling, Fujiwa turned to pat Akane on the head. Ruki growled, but Fujiwa ignored his shikigami's jealousy. Turning to the woman, he said, "Let me through. I'll take responsibility for this."

Fear flashed across the woman's face. Muttering beneath her breath, she stepped aside. Kurara tensed. She had come this far, she did not want to leave empty-handed, yet, now that she was here, a thousand worries

265

plagued her thoughts. When Kurara had imagined meeting Princess Tsukimi, she had always thought she would have Haru's core with her, that Himura would be by her side to advise and encourage her every step of the way. In her mind, she had not been this afraid.

Kurara steeled herself. Nothing ventured, nothing gained. She nodded to Fujiwa.

"Let's go."

Following the Crafter up a flight of stairs, Kurara stepped past a balcony overlooking the gardens and into a long, expansive hallway. Her footsteps echoed against the polished wood. Small lights dangled from the high ceiling, mimicking a path of stars. A gold leaf trim bordered the circular windows and the frames of the sliding doors. Painted murals covered the walls: scenes from famous stories approved by the Patriots Office. Armed guards were posted at the entrances, their only emotion one of chiselled displeasure.

"This is the throne room." Fujiwa pushed open a set of ornate doors. "It is empty at the moment, but inside you can see where the princess conducts most of her duties."

Kurara stepped through the arched entrance. The hall was larger than any she had ever seen. A sunburst chandelier cast a constellation of small lights across the floor. Red and gold pillars supported a cavernous ceiling of stars. Statues of dragons lined the walls all the way down to the end of the room where marble steps led up to a large dais. Upon it stood a canopy of black silk, the curtains pulled back to reveal a golden throne. Silver dragons curled up the legs and across the top of the backrest.

Kurara kept a tight lid on her awe. There was a cold grandeur to the way the throne loomed over anyone who entered and the dragon statues seemed to follow you with their stony eyes. The décor was at once marvellous and horrific; the kind of splendour meant to intimidate.

"Tokiyuki? Fujiwa Tokiyuki? Is that you?"

A woman poked her head around one of the dragons. Kurara had not noticed it at first, but there was a door to the side of the throne hidden by the statues.

"Ah, Tokiyuki, just as I thought!" The woman ducked beneath a stone wing as she approached Fujiwa. She had a round, curious face. Her dark eyes seemed to cut straight through the heart of the room.

"Princess!" Fujiwa bowed.

Kurara froze.

Standing before her was Princess Tsukimi, and behind her was Himura.

THIRTY-TWO

KURARA stood rooted to the spot. Of all the places she had expected to see Himura, this was not one. Cold shock thawed into relief. Now he could return Haru's core to her and they could ask Princess Tsukimi to save her friend.

Himura stared back at her, wide-eyed. His face drained of all colour. He looked as though he had seen a ghost.

"*Master!*" Akane bounded towards him, happy to be reunited. Kurara wanted to say something, too, but she remembered where she was and quickly dropped to the floor, prostrating herself.

"Is this your shikigami?" The princess looked upon Akane as one would a small pet. "Adorable."

"A headache," said Himura, stiffly.

With her forehead against the cold floor, Kurara peeked at the princess through the curtain of her hair.

Princess Tsukimi's skin was so pale there was something not quite human about it. Her moon-shaped face, the same colour as Kurara's ofuda, stood in stark contrast to the deep, ink-black of her hair and the rouge that painted her lips blood red.

If Kurara had dared to move, she would have shuffled back. The princess's beauty was a cudgel, just another trapping of power to beat people into submission. She did not wear the grand, twelve-layered robes Kurara would have expected from royalty, but the fact that she dressed like a commoner only made Kurara feel the difference between them all the more keenly. There was a chasm between them, folded into the creases of the princess's navy kimono and the crooked lines of her hakama.

"Your Imperial Highness" – Fujiwa cleared his throat – "may I present to you—"

"A Crafter!" The princess's eyes lit up. She paced around Kurara, eyeing her as one would a rare specimen. There was something manic, almost overbearing, about her sudden enthusiasm. Like a collector who could speak of nothing else but their hobby. The pressure of her gaze was a weight against Kurara's chest. The longer she stood before the princess, the more it crushed her.

"*Humans are hungry. Eat your flesh with their mouth; eat your soul with their eyes. Consume, consume.*" The eagle's words rang through Kurara's head. At the time, it had just been the crazed ramblings of an insane beast. Now, Kurara understood. Just being in the princess's presence made her feel like prey about to be hunted down.

"My, and what a fine specimen you are." Princess

269

Tsukimi ran a pale finger over her blood red lips. "Little Crafter, why did you come here? Do you wish to demand my royal favour like so many other fools and dead men?"

"She is one of my comrades, Your Imperial Highness…" croaked Himura. "We both fly with the *Orihime.*"

"Princess Tsu— Your, uh, Your Imperial Highness!" Kurara stammered. She was going to make a fool of herself, she just knew it; she would say something rude by accident and then – well, there were so many awful things that could happen, she did not know which one to fixate upon first. "I didn't come here to demand anything, but I do beg your royal favour!"

Again, that slightly manic gleam entered the princess's eyes. She laughed. "Good! Good! I do like it when people beg! And what will you give me in return, little Crafter?"

"I – I can impress you," she said.

Princess Tsukimi's eyes lit up with delight, though something about her amusement felt far too dangerous.

"A lofty claim! Are you sure? I also accept payments in fingernails and body parts, you know," Princess Tsukimi said with a tinkling laugh, though Kurara was sure she was being serious.

To the side, Fujiwa cleared his throat. "Your Imperial Highness, if you have no need of me, Inui has still not returned. I fear something has happened."

Princess Tsukimi gave Fujiwa the same look she might give to birds that refused to sing, or dolls that broke when she played with them; it was a face irritated by a world that did not quietly dance to her tune.

"If she is gone, she is gone. Why should I or any of my Crafters waste their time on something this unimportant?" She waved a dismissive hand.

"But…" Fujiwa wrung his hands together, upset by the princess's frostiness.

"What's with that face, Tokiyuki? You look displeased." Tsukimi caught the hurt in his expression. She stepped forward, daring him to speak.

"N—no, not at all, Your Imperial Highness," Fujiwa stammered in response. His handsome face no longer looked quite so perfect, twisted in unease.

As if on cue, another Crafter stepped out of the side room. He was as tall as he was broad, bald, with a white crow perched upon his shoulder.

"Your Imperial Highness, it is done," he announced.

Princess Tsukimi's eyes lit up. She was a child, flipping between anger and delight at a moment's notice and forgetting both just as quickly.

"Excellent, Goro! Get some rest. Fujiwa, I must show you something. It's *fascinating*! My finest work yet! You two…" Her lips twisted into a frown as her gaze fell upon Himura and Kurara.

"I would love to see Your Imperial Highness's greatest work! I've heard that no one knows more than the great Princess Tsukimi when it comes to Crafters or shikigami!" Kurara leapt to her feet before the princess could even *think* about sending them away. It was a risk to interrupt the princess, but Kurara had watched entertainers on the *Midori* appease even the most aggressive drunk by stuffing them full of compliments.

271

The princess preened. "Very well." She gestured for Kurara and Himura to join her. "Follow me."

Himura looked as though he was swallowing a cumulous whale.

The room behind the throne was nothing more than a large storeroom, bereft of any furniture. Watercolour paintings adorned the paper doors surrounding them.

"There, take a look at that." Princess Tsukimi grinned.

Kurara's gaze fell onto the futon in the middle of the room and the figure lying there.

She stopped in her tracks.

Her breath fell short.

She knew that sweep of black hair, those gangly limbs, that slightly crooked nose. The boy lay motionless, eyes closed, his limbs arranged to make it seem as if he were only sleeping. For one terrible moment Kurara was sure that he was dead. She had to remind herself that he was a shikigami, that death meant different things for his – for *their* – kind.

"Fascinating, isn't it?" Princess Tsukimi brimmed with excitement. She drew back the sheet covering Haru's legs and torso. His chest was open. Paper bones and organs lay on display for all to see. In place of a heart lay the reattached core. It was slightly dented, and the markings faded, but threads of paper connected the sphere to his limbs all the same.

"Himura, you took Haru to Princess Tsukimi? Thank you!" Kurara's lips tugged upwards in a grin so bright that she could not fight it off her face.

Ever since entering the summer palace, her nerves had been wound as tight as a string. To discover that

Himura had spoken to the princess on her behalf made something unspool inside her. She was so relieved she thought her joy would crush her.

Himura did not look at her. Here, inside the plainest room in the palace, he couldn't take his eyes off the wall.

"Himura?" A subtle sense of wrongness nagged at the back of her mind, growing with every second. Kurara could feel the panic rising inside her. "What did the princess ask from you in exchange for fixing Haru?"

"What did *I* ask?" Princess Tsukimi's laughter was as soft as silver bells. "I believe there's been some mistake here, this shikigami belongs to me. I asked for nothing. Your comrade" – she pointed to Himura – "sold him to me. In exchange for some books in my library."

It took a moment for the words to sink in before it all came crashing down.

Kurara whirled around to stare at Himura. It hurt. More than she ever thought anything could hurt.

There must be some mistake. Himura wouldn't do this. There's been a mistake. I am a lotus, I am a lotus, a lotus.

At last, Himura met her eyes, and any doubt disappeared.

THIRTY-THREE

KURARA had never imagined that Himura could do something so cruel. He knew how much Haru meant to her; he had seen her when Haru's body gave out. Though they had argued and disagreed on many things, Himura had promised to help her save Haru.

The daruma pendant lay heavy against her collarbone. Did being a shikigami change his opinion of her that much? Did he care for her so little now that he would do this to her without a hint of remorse?

Hurt gave way to anger. He had trampled upon her hopes as if they were nothing. As if she meant nothing. As if she were no more than a tool with no will of its own.

"Isn't it amazing?" Princess Tsukimi placed a hand against Haru's chest, oblivious to the storm raging through Kurara's. "Under my instructions, my Crafters followed the blueprint of its core to remake its physical appearance. Records suggest that the very first shikigami were more ... natural-looking than they are today. It is possible that it is one of the very first shikigami ever created! Can you imagine? What a priceless piece of history has fallen straight into my lap!"

Kurara shook her head. Haru had always been Haru – the boy who loved adventure stories and stealing paper from the entertainers for Kurara to make into origami. He – no, *they* – could not possibly be anything that special. Besides, Kurara was familiar with all the stories about special people – heroes descended from Gods, half-immortals, children blessed by friendly yōkai. Special people lived special lives and did special things. Kurara had spent half of *her* life scrubbing pots on the *Midori*.

"What – what do you plan on doing with him?" she asked.

Something shifted in Princess Tsukimi's expression. She smiled, but there was something cruel about the angle of her mouth.

"Who knows? Perhaps I will have him serve me."

"Against his will?"

"You want to hear the shikigami's opinion? I suppose you also ask your bed sheets whether they want to be slept on?" Princess Tsukimi stood up. She appeared irritated by Kurara's questions.

"Kurara," Himura hissed a warning.

"Now, you said you wanted something," said the princess, taking a step closer to Kurara. "What?"

Kurara tensed. Everything she wanted depended on

the princess's whims. Kurara had hoped she could weather the storm of the princess's temper, that Tsukimi would be more generous with someone who she thought was a Crafter. Listening to her talk about shikigami, Kurara understood that nothing she could say would sway her. The princess was like a child with a rare toy. Nothing in the world would make her give Haru up.

She did not bother with words. If she did not act quickly, it would be too late. Kurara ripped off her necklace in one, fluid motion. In the blink of an eye, it formed a chain that shot towards Princess Tsukimi. Fujiwa reacted without hesitation, pushing the princess behind him. As he moved to block the attack, Kurara's ofuda suddenly curved around him, snaking past his defences and towards Haru's unconscious form.

"Kurara! Stop!" Himura grabbed Akane to keep the fox from jumping into the fray. His ofuda slipped from his wrist and circled around him, but he did not strike. His eyes darted from face to face.

Fujiwa deflected Kurara's ofuda. As she backed away, Ruki lunged for her. She avoided its massive, sweeping paw, hurtling through one of the paper doors and into the next room. Her ofuda regrouped around her and hardened like rocks. With a roar, she sent them flying towards Fujiwa and his shikigami, pelting them both with ofuda that smashed holes in the tatami and left dents in the walls. While Fujiwa jumped behind Ruki, she made a run for Haru.

"Kurara!" Himura's harsh cry distracted her for only a moment, but it was long enough for Ruki to pounce.

The shikigami latched on to her left arm, its teeth sinking deep into her would-be flesh.

She smirked at its attempts to stop her. She had no feeling in that paper limb. Without any pain to distract her, Kurara grabbed a fistful of the tiger's paper fur and aimed a shard of ofuda at its flank. Before she could hit her target, Fujiwa's paper turned into a long, white blade that lanced down her left arm, severing it at the elbow.

Ruki threw her to the ground. Its paw crashed on top of her chest, cracking her ribs and pinning her down like a butterfly impaled inside a glass case.

Kurara screamed. The pain was excruciating. Her chest burned; she was sure her bones were scraping against her lungs. The cut to her arm was clean, severing it right at the elbow where it had previously fallen off.

"Why isn't she bleeding?" Fujiwa's voice drifted over her.

Her arm. Kurara could see it lying a few feet away from her. A thought struck her.

With a tug of her mind, her arm crumbled. The glove deflated as the limb inside it separated into squares of paper that swept across the floor. They swirled over Ruki's head and reconnected to her elbow, reforming her lost limb. As they did, her hand morphed into a claw the size of a dragon's. Straining, she knocked Ruki off her and rolled to her feet, her broken chest screaming in pain.

"Not so fast!" Ruki growled as she made a dash for the exit.

Princess Tsukimi drew a pistol from the waistband of her hakama and fired.

The bullet hit Kurara's stomach. Pain exploded through her body, but she ground her teeth together and bore it. Stumbling forward, she continued to run.

Without warning, the bullet in her stomach exploded.

The casing broke apart and a wide spike burst across her back. It curled, tendril-like, around her torso and up her arms, binding them to her side.

Kurara toppled to the ground with a crash. As the bullet casing hit the floor in front of her and rolled across the ground, she understood what had happened. There was no gunpowder inside the metal casing but a roll of paper. Fujiwa, not the princess, had control over the bullet.

In one last desperate attempt to break free, her ofuda turned into knives. Hovering above her, they formed a desperate barrier, telling Fujiwa and the others to stay away.

"Himura," she croaked. Surely he would not let her die. As strict and unfeeling as he was, there were lines even Himura would not cross.

"Enough!" Himura towered over her, balling his hands into fists. "That's enough, Kurara. Stop it."

His words cut her deeper than any knife. Kurara flinched. His anger was like a storm. She could see it build and build from a distance and yet she could do nothing but brace for impact.

"I will not argue with a shikigami!" His voice cracked as he yelled. He held himself like a tightly wound spring, his eyes wild and distraught. "You are not really human. You may think that you have emotions, dreams, wishes, but you do not. Everything that you feel, everything that you want, was decided for you by the person who made you. Do you not see? Do you not understand?"

Himura blew through her hopes like a tsunami. The weeks that they had spent training together, the paper daruma doll hanging from her necklace, his promise to help her. Despite everything, Kurara had still believed that, deep down, Himura cared about her in some way.

She knew better now.

THIRTY-FOUR

KURARA could do nothing but struggle as Himura turned and bowed to the princess.

"My humblest apologies. Please know that I did not plan for this to happen."

Tsukimi gave him a foul look. Ruki moved to circle him, glowering.

"I could have you and your entire crew executed. You say you did not plan this, but she is your shikigami, isn't she?"

"She is not. She does not obey my will. The two came as a pair. I sold that one without her knowledge. That is why she is angry."

Tsukimi was silent as she digested this. She glanced down at Kurara.

"Give her to me."

"No!" Kurara thrashed against her restraints. They held fast.

Princess Tsukimi crouched in front of her.

"Your Imperial Highness!" warned Fujiwa.

She silenced him with a wave of her hand. Though Kurara's knives remained levitating in the air, they did not worry the princess in the slightest. They both knew that if Kurara attacked, it would be the last thing she did.

The princess leaned in and placed her cold hands over Kurara's face, tilting her head upwards. The hard edges of her nails dug into Kurara's skin ever so slightly.

"Fascinating," she whispered, her face close enough that Kurara could count every eyelash as they fluttered against the curve of her pale cheek. "You really don't look anything like a shikigami and you can use ofuda too."

Kurara could see her own reflection in Tsukimi's eyes: her bruised forehead and busted lip.

"Give me a knife." Princess Tsukimi held out her hand to Fujiwa. He handed her a tanto made from ofuda.

There was no time to move. Kurara's mind did not even register her panic before the blade pierced her gut. It hurt. No blood spilled from the wound, but that did not ease the agonizing pain of being cut open.

"Fascinating! Fascinating!"

Kurara tried to twist out of the way but the more she writhed, the tighter her restraints became. If she strained her head forward, she could see her open chest. An off-white core lay between her ribs, her organs pumping without blood, liquid remains of what she had last eaten lying in her stomach immersed in a strange greenish fluid.

Just like Haru.

With the last of her strength, she released the knives floating above her.

Princess Tsukimi did not move. Fujiwa threw a barrier of paper over her and the knives bounced off, skidding away to one corner of the room, where they unravelled.

Tsukimi's cold fingers entered her chest and cradled her core. It felt as if she were touching her heart.

"The other core was slightly damaged. It looked like something had nicked it and the markings were scuffed. This one is perfectly intact. Perhaps that is why this one can use ofuda." She spoke with the fascination of an explorer discovering new ruins.

"They found you and Haru lying together in an empty barn. There was a great big shaft of wood sticking through his chest." Kurara remembered Madam Ito's words. Had Haru once been able to use ofuda? Had that piece of wood scraped his core and destroyed his ability to manipulate paper?

"It is amazing that it has not gone mad after all these years," said Fujiwa.

Not mad? No, maybe she was. Kurara certainly felt like she was losing her mind right now.

She glanced at Himura, but he was not looking at her. He stood in the same position as before, hands clenched. His face was pale, but his eyes were full of steel.

He cleared his throat.

"Ah, of course. You want to see my library, don't you?" Tsukimi smiled.

"Himura, you can't just leave me like this!" Kurara fought against the paper binding her.

Himura met her gaze, but looked away so quickly that Kurara did not know if she had imagined it. Without a word of farewell, he turned to walk out of the room.

"Akane!"

The fox looked back. Kurara's heart soared. Akane would not abandon her.

"Come, Akane!" Himura snapped. The fox bobbed its head – a brief bow – and turned its back to Kurara.

It trotted after its master, leaving her to her fate.

Interlude

Then the demon asked:
"How much must you devour
to be satisfied?"
And, smiling, you then whispered:
"This entire, rotten world."

– from *Conversations with Yōkai*
(banned by the Patriots Office)

The best death a Sorabito could hope for was death by falling – the brief euphoria of flight, the rush of the wind, the scream of the air, the freedom of the sky. Falling was nothing more than flying downwards to an abrupt stop.

It was a small comfort to Rei that most of the Sorabito that would die today would probably plunge to their death.

It was a greater comfort to know that groundlings would count among that number.

The sound of fireworks echoed through the walls of

284

the warehouse. A mere three feet away, the dragon lay coiled in knots. It glowered at Rei. The claws of its front legs scraped at the ground. The orders Inui had imposed upon it to keep it calm were wearing off. It would not remain manageable for long.

"It's almost time." He checked his watch and smiled.

"Do you expect me to fight a shikigami on my own? When we hunt, it takes the whole crew just to bring down one! If you want me to stop it after – after it's done what you need it to – then let me talk to my crew." Tomoe did not beg. She knew that he did not respect anyone who would throw their pride away and plead.

Rei shook his head. "I don't trust your crew. I only trust you, my daughter. My flesh and blood."

Tomoe looked at him in disgust. He knew that she did not want to believe that any part of him had gone into making her.

"It's not a matter of trust! You're asking for the impossible! I can't take down a shikigami on my own!"

Rei did not believe her. Perhaps it would be harder without her crew's support but Tomoe was his daughter. His blood ran through her veins. He was sure that she was capable of more than she wanted him to believe.

"You can either help or you can stand back and watch." He smiled at her and was pleased when Tomoe's shoulders stiffened.

Though she looked at him as though she would like nothing better than to see the dragon rip him to shreds, Rei knew that Tomoe would do as he wished. She would

not allow the city to be destroyed just so that she could say she had nothing to do with Sohma. She would not let innocent people die.

"I do not wish to hurt our fellow Sorabito any more than you do. But something must be done about Princess Tsukimi." He walked towards the dragon.

It was time.

The shikigami snapped as he drew closer, but the chains held it back from sinking its fangs into his skull.

"Don't you dare!" Tomoe burst into a run, but she was too late to stop him.

Rei moved to the side, towards the side of the warehouse, where a long metal contraption pulled the dragon's chains tight, keeping the beast tied down. He yanked the lever and the chains fell away. The creature blinked its massive, colourless eyes and a film of white shuttered over its protruding eyeballs. Then its body began to jerk. Its writhing tail smashed into the walls.

Tomoe stepped back in alarm. The shikigami's claws dug deep trenches into the stone floor, mouth parting in a silent scream. It rose to its feet like a tidal wave. Its mouth snapped as it lunged for Rei, missing only when its tail caught in the tangle of chains spooled around its legs.

Rei's laughter echoed through the warehouse. He danced back as if the dragon was just a playful dog nipping at his heels and not a monster capable of devouring him whole. Now this was power! He could get used to this feeling. Perhaps this was why Crafters had made such beasts. This giddy rush of invincibility.

The dragon wriggled its way out of its chains, but before it could attack Rei again, Tomoe launched herself at the beast. For all her hatred of him, Rei knew that she would not stand by and watch him die at the claws of a shikigami. Just as she would not step back and let the city be destroyed.

Her tanto ripped into the side of the shikigami's face, cutting through paper scales to tear apart its cheek. The dragon's tail knocked her back in retaliation, but Tomoe had anticipated the blow and braced herself against impact. Rei had to admit, he was rather impressed with the way she protected herself from injury as she was sent rolling across the ground.

Perhaps annoyed by Tomoe's refusal to stand still and be crushed, or perhaps enticed by the sounds of the festival above ground, the dragon reared back. It bolted into the air, hitting the ceiling and punching through the jungle of cables and pipes above it until it reached the surface. Bursting out of the warehouse, it erupted into the city.

Screams of alarm rang through the air. With her tanto pressed against her obi, Tomoe watched the dragon soar free.

Rei turned to meet his daughter's gaze. She had not looked at him with such hatred since the day she had left for the *Orihime*. He grinned.

"Well? Get going."

It was time for a hunt.

THIRTY-FIVE

THE village was burning. When Kurara opened her eyes, it was to the sight of broken houses and blazing fields. She stood in the middle of a wide dirt path, cracked and littered with lost possessions. Ash blew on the wind.

Her first response was panic. Where was she? What was happening?

At the back of her mind, she was sure she had experienced something like this before, though she could not quite remember when. Someone shouted her name. Kurara turned to see Haru running towards her. Though he looked no different than usual, he was wearing a long cloak of woven grass that fell down to his ankles. The cloth bracers on his arms and legs were stained with dirt and blood.

"Aki! Come quickly!" Haru grabbed her hand and

pulled her through the village, past broken fences and gouged storehouses. "It's Seiryu! It's losing its mind!"

Despite the heat of the flames, Kurara felt as if someone had doused her in a bucket of ice water. The name "Seiryu" did not sound familiar, yet it conjured up images of a giant, snake-like dragon as large as a cumulous whale.

She remembered now. In the last battle, Seiryu's Crafter had died. It had been a chaotic and frenzied fight across the muddy slopes of the Irio Mountains. The loss of such a powerful Crafter had hit everyone in the village hard.

"So soon? But it's only been a day!" There was a new Crafter lined up to become its master. A new master to tie its soul to this world.

If only Seiryu had been given one immediately. But then, how were they to know that it would lose itself so quickly? Was this her fault? She had asked the Crafters to wait. It was cruel to thrust a new master on a shikigami so soon. "Give them time to mourn," she had begged.

Beneath the darkening sky, razed fields rose into rolling hills. At the bottom stood a crowd of men dressed in long grass capes. Shikigami of all shapes and sizes milled around them.

As Kurara and Haru caught up with the crowd, a lookout's cry alerted them to the dragon's approach. Seiryu flew overhead. Its body was a giant river of snow streaming across the sky. The men raised their bows, shooting flaming arrows into the dragon's side.

"Seiryu!" Kurara shouted, hoping the wind would carry her voice to it. "Come to your senses!"

She was sick of watching other shikigami die.

The sky trembled. Men shouted, rallying for another attack.

"A dying star fell from the heavens ..." she sang, though it was half shouted and without a melody.

It was a lullaby everyone knew. Kurara hoped against all odds that it would calm the dragon. That there was some way she could still save it.

"... and from that star grew a tree. The people of the village cut down the tree to make paper."

Above, Seiryu roared and dived at them.

———————o———————

Kurara jerked awake. She was lying on a futon inside what looked like a meditation room. The only decorations were the watercolour paintings on the sliding doors that covered all four walls. Wooden pillars held up the tall, arching ceiling. From somewhere beyond the doors she could hear the sound of running water.

"It is a shame about the eagle..." Princess Tsukimi's voice drifted over her. Though the room was dark, Kurara could see the princess sitting at the end of her futon. "But I was going to destroy it anyway. There is no point in a shikigami that cannot obey."

Kurara looked down. Her restraints were gone. She was free to move but she did not dare. Though Tsukimi did not look at her, the princess was probably aware that Kurara was awake.

Electric lights flickered on, illuminating the room. Kurara flinched at the sudden brightness. Only after

290

a few moments did she dare to peel one eye open.

Haru lay on the other side of the room. He was pale, but his skin was not like paper any more. The eyelashes falling against his cheeks matched the dark sweep of unruly hair fanning against the pillow. Fujiwa knelt at the foot of Haru's futon, Ruki next to him. He held a knife in one hand. His other was freshly bandaged and damp with blood.

"What are you doing?" Kurara tried to sit up.

Himura and Akane were gone. She really had been abandoned. Though she tried to keep the hurt from reaching her heart, it managed to creep in, anyway. Was being a shikigami such an awful thing that Himura would turn on her so quickly?

"Fascinating." Tsukimi crouched in front of Kurara. The tip of her fingernails touched the edge of Kurara's jaw. "You're different from all other shikigami – so ancient, so long without a master, yet you still have a hold of your mind. Perhaps you do not need to be tied to a Crafter."

The princess's eyes flickered up to meet Kurara's gaze. The smile of a cruel God painted her lips.

"In that case, tie yourself to me. I have always wanted a shikigami for myself. If only I could have been born a Crafter."

Kurara was only half paying attention to the princess. She felt as though she was a spectator in her own skull, staring down at a body that did not belong to her.

There's a hole in my chest. Kurara's head spun. She looked down at her open ribcage, at her core nestled in threads of paper like a cocoon resting upon a web of spider silk. Was this really her?

291

Sensing her lack of attention, Tsukimi pushed Kurara's chin up, forcing her to meet the princess's eye. "My father and brother don't appreciate my hobbies. They don't understand, but you do, don't you? That power inside you is captivating."

Clenching her teeth together in anger, Kurara fought the urge to try and bite the princess. She would not be touched and inspected like an animal!

"You people are all the same!" she spat. "Shikigami are not objects to possess! We may be different from you, but that doesn't mean we're not able to think or feel. Putting a collar around our necks and forcing us to obey you won't change that. It won't make us love you!"

Princess Tsukimi's cruel laughter dominated the room. "*Love?* Why should I care whether you love me or not? There's only one thing in this world that matters to me." Her red lips split into a wide grin. She would eat Kurara alive. "Are you interesting to me or aren't you?"

Shoving Kurara back onto the futon, she stood up.

"Lucky for you" – she tossed Kurara a haughty look before making her way toward Fujiwa – "I find you *very* interesting."

Closing her kimono over her open ribcage, Kurara glowered at the princess's back. She had to escape somehow, but first she needed ofuda. The doors were made of paper. Could she use those?

"Fujiwa, are you done with him yet? Wake him up." Tsukimi nodded towards Haru's prone form.

Kurara panicked. She realized why Fujiwa's hand was bleeding, why he had closed the hole in Haru's chest.

His blood was on Haru's core.

Fujiwa had made himself Haru's master. The moment he awoke, Haru would belong to Fujiwa, his free will leashed to someone else.

"Ruki!" she called out to the tiger. "Are you happy with this? You'll have to share your master with another shikigami. Doesn't that mean you're only half as important to him as before? Maybe one day you'll be replaced completely!"

Something in Ruki's face twitched. Kurara swore that she saw the hesitation in its eyes, but then the tiger turned its face away, as unmoved as stone.

She had to do something. She knew that she could not take on both Ruki and Fujiwa at the same time, but perhaps if she was quick enough, she could gain the advantage of surprise. If she used the paper doors as her ofuda, she could take Princess Tsukimi hostage. As long as she had the princess, there was nothing anyone could do to her.

Steeling herself, Kurara rose to her feet and took a step back, closer to the southern doors. She concentrated on pulling the paper towards her, imagining the kind of knife that it would transform into.

Nothing happened. The doors did not budge. Even as Kurara put all her effort into summoning the paper to her, the watercolour doors did not even quiver.

Tsukimi's shrill laughter broke the silence. "Nice try. Unfortunately, the doors in this particular room are not made of paper but parchment. Parchment made from animal skin." She gave Kurara a haughty, knowing look.

Kurara's cheeks burned, humiliated. Ruki had not even moved when she stood up, so certain that Kurara was completely powerless.

A soft groan stole her attention. Haru's eyelashes fluttered against his cheek. His eyes opened to stare at the ceiling. Kurara watched as if in slow motion as Haru slowly realized that he was not on the *Midori* any more. Confusion filtered into his gaze. Kurara saw the sharp hitch of his chest as he took his first breath, and heard the sound of air being sucked between his clenched teeth.

"Ha—" Kurara began to speak, but before she could even say his name, something crashed into the ground with a bang that echoed through the walls.

Ruki jumped to its feet as Fujiwa dashed to the princess's side, his ofuda flitting around him at the ready.

A guard burst into the room.

"Your Imperial Highness, we're under attack!"

Not a moment after he spoke, something swiped the roof clean off, tearing the ceiling away. Ceramic tiles, wooden beams and support ropes crashed over the tatami floor.

A beast towered above them, its claws clinging to the edges of the room. Kurara's mouth fell open at the sight.

There was no mistaking it. It was the dragon that had attacked the *Midori*.

THIRTY-SIX

THE dragon stared down at them.

Kurara barely drew a breath. There was something wild and frantic in its eyes, just like the dragon in her dreams. She wanted to reach out, to comfort it.

"A—a dying star..." The words escaped her lips. She clamped her mouth shut. It had not worked in her dream; it would not work now.

The dragon's talons cracked the palace walls. With a snarl, it lunged at them.

"Stop!" Kurara flung her arms out. She did not care about the princess, but she knew that if the shikigami remained here, it would be torn apart.

Claws stopped inches from her face. Kurara stared up at the folds of the dragon's face. Their eyes met for moment, but before she could speak, Ruki lunged for the dragon's neck. With a flick of its tail, the beast sent part of the wall crashing to the ground, almost burying Ruki in the rubble. As the dust rose, the dragon took off towards the west side of the palace.

Princess Tsukimi grabbed the sword at the guard's waist, pulling it free of its sheath.

"Your Imperial Highness!" The guard looked like he was going to have a heart attack.

Tsukimi spun on her heel and grabbed Kurara's face in both hands, yanking her forward so suddenly that Kurara feared the princess would rip her head from her neck.

"Shikigami, will you follow me? Will you be mine after all?" Her eyes were alive with a manic fire that threatened to consume everything in its path. Kurara could not meet Tsukimi's gaze. Those eyes would burn her alive.

She shoved the princess as hard as she could and made a break for the door, but before she could take more than a few steps, Ruki's paw came crashing down against her back, slamming her into the floor and knocking the wind right out of her.

She gasped in shock, but Ruki's weight was so crushing she feared her chest would cave in. Kurara struggled to crawl free, but the tiger's paw had her pinned. She tilted her head to see Haru scramble to his feet. He called her name. At least, she thought that she heard him call her – her head was swimming and her ears ringing so loudly she could not be sure.

"Stop!" Fujiwa ordered.

Haru jerked to a halt, as if his legs had suddenly frozen.

Princess Tsukimi glared at Kurara. Her expression

was steely. She looked as though she wanted to devour the world.

"Tie her up," she ordered. "Tie her up and leave her here. I'll come and fetch her when this is over."

The weight lifted from her body, but before Kurara could run, Fujiwa grabbed the ropes that had fallen down with the roof and tied her chest and legs to the nearest pillar.

Kurara thrashed, screaming, until Fujiwa shoved another rope between her teeth. It tasted like dust and burnt hair. He yanked the knots tight. To one side, Haru remained motionless, but Kurara saw a flicker of something cross his face.

Fujiwa turned away from her to address him. "Do you know who I am? I am your new master, Fujiwa Tokiyuki."

The ropes bit into Kurara's skin as she struggled.

Haru's gaze met her own.

"Leave her. She means nothing." Fujiwa placed a hand on Haru's shoulder. "Come, follow me."

"No, don't go!" she wanted to scream.

Haru said nothing. With one last glance at her, he followed Fujiwa and Ruki out of the room.

———————o———————

Kurara's body screamed at her. She struggled against the ropes binding her to the pillar, but no matter how much they cut into her flesh or bit at her skin, they did not loosen. Panic nipped at the edges of her thoughts. She had to escape. She had to find Haru. The sound of battle echoed around her. The ground shook and the walls trembled. How much time was she wasting tied up here, unable to do anything?

I am a lotus, she repeated to herself over and over. *I am a lotus, I am a lotus feeling nothing at all. I rise to the top of the water, leaving the earthly mud below me.*

She had to calm down. Tugging at the ropes did nothing. If she really wanted to escape, she had to stop and think.

My body is paper. I can control it however I want.

Taking a deep breath, Kurara concentrated. The stub of her elbow stretched downwards to remake her missing forearm. The limb was thin and weak, but it was there – a paper white arm that ran down from her elbow to her wrist, fanning out into her hand. Concentrating, her fingers melted together to form a paper blade. She squirmed. It was difficult, but she managed to lift her hand to the ropes.

Her fingers cut through the thick knots like butter. As they fell away, she leaned down to free her legs and stepped away from the pillar. The blade transformed back into a hand. Kurara gave her fingers an experimental twitch. They worked, though they were still as white as snow.

Well, that was something she could worry about later. Picking up the glove left on the ground, Kurara slipped it on. Giving her arm a quick shake, she was satisfied that it would not drop off again.

Swiping her fingers over her chest, the paper knit back together, closing the wound from Princess Tsukimi's knife. Kurara shuddered as she remembered how the princess had touched her core, those icy fingers pushing inside her chest.

Another rumble shook the panelled doors around her. There would be time to dwell on it later. For now, she had to find Haru and escape.

To where? An unwelcome question crossed her mind. Could she return to the *Orihime*? After everything that happened with Himura, did she want to? But where else could she go? Both the sky and the ground felt as unfamiliar as her hazy memories. Her home had always been Haru.

She could think about it later. Pushing aside her worries, Kurara dashed towards the hallway. Cannon fire echoed through the air. The guard towers along the edge of the palace grounds were likely shooting at the shikigami, though their aim was sloppy. A cannonball blew through the roof and smashed into the floor in front of her. The ceiling began to collapse, leaving jagged pieces of wood, like shattered bone, poking in the air.

Covering her head, Kurara closed her eyes and ran out into the hallway. She summoned sheets of paper from the doors that she passed, wrapping them into a chain around her neck. The weight of her new ofuda was like a warm blanket on a cold night, an oasis in the desert. Her fingers played against it, enjoying the familiar feel of hardened paper.

As she rounded another corner, Kurara slammed into someone coming from the opposite direction. The impact almost sent them both flying. Without waiting to see who it was, Kurara formed a knife from her ofuda to protect herself.

The man raised his hands in surrender, though there was nothing submissive about his expression. He looked familiar in a way she could not put her finger on. His clothes were distinctly Sorabito-made. His head sat upon his neck like an egg balanced upon a stick. "You'd better run along and protect your master. She's going to be eaten alive."

He thought that she was an imperial Crafter. Kurara did not care to correct him. It did not matter to her if he was an intruder or an assassin or just an opportunist looking to ransack the palace of its jewels while everyone was busy with the shikigami.

"Which way did she go?" The princess would certainly be with Fujiwa … and Fujiwa had taken Haru.

The man pointed down the hallway, to the exit. "Tell the princess that her dear Inui is dead."

Kurara did not know what he was talking about and did not care. Without a second glance, she raced out of the palace.

THIRTY-SEVEN

OUTSIDE the throne room, a servant led Himura away.

He was not wrong, Himura told himself, as he fought the temptation to go back. He could not be wrong. After everything that he had done, he could not allow himself to be wrong.

It was too late to regret it now anyway.

Princess Tsukimi's library was in a converted storeroom. There was no lock, no indication that they were anywhere special, but this single room contained items more precious to Himura than any of the jewels in the empire. A gas heater stood in the middle of the floor. The low bookcases were occupied by large, leather-bound books that lined the shelves. At the end of the room, a reading table and chair stood in front of a long slit of a window, a single beam of horizontal light striking the ground and throwing harsh shadows against the bookcases.

"Have you read anything from here?" Himura stepped into the dimly lit room.

"No one is allowed to read Princess Tsukimi's collection but the royal family. I would never betray the princess's trust," the woman replied in a monotone.

Himura could not understand how anyone could live in the summer palace and not feel even the slightest pinch of temptation. That was like putting a raw steak in front of a starving wolf and expecting it not to devour it. He certainly knew what he would do in that situation.

The servant took his bracelet from him before leaving. Alone, Himura inhaled the library's musty scent. How his parents would have loved to see this. Had they still been alive, they would have trembled and wept with joy.

"A long time ago, we Crafters ruled this land. A long time ago, we were so much more than what we are now."

They had lived and died dreaming of the past, of a golden age when Crafters lived in glory. Now, Himura would find the truth his parents had so desperately sought.

All the books and scrolls were made from dried animal skin rather than paper. This was, he supposed, to stop Crafters from shifting around the pages. He turned to one of the shelves, his eye catching on a slim tome with a red leather cover. It was the same book Princess Tsukimi had been reading when he crept into her chambers in search of books to steal all those years ago. It was here.

Himura pulled it from the shelf and opened it to the first page.

He had been just a child when he first approached Princess Tsukimi, too young to realize his full potential, but he had fought her with everything he had, hoping to show off his skill. His ofuda had formed swords and shields and wolves with gnashing teeth and when his paper failed him, he had tried to claw at her until the princess grew bored of toying with him and kicked him away.

"*Too bad*," she had sighed. "*But if you cannot impress me, you can at least entertain me.*"

Standing above him, she had dangled the red leather book in front of him. With two finely manicured fingers, she began to tear it in half. The sound was much like the ripping of Himura's heart.

He thought she had destroyed the book. There were rips in the crinkled parchment where the princess had torn through the pages. He flipped through the book only to see the faint stitches where the skins had been sewn back together. Himura shoved the memory from his mind as he concentrated on the words – and the illustrated diagram – before him.

His breath caught in his throat. He set the book down on the table, flicking on the reading lamp without tearing his eyes away from the page.

This was it! The knowledge of the past that had been cruelly kept from him. The knowledge that was his to know by birthright.

Himura needed paper. He wanted to take notes. He could not risk Princess Tsukimi destroying it.

"Akane." He called his shikigami over. The fox dropped what it was doing and obediently trotted over.

"Don't move," he ordered as he placed one hand on Akane's back. He gripped the tail in his other hand, took a deep breath and pulled.

The squawk from Akane's mouth was unlike anything he had ever heard – a shocked squeal and a gasp of confused hurt. Himura sometimes forgot that shikigami could feel pain. Once he fully understood how shikigami cores worked, he could fix that.

"Master! What are you—?"

"Shhh!" Himura pulled again.

After three or four vicious yanks, Akane's tail began to tear. With one last heave, Himura ripped it clean off. Akane stumbled forward, panting and wheezing, legs shaking so hard they threatened to collapse. The ofuda that made up its tail instantly reverted into two dozen perfect squares of paper.

Himura gave the fox a conciliatory pat. "Good. You did well."

Whimpering, Akane limped to the corner of the room to nurse its wound.

"Do you hate me for that?" Himura watched as it curled into a ball. He asked the question without thinking and immediately wondered why he had bothered. A shikigami was a shikigami. It could not hate him any more than a nail could resent a hammer.

"I love you, Master," Akane replied, though it sounded distinctly glum about it.

Himura turned back to the desk.

An almighty explosion ripped through the palace grounds.

Books toppled and plates crashed to the ground. Something shot past the window, blocking the sky from view as it was catapulted heavenwards.

"*A shikigami!*" Akane ran up to the window.

Time seemed to stop for a moment. Himura felt as though he had been hit by a speeding kohane. He looked from the shikigami to the library then to the chaos it was causing as cannonballs struck the ground near the dragon.

He knew that there were guards outside the door, ready to check him for any hidden pages, but with everyone distracted by the shikigami now was the perfect opportunity. Turning away from the table, Himura plucked a scroll from the nearest shelf and tucked it beneath his arm.

"Grab as many books as you can!" he instructed Akane as he made his way to the door, where the larger tomes were. "I want them!"

They belong to Crafters anyway, he told himself. *Why shouldn't I have them?*

The idea of giving Himura something he wanted excited Akane. "*Whatever Master wants, Akane will get!*" it said as it knocked the scrolls off the shelves.

A battle raged outside, shaking the walls. Cannon fire pounded through the air. Suddenly, something hit the building, crashing through the roof with a crack that brought down the ceiling.

"No!" yelled Himura as debris fell onto the gas heater, splitting it open.

Fire burst in all directions. In a matter of seconds, the bookcases were alight. Flames swallowed the books and scrolls with indiscriminate glee, eating away at the parchment and the centuries of knowledge contained within.

Himura swore he could hear them scream.

Smoke rose as quickly as the flames. It burned his eyes. Without a second thought he lunged for the books that were only partially burning, grabbing them and stamping on them to put out the fire even as flames crept above him and the rafters came crashing down.

There was not enough time. Almost everything was aflame. The smoke was becoming unbearable. Himura grabbed what he had managed to save and beat a swift retreat.

"Akane!" He gestured for his shikigami to follow him before the entire building collapsed.

The fox did not move.

"Akane!" Himura shouted, louder, over the crackling flames and the almighty groan of snapping wood.

His shikigami stood in the middle of the library, surrounded by burning shelves, and illuminated by the soft rays of starlight that shone through the hole in the roof. Akane's eyes were locked on the book at the very end, the book that Himura had been reading and had left open on the far table. There was no way he could reach it any more.

He looked down at Akane. The fox stared back at him as if he hung the moon against the sky and set alight the stars.

A thought crossed Himura's mind. The body of a shikigami was just a shell, easily replaceable, but that book – all these books – there was no replacing them. If he let them burn, centuries upon centuries of knowledge would be lost in an instant.

"*Shikigami were created to serve Crafters. That is the reason they exist.*" His parents had died dreaming of knowledge they would never possess. Himura would not end up like them.

Why did he need to convince himself? This was the right decision. He was sure of it.

"Akane!" Himura felt light-headed, but there was no time to dither. "Retrieve that book for me, Akane."

Without a moment's hesitation, his shikigami leapt through the flames. The fire caught and set its fur alight, racing up its back. Reaching the table just as one of the bookcases collapsed, Akane grabbed the book in its mouth and leapt back. The fox jumped over the fallen cases and darted around the holes in the floor caused by the collapsed debris. Flames climbed over its body. Its right foreleg crumpled, then the opposite back leg.

Himura's heart froze as Akane stumbled and fell. The book slipped from its mouth and tumbled across the floor. With all the strength it could muster, Akane hauled its body forward even as its back broke and its hind legs turned to ash. Grabbing the book between its jaws, the fox flung it at the doorway.

It landed at Himura's feet. He wasted no time in grabbing it, holding it close to his chest as the smoke pushed him back.

"*Master, I love you.*" He looked up just in time to see Akane grinning at him with the same adoring look on its face that it always wore.

"*Shikigami were created to serve Crafters. That is the reason they exist.*"

307

Dread and horror climbed as quickly as the fire. He had not expected it to feel like this.

"Akane! Come here!" Himura reached out a hand, but the heat of the blaze forced him back. It was too late.

Flames swallowed Akane's body whole.

THIRTY-EIGHT

$OUTSIDE$, the gardens were burning. Flames engulfed every tree and building, making blazing pyres out of the watchtowers. Servants and guards ran for cover as explosions ripped apart the ground.

In the distance, chains of paper lashed around the dragon's body, pulling it towards the ground. Kurara sprinted towards the shikigami. Fujiwa and the bald Crafter from before were working together while their shikigami darted about to shield them from the dragon's attacks.

"Stop it! It's not its fault!" Kurara wanted to shout. There was something wrong with the world, something wrong with the relationship between shikigami and Crafters that led to them losing their senses. It wasn't their fault. Why were shikigami always paying the price for something they had no say in?

She jumped over the debris in her path, avoiding bursts of stone and wood that showered over her as cannonballs crashed into their own towers. The Crafters were too preoccupied by the attacking shikigami to notice her. Beneath the smoke and the sounds of gunfire, she rushed towards Fujiwa.

Her ofuda formed a long spear. She grabbed it and hurled it at his head with all her strength, but Ruki noticed the attack just in time and blocked the blow. The tiger leapt at her, its massive paw ready to swat her into the nearest piece of crumbling wall.

"You," it rumbled, its voice enraged yet clear, eloquent compared to the dragon's crazed ramblings, *"need to learn your place."*

She jumped back, avoiding the blow. Where was Haru? Her eyes searched the smoke-swept battlefield. Above, guards on qipaks soared around the dragon's head, crashing back to the ground as the shikigami snapped off the wings and crushed the vehicles' tails between its powerful jaws.

Kurara summoned all her ofuda to her, weaving each piece together. She thought about Akane; how the shikigami had moved, the way it jumped and twisted its body and got to work creating her own paper beast.

Stitching muscles together, forming a spine, then a head, raising the fur on its back and shaping its paws, Kurara created a paper fox the same size as Ruki. Though one was very much intelligent and the other nothing more than a paper puppet moving to Kurara's will, the two beasts circled one another, snarling and snapping at each other's heels.

"Ruki!" she shouted. "Where is Haru? Let me have him and you can be your master's one and only shikigami. That's what you want, right? You don't want to share Fujiwa."

"Silence!" The tiger swiped at Kurara's paper fox. *"I will fulfil my master's wishes!"*

"And what about *your* wishes?" Kurara demanded, but Ruki was not interested in talking any more.

The wind whistled around them. The fox leapt. Its claws pierced the tiger's flank and they barrelled across the ground, breaking apart for a moment before lunging at each other again. Sinking its fangs into Ruki's shoulder, Kurara's fox tore off a huge chunk of paper. With a howl, Ruki whirled around to swat at it. Before the blow could connect, Kurara collapsed her ofuda. The fox crumbled, paper swirling past Ruki's lashing tail, then reformed around the tiger's back.

Bursts of fire exploded overhead. Someone gave a shout of alarm. The dragon had broken free from its chains and was soaring up into the air.

"Kurara!"

Kurara turned just in time to see a flash of dark red hair. "Tomoe?"

Tomoe's face perfectly mirrored Kurara's shock. Her hair had slipped out of its usual neat plait to whip wildly around her face like tongues of fire. Her eyes were blown wide, her mouth parted and her lips cracked.

"What are you doing here?" the girl cried.

Kurara wanted to ask the same thing when suddenly, Tomoe pushed her out of the way.

A blade swung at Kurara's head, missing only by a hair's breadth.

Haru stood between two pillars of broken wood. In one hand, he gripped a sword the length of his body, the tip of the blade resting against the cracked earth. Kurara pulled her ofuda back, collapsing the paper fox. She wanted to run to Haru, but the strange look in his eye and the sword in his hand held her back.

He lifted the blade.

"Haru, stop!" Kurara lifted her arm just in time to block the blow. Though she knew he was only attacking her on Fujiwa's orders, the wrongness of it set a tsunami inside her chest.

The blade sliced into her left arm, almost severing her wrist, but as the edge of the sword cut into her, she hardened her paper arm to stop the blade cutting clean through. Trapped inside her wrist, she knit the fibres of the paper around the metal, sealing the tip of the sword within her arm.

"I cannot let you hurt my master!" He tugged at the sword, but it remained firmly lodged in Kurara's arm.

"He's not your master!" Anger made her voice crack. "His blood is on your core, but that doesn't mean he owns you!"

She did not want to hurt him. Here they were, standing inside the city of their dreams and they were fighting. Why did things have to be like this? Had all her struggle and toil only led her to this?

No, it was not her fault. It was not Haru's fault. It was the world. It was Crafters. It was the way shikigami were made to obey their masters. Everything about it was rotten.

Tomoe unsheathed her tanto and prepared to jump in between them.

"Wait!" cried Kurara. Now that Tomoe was here, maybe they could work together to rescue Haru.

"Oh, I'll be gentle!" Tomoe swung her knife at him.

Haru abandoned his weapon to leap clear of her attack. The moment gave Kurara time to recover, but just as they were about to pin him down, Ruki emerged from the chaos.

Kurara did not register the blow until she was thrown across the ground, rolling over rock and splintered wood. Haru's sword dislodged from her arm. Her cheek scraped against the earth, searing with pain.

She staggered to her feet in frustration. Of all the things she did not want to deal with right now, Ruki was at the top of that list. She had to get Haru away from here before the imperial Crafters dealt with the dragon and turned their attention back to them.

As Kurara wracked her brains for a way to escape, something caught her eye, glinting above her. She looked up. A copper-coloured kohane soared overhead.

"Tomoe!" she shouted. She had an idea.

"Not so fast!" Ruki charged.

With a wave of her hand, Kurara's ofuda streamed towards Tomoe and Haru, wrapping them both in vine-like strands of paper and binding their arms to their sides. With a yelp, they both flew across the ground towards her. Kurara lassoed a paper rope around the wing of the kohane flying above them. As the craft soared by, all three of them were yanked into the air.

The tiger's claws raked against the earth, cracking the ground in the exact spot where Kurara had stood just moments before. Furious, it looked up to see Kurara and the others soaring through the sky.

Haru struggled to slip free, but once they were high enough, he stopped like a puppet whose strings had been cut.

As the length of Kurara's makeshift rope shortened, the three of them were pulled up and up until they were close enough to clamber onto the kohane's wing.

"Y–you bloody, pigeon-guzzling Crafter!" the pilot screamed into her face. "Are you trying to tear off the wing?"

Kurara blinked. Her chin was barely level with the wing, her right hand holding on to what little purchase she could find while her left arm remained tied to the others.

She stared at the pilot's livid expression in shock.

"Sayo? What are you doing here?"

THIRTY-NINE

SAYO burst into a litany of curses. "What am I doing here? What about you? Bloody Crafters thinking they can just grab on to any craft they fancy! You lousy—"

"Sayo?" Tomoe's muffled voice came from somewhere below. Kurara wriggled aside, still hanging from the edge of the wing, so that Tomoe's red head could pop into view. "Sayo? Where did you get this kohane?"

Kurara did not care why Sayo was here; she was just glad that they could finally escape from the summer palace.

Sayo huffed. "I was waiting for you. When you didn't return to the *Orihime*, I went to look for you. Then the explosion happened and … well, I'm a hunter, aren't I? It's my duty to fight shikigami!"

Now that she had a good look at it, Kurara recognized the copper-coloured kohane from the shop where she had last seen Sayo. She pulled herself up, dragging Haru with her. His brows were furrowed and his expression pinched. Settling onto the wing, Kurara gently pushed strands of black, tangled hair out of the boy's face.

"Who in the blue skies is that?" asked Sayo, her expression tight.

"A friend." Kurara did not have time to explain everything.

"Isn't he a shikigami?" Tomoe swung around and crawled onto the opposite wing. She stared at Haru, eyes wide. "You shouted something about a core. But he looks—"

"You *stole* a shikigami? From an imperial Crafter?" bellowed Sayo.

"I didn't steal anyone! Haru doesn't belong to anyone!" Kurara did not think Sayo had any right to accuse her of theft. Especially since she was currently flying in a stolen kohane. She secured Tomoe and Haru to the wing with paper ropes before trying herself to the kohane as well. "We need to deal with the shikigami first."

No matter what, she would not let the princess have its core. She would not allow another shikigami to become a slave.

A few feet away, the dragon snapped free of its chains once more. Triumphant, it pulled a qipak from the sky, swallowing both the vehicle and the rider whole. The Crafters on the ground tried to contain it again, but it slipped from their reach and soared towards the city.

"For once, we agree on something." Sayo ground her teeth together as she kicked the kohane into full speed, racing after the shikigami as it hurtled towards the streets.

The dragon knocked a building stack into the road. Like a domino, it crashed into its neighbour. Row after row, street after street, the stacks collapsed to the ground. Washing lines snapped. Staircases splintered. People screamed, fleeing from the tidal wave of debris hurtling towards them. Fires erupted from overturned kitchens and demolished fuel stores. The military police who had been stationed around the summer palace took off in pursuit, leaning out of their motor cars and firing up at the dragon with bullets that barely seemed to dent it.

Sayo forced the kohane to dive after the dragon. Wooden beams rained over them. The craft swung like a pendulum to avoid the rubble falling from the building stacks. Scattered belongings bounced off the wings: china plates, children's toys, bottles of pickled preserves. A full wardrobe almost crashed on top of the cockpit. Sayo veered hard left and it hit the ground right next to them.

Haru jerked awake.

"K–Kurara?" He stared at her, eyes wide. "Where are we? What's going on?"

His voice. His eyes. It had been so long. Kurara wanted to stop everything and just cry, but she had to focus on the dragon.

The dragon twisted its body into a knot and dived not just to the ground, but through it, punching past the stones and into the metal foundations of the dome, burrowing through the city depths.

Kurara's breath stopped short.

The screech of metal being ripped apart tore through her ears. A groan, like a dying cumulous whale, echoed through the air. The shikigami ripped through the infrastructure holding everything in place; the metal plates that served as a foundation for the ground, the sewer system, the rain catchers, the power grid, the engines and floatation devices. Everything screeched to an almighty halt.

The roads erupted as pipes ruptured below the pavement, sending jets of water spraying into the air and flooding the streets. Broken wires fell into water, the power surging and exploding. The dome suddenly tilted, its foundation cracking. It sloped at an angle from its neighbouring domes.

Sayo's hands gripped the gearsticks, knuckles white. She pulled the kohane into a sharp ascent. It spun as it soared, pirouetting towards the heavens for a brief moment, before changing gears and spiralling down again, diving through the hole left in the dragon's wake.

Kurara barely had time to make sure they were all secured to the kohane before they were swooping past the broken pipes and bisected tracks of the city. They plunged past the foundations that held up Sola-Il's domes, out of the sky city and into the open sky below it.

The kohane sped forward until the cherry-blossom domes of Sola-Il were safely behind them. A long shadow fell over the craft. Directly above them, the dragon hovered in the air.

FORTY

"GREAT, what do we do now?" Tomoe clutched at the edge of the cockpit. Here they were, out in the open sky, with no weapons to speak of and no way of starting a fire needed to destroy a shikigami.

Kurara remembered when the dragon had first appeared on the *Midori*, how it had felt like staring at an oncoming avalanche. She had come a long way since that first encounter. Although that feeling was not completely gone, she managed to swallow back her fear and lean towards the dragon.

"Leave this to me," she said. "Just get me close to it."

Knowing what Haru was, what *she* was. Watching Akane's sunny enthusiasm for everything and even Ruki's sombre devotion, she knew now that she could not fight shikigami as if they were just monsters that needed to be stopped.

She would fight the shikigami, she would take it apart, but not for the people of Sola-Il. She would do it for the shikigami's sake. If she could give it nothing else, she would give it a dignified death.

"Lure the dragon in and I'll cut its core out," she said.

Haru stared at her in disbelief. "By yourself?"

"I can do it!" Kurara insisted. She had to.

The dragon turned towards them. The skin on the back of Kurara's neck prickled. She was not looking at a mere beast made of paper, but an intelligent creature caught in the throes of its suffering.

"Hang on!" Sayo pulled the kohane downward into a sharp nosedive.

As they barrelled towards the scarred earth below, the dragon gave chase. It quickly closed the distance between them, coming so close that its snout almost touched their tail. Fangs as large as a kohane's wings snapped at the air behind them.

Just as they came dangerously close to the ground, Sayo pulled the craft up. The kohane climbed again, twisting in spirals that made Kurara's stomach churn. The kohane's metal frame rattled and blackened trails of ribbon-like smoke spluttered from the engine.

"If you want to do something," cried Sayo over the roar of the engine, "now's the time!"

"I'm trying! Can't you keep this thing steady?" shouted Kurara as the kohane lurched out of the way of the shikigami's snapping jaws.

Sayo made a rude gesture in the rear-view mirror before dropping them into another stomach-churning nosedive.

Grabbing hold of the wing, Kurara gathered her ofuda and formed a trident the same size as the kohane beneath her. Her teeth were clenched in concentration as she levelled the weapon at the dragon's furious eyes.

The sound of drums beat through the air. Above, a red and gold airship soared across the sky. Its long sails streamed in the wind like war banners. What little light remained glinted off gaudy red masts. The faces of snarling ogres etched onto the side of the ship were twisted into ghoulish expressions.

Haru grabbed Kurara's wrist. He looked frantically from Kurara to the airship's broad flank. "That's one of Princess Tsukimi's warships. Master Fujiwa is on the deck. I can sense him!"

A sudden volley of ofuda rained from the sky. A hail of swords arched past the shikigami and towards the kohane.

"Are they aiming for us?" cried Kurara as Sayo yanked the craft out of the line of fire.

"It's me. I'm betting the princess wants me back," said Haru, miserably. "Keep your distance. If you let Master Fujiwa give an order, I have no choice but to obey."

"Humans are hungry. Consume and break. Break and consume. They'll eat you with your eyes, eat you with their hands. Run, run, run!" The dragon's inane jabber spilled from its throat as it twisted its body around and around in circles, unable to decide who it should attack.

After a moment, the dragon settled for them.

It lunged. Ofuda swords hurtled towards them at the same time. Sayo veered the kohane to one side as the paper weapons gave chase, hounding them as they swooped and dived through the air, out of range of the shikigami's thrashing tail, dodging the barrage of paper projectiles, avoiding the cannons that boomed from the ship's side.

As the kohane rose through the sky, Kurara spotted Fujiwa standing at the edge of the ship with an arsenal of paper swords behind him.

Without a second thought, she lifted her paper trident and flung it straight at the ship's hull. It soared true, but as it reached the ship, Fujiwa's ofuda batted it out of the way, sending the weapon tumbling back down through the sky.

Haru threw himself against the back seat. "Kurara!" he shouted as she pulled the trident back and sent it soaring towards the ship once more. "The dragon! Aim for the neck!"

Kurara turned just in time to see a giant tail bear down upon them. Her ofuda returned to form a shield between the shikigami and the kohane. The dragon's tail smashed into her ofuda, denting the protective paper barrier.

"Master, where are you? Why did you leave me alone?" the shikigami shrieked, its ramblings like a storm drowning out everything else.

"Leave me. Stay with me. I don't want anyone but you."

Kurara wanted to reach out her hands and comfort it as she would a crying child, though she knew it was far too dangerous. There was only one way to give the shikigami peace now. Through gritted teeth, she turned her shield into a giant spear.

With a roar, Kurara sent the spear flying. The dragon twisted out of the way, but it could not escape. Kurara's ofuda was locked on to its target. Cutting through the air like a blade through silk, the spear shot through the bottom of the dragon's jaw, severing the beast's head.

The shikigami's body crashed to the ground with such force the cloud of dust that rose in its wake almost reached Sola-II. Like ice melting into sludge, a tide of paper washed over the mines where it had fallen, slamming into the sides of rickety barracks and sweeping away storehouses. Its tail stretched far enough to touch the forest that skirted the cracked ground.

The head tumbled high into the air before gravity pulled it down. Its colourless eyes rolled back.

"Humans will have your soul, little one. Run, run, run, before they can catch you."

FORTY-ONE

KURARA did not let herself look away. She had done this. It was only right that she witness its final moments.

It had to be stopped, she told herself. *I had no choice.* Now it could finally rest in peace.

As the dragon's head began to disintegrate, Kurara could see its core and the threads of paper muscle nestled around it. It tumbled through the air between Sayo's kohane and Princess Tsukimi's warship. In the corner of her eye, Kurara noticed Fujiwa leaning over the deck.

The sight jolted her from her sombre thoughts. In that moment, she only had one thought: grab the core before anyone else could. She threw a paper chain into the air toward it, but Fujiwa was faster. His fluttering ofuda darted through the sky and snatched the core out of the air.

"No!" Haru shouted. Tomoe had to stop him from climbing out of the cockpit.

"Rara!" cried Haru. "The core – don't let them have it!"

Kurara's head whipped back to the warship. If she left the core with Fujiwa and the others, they would revive the dragon, bind it to one of them and force it into a lifetime of servitude. She had not destroyed the shikigami just to give them a new slave. That was the kind of fate she would not wish upon anyone.

Paper whipped around her, brewing up a storm. Her eyes met Fujiwa's. Across the short stretch of open sky, she could read the determination in his gaze.

"No," Sayo snapped, "we're done here. We need to—"

Cannon blasts shattered the air. The airship's gun port angled itself in line with the kohane – and opened fire.

Sayo cursed as a cannonball barely missed them.

"Head for the city. I'll distract them." Kurara pulled off the ropes keeping her tied to the wing and prepared to jump. For a moment, Sayo looked as though she would protest; though her expression remained obstinately unhappy, she did not speak.

"Wait," said Haru. "It's me they want. If I leave, you three can escape."

"No!" cried Kurara. She would rather take on all the imperial Crafters and their shikigami than be separated from Haru again.

"Well, he is right," said Sayo.

"I said no!"

Kurara was just about to jump when cannonballs arched across the sky. From the edge of the imperial warship, Fujiwa joined the barrage. A stream of paper projectiles sailed toward the kohane, each one capable of knocking them out of the sky.

Kurara spread a shield over the entire craft, concentrating on keeping the cockpit protected as cannonballs and ofuda alike pelted them like an iron fist to the ribs. Each blow knocked a dent her shield. She felt the moment Fujiwa's ofuda ripped through her barrier. A paper rock the size of her fist tore past her ofuda and through the kohane's tail, destroying the engine.

"We're hit!" shouted Tomoe.

Like a falling meteor, the kohane nosedived towards the ground, falling directly over the forest that skirted the ruined levistone mines. Trees shook at the sight of them, their branches gnashing together in the wind like monsters waiting for them to plunge into their hungry mouths.

"No, no, no, no!" Sayo wrestled with the controls, but the kohane continued to hurtle down.

The wind buffeted Kurara's body, cold and sharp. She felt it pierce her as she clung to the edge of the wing. There was no time for anything fancy. She made the first thing that she could think of – a paper ball. Cushioned on the inside with a hard metal-like shell on the outside, she wrapped herself in the comfort of her ofuda, her body sinking deep into its pillowy interior.

"Get in!" Kurara reached into the back seat to pull Haru and Tomoe up. "You, too, Sayo!"

With one last, frantic glance at the ground, Sayo abandoned the controls and climbed towards her. Kurara hauled her inside, closing the ball around them just as the engine exploded into flames, flinging them into the air.

Round and round, they were buffeted about. The ball hit something with a crunch, dislodging bits of paper from its tight formation. They were falling, plunging downwards for miles. Fire ate at the edges of Kurara's ofuda. Part of the engine must have hit them as it had exploded – her paper ball was crumbling to ash. As the star-swept sky crept in between the holes, Kurara stretched her hand towards the clouds.

The ball smashed into the trees. Kurara felt it break apart around her. She reached for a hand – she could not tell whose – but her fingers wrapped around nothing but thin air. With what little control she could muster, she pushed her ofuda towards the others, the paper billowing out in the hope that it would cushion their fall.

Please, keep them safe! she prayed as her body hurtled towards the ground.

FORTY-TWO

TREES broke her fall as Kurara tumbled down. Something snapped – a branch, a bone. Twigs scratched at her face and leaves cut at her skin until at last she landed among the ruins of her paper ball, flat on her back beneath a curving oak tree.

She was distantly aware of someone groaning next to her, but she was too dazed to turn her head and see who it was. The stench of levistone filled the air. In the distance, a column of smoke rose above the trees. Likely, the spot where the kohane had crashed.

Kohane. Crash. Those words floated around Kurara's brain until they finally sunk in. She leapt to her feet, stomach lurching. Black spots danced over her eyes as the world tilted into focus.

"Tomoe? Sayo?"

Kurara turned to see the two girls lying on the ground

near her. The sleeves of Sayo's kimono were torn and Tomoe's legs were tangled in a bush, but they did not appear badly hurt.

"Where's Haru?" Fear wrapped its cold hands around her chest. Had he landed in the forest as well? Was he injured? Her thoughts spun in circles, trying to avoid the memory of the first time she had crashed to the ground. The memory of Haru burning.

Picking herself up, Sayo brushed the leaves from her clothes. Her cheeks were bleeding and her arms were covered in scratches, but nothing was broken. After a quick inspection of her bruises, she said: "Haru? That's the name of that boy, right? That shikigami from the palace?"

"He didn't look like a shikigami." Tomoe sat up with a groan. "Oh blue skies, look what the ground has done to my boots!"

"Is he a new type perhaps?" asked Sayo. "One of Princess Tsukimi's experiments?"

Exasperated, Kurara opened her mouth to set them straight when Tomoe suddenly drew her tanto from its sheath and whirled around to face a clump of thick bushes. "Who's there?"

"Stop!" Haru scrambled to his feet, his hands raised in surrender. "It's just me!"

Time stopped. Kurara's breath caught in her throat as a wave of relief threatened to overwhelm her. She could not remember how to blink. Or how to breathe.

"Haru!" Kurara flung herself at him. Her legs buckled as she wrapped her arms around him in a furious hug.

Haru did not catch her in time and her knees hit the ground, dragging him down with her.

Tears rolled down her cheeks, her face scrunching into an ugly mess as she sobbed.

Finally. After everything she had been through. *Finally*. She had no other words than that. An immense weight lifted from her shoulders. Her lungs could breathe again. *Finally*.

Haru's hands gently curled around Kurara's wrists, holding them tight. "Rara. I'm fine."

"Why is he here?" demanded Sayo. "Isn't he the shikigami you stole from Princess Tsukimi?"

Kurara got to her feet. She suddenly felt so very tired.

"I didn't steal anyone. Haru was my friend from the *Midori*. I… We…" She struggled to explain everything that had happened to her from the moment the *Midori* had been destroyed to encountering the soldiers in the forest to the deal she had made with Himura.

Haru listened with a solemn expression as she spoke about what had happened on Sola-Il and how Himura had sold Haru's core to the princess. As she reached the moment when Himura had betrayed her, she paused and took a deep breath.

She did not want Tomoe and Sayo to look at her like Himura had, she did not want to risk being hurt again, but she did not want to lie to them either. They had fought together. They deserved to know the truth.

What they decided to do once she told them was another matter.

"There's one more thing…" Bracing herself for a storm, Kurara pulled back her sleeve and rolled down the black glove covering her left arm. She lifted her paper limb to her face. "I'm a shikigami too."

A thousand emotions flickered across Sayo's face, too fast to catch, before settling into a stony look. Tomoe's eyes grew impossibly wide. Her mouth parted into a slack-jawed gape.

Kurara tensed, steeling herself for the explosion of questions that would surely come, but before anyone could speak, a familiar shadow passed overhead.

She gaped. The *Orihime* was leaving Sola-Il. Leaving them.

"The ship!" Sayo took two sudden steps forward, as if to run after it. She turned to Kurara, panicked. "Quick! Use your ofuda to get their attention! They don't know where we are."

"No, don't!" Tomoe lurched forward to grab Kurara's wrist. "The princess is after you. If you signal the ship, you'll only give away your position. After that attack, it's best if they leave before the city is locked down."

"So they'll leave without us?"

"If that's what they have to do."

Sayo made a noise halfway between an agitated scream and a groan. She carded her shaking fingers through her hair.

"Kurara." There was steel in her eyes. "I have never asked you for anything, but if you ever do anything for me, you'll do this—"

"Sayo!" snapped Tomoe.

Haru hooked his fingers over Kurara's. "What do you want to do, Kurara?"

331

She looked at him. "I want to protect you from Princess Tsukimi and Fujiwa, and..."

He shook his head. "Forget about me. Forget about your duty to your ship. Forget about everyone else. What do *you* want?"

It was a question Kurara rarely had to answer. It was difficult to put into words. Her desires were so tangled that she did not know where one began and the other ended. She wanted Haru to be safe. She wanted to return to a ship and a crew that could accept her no matter what. She wanted to confront Himura and punch him in the face. She wanted a better life for the shikigami.

Above, the sky rumbled. The *Orihime* was moving further and further away, its ragged sails fluttering in the wind. It looked so pitiful from a distance – the canvas covering the holes in the hull was visible even from the ground. Kurara summoned the remains of the paper ball towards her. The bits of ofuda scattered over the ground and in the trees and bushes floated back to her. She did not have much left but maybe she could use what paper remained to signal the ship.

Is that a good idea? An uneasy thought stole through her head.

She wanted to help Tomoe and Sayo. She did not want to be stuck in the middle of the forest, alone, and at the mercy of whomever Princess Tsukimi decided to send after her. The *Orihime* was safety. It was freedom, and the comfort of a soft bed and a warm meal. It was home.

But Himura was probably on the ship. Akane too. And the crew... Would they accept her if they knew what she was? Would they accept Haru?

What if the princess attacked the ship because they were sheltering her? The military were the *Orihime*'s biggest customer, but if Princess Tsukimi wished it, she could make sure no one in the army ever bought cores from them again. Or worse, she could have them hunted down as traitors to the empire.

Kurara's thoughts began to run away with her, as she imagined all the awful things that could happen to the crew. She couldn't do it. She couldn't risk it.

Her ofuda returned around her neck.

The *Orihime* sailed on.

FORTY-THREE

KURARA could no longer see the ship. The *Orihime* dwindled into a black dot upon the horizon. As it disappeared, so did their last chance of rescue.

Sayo turned and slammed her fist against the nearest tree. Without a word, she pushed her way past the others and into the forest, smacking away the low-hanging branches that obstructed her path.

"Sayo? Where are you going?" Tomoe scurried after her.

"To catch up with the ship!" she shouted back.

No one said anything about how it was impossible to do that on foot. Or that they were likely not out of danger yet. They were not thinking straight, still coming down from the rush of fighting and crashing into the forest, still full of nervous energy and a need to do something, anything.

There was nowhere else to go but south, picking their way beneath the tangle of branches that formed a cage between the ground and the sky. The air, rich with the scent of pines, had an otherworldly quality to it, marred only by the stench of destruction. Kurara could smell smoke on the wind.

Twigs scratched at her face and legs. For a while, the only noise was the sound of their footsteps and the rustling leaves. She glanced to her right. Haru's arms swung at his side, gangly and uncoordinated as always. His clumsiness was reassuring. He was back. It felt like a dream. He was really here, wasn't he? He would not disappear the moment she turned away? Despite everything that had happened, she allowed herself a small sigh of relief. They were together. They were safe, at least for now. The dragon had not destroyed Sola-Il and the *Orihime* had managed to escape.

But – worries crept at the corner of her mind – *what do we do now?*

"A dragon inside Sola-Il! And human shikigami too! What in the blue skies is going on?" Sayo grumbled as she stormed ahead.

Both she and Tomoe were taking Kurara's news rather well, considering everything that had happened. Although Kurara was sure that was only because they had so many other things to fret about.

They had to part ways soon. As soon as they were out of the forest, Tomoe and Sayo would try to rejoin their ship and Kurara would ... well, she did not know what she would do, only that she could not go with them.

Princess Tsukimi was only interested in *her*, after all. She would not bring her troubles to the ship. If Tomoe and Sayo were thinking straight, they would acknowledge that too. Kurara wondered if it was cowardice that she did not bring it up first. The thought of parting with her friends hurt more than she had anticipated.

It would be her and Haru again. Just as it had been from the very beginning.

Slowing down to match Haru's pace, Kurara whispered, "How are you feeling?"

"At the moment, I only have orders to defend Master Fujiwa." Haru lowered his voice. "As long as you don't try to hurt him, I won't try anything. But it's strange. When he gives me an order, it doesn't feel as though I'm being forced to obey. Whenever he tells me to do something, I think, *Oh, that's a good idea!* So I do it, but afterwards, I wonder what came over me. It's like for a moment I'm not really myself. I almost forgot how it feels to have a master again."

"Again?" Kurara pounced on Haru's slip-up. There were things he was keeping from her, and she needed to know what they were.

His expression shuttered, which in turn made Kurara falter. She knew that Haru could be secretive; she was just not used to him acting like that around her. On the *Midori*, he would tell her everything from a silly crush on one of the entertainers, to his plans to steal chocolate from the kitchens, inviting her into his mind with no care for what she would find rattling around in there.

This time, when Kurara tried the door to his thoughts, it was firmly locked.

"Since when do we keep secrets from one another, Haru?"

A surprised laugh escaped Haru's mouth, sharp and harsh. "I've been keeping secrets from you for years, Rara." There was no triumph in his reply, only a sad and bitter truth.

"Then you've always known that you – that both of us – are shikigami? You remember everything from before the *Midori*? When we were children?"

"We were never children, Rara." Haru's gaze flicked across her face as they trailed behind Tomoe and Sayo. "Our physical bodies changed, but we did not really grow up. Not the way real children do."

"Why can't I remember any of this?" Madam Ito had called it trauma, but Kurara was beginning to wonder if that was true.

Haru kicked a stray stone out of his path. It bounced across the ground and rolled out of sight.

"Aki. That was my name before," she said.

He shot her a sharp look. "You shouldn't know that."

Kurara pressed her lips together in a thin line. How could Haru irritate her already? She had only just got him back. A few minutes ago, she had wanted to cry and hug him, and now she wanted to smack the back of his head.

"I want the truth, Haru."

"I promised you that I wouldn't say anything."

Kurara lifted her head to the sky. She recalled the story Madam Ito told her about how she and Haru had been found among the ruins of their burning village,

337

the strange dreams that she could not quite remember. There was something missing, something important had happened to her, but she could not quite put her finger on it.

"Did you...? Did you erase my memory?" If not trauma, then what else could it be? The symbols on a core contained everything about a shikigami. Just like Akane, how easy would it be to blot out a few years? She did not want it to be true, but the more she thought about it the more it made sense.

Haru sighed and nodded. "Erasing symbols is easy. Even I can scrub away parts of a shikigami's core."

Like an axe falling, Kurara saw the blow coming but failed to dodge it. When it struck, she its full force knocked her off-kilter. Her body moved on automatic through the forest, but her brain stuttered to a stop.

"Did I ask you to do it?" She wrestled back some semblance of thought.

"You did. I didn't want to, but you begged me to," said Haru.

"Which memories did you erase? What am I forgetting?" How much had she lost? How many memories had she traded away? The people that she had met, the things that she had seen and the experiences she had lived through – would she ever get those memories back?

Haru said nothing. The silence was broken only by a distant rumble of thunder.

"I can't tell you that. I promised."

"You promised Aki, not me," she said.

338

A flicker of hurt crossed Haru's face. Grey, drizzling rain began to fall against the crowns of the trees, trickling through and turning the earth to mud. With every step, Kurara's feet sank into the mud as though the ground were trying to chain her down. The rain grew into a roaring downpour. Ahead, Tomoe shrieked and ran for cover, pulling Sayo with her.

"Fine. Don't tell me. I'll find out by myself!" Kurara raced past him.

"Rara!" Haru called after her. She stopped. He looked at her, his expression sombre for a moment before his face broke into a smile. "I'm glad I'm back."

There was the Haru she knew: the curious, kind boy that she had grown up with. The stars were hidden by clouds, the wind howled. Rain plastered his hair to his face and soaked through his clothes, yet Kurara had never seen him look so bright.

A dying star fell from the heavens, and from that star grew a tree.

Haru was her star. She had travelled across the country, fought against shikigami, battled imperial Crafters and defied the princess of the empire just to bring him back. As long as they were together, she could face whatever tomorrow would bring.

GLOSSARY OF TERMS

Crafters – People who can control paper at will.

Hakama – Clothing tied around the waist, which falls to the ankles.

Katana – A type of sword with a curved, single edged blade, wielded with two hands.

Kimono – Clothing made from straight cuts. Wraps around the body and must be tied and folded securely into place.

Kitsune – Fox yōkai known for their intelligence and cunning. They appear in mythology both as faithful guardians and as tricksters.

Ko – The common currency of Mikoshima.

Kohane – A common type of aircraft used for transport, fighting and scouting.

Koto – A musical instrument made of thirteen strings across a board of wood. Sound is made by plucking at the strings.

Obi – A sash worn with a kimono.

Ofuda – Paper used by Crafters. Though traditionally one should write a blessing or prayer onto ofuda, many Crafters these days skip this step.

Okayu – Savoury rice porridge, also known as congee.

Qipak – A type of aircraft typically used for short flights. It resembles a small fishing boat with wings.

Ronin – A masterless samurai.

Shikigami – Creatures made of paper. Not much is known about shikigami, and the truth of their origins has been lost